A SUPERNATURAL BAR

"You say the animals from his d.t.'s came alive?" said Witherwax. "I'd like to hear about this. I was just reading in a book about something like that. They call it materialization."

"Well, I don't know," said Willison. "The few of us who knew him have always rather kept it quiet . . ."

"You can tell them," said Mr. Cohan. "No harm to anybody now the poor young felly is dead and gone, and his animals with him."

"Mmm. I suppose you're right," said Willison. "Well—fill me up another rye and water, Mr. Cohan, and let's see. I want to get this straight."

TALES FROM GAVAGAN'S BAR

(Expanded Edition)

L. Sprague de Camp
and Fletcher Pratt

To John Drury Clark, Ph.D., a longtime friend of both authors.

This low-priced Bantam Book has been completely reset in a type face designed for easy reading, and was printed from new plates. It contains the complete text of the expanded edition.
NOT ONE WORD HAS BEEN OMITTED.

TALES FROM GAVAGAN'S BAR
A Bantam Book / published by arrangement with the authors

PRINTING HISTORY
Originally published by Twayne Publishers 1953
Olswick Press expanded edition published June 1978
Bantam edition / January 1980
2nd printing

ISBN: 0-553-13127-3

Published simultaneously in the United States and Canada

Bantam Books are published by Bantam Books, Inc. Its trademark, consisting of the words "Bantam Books" and the portrayal of a bantam, is Registered in U.S. Patent and Trademark Office and in other countries. Marca Registrada. Bantam Books, Inc., 666 Fifth Avenue, New York, New York 10019.

PRINTED IN THE UNITED STATES OF AMERICA

ABOUT THE AUTHORS

L. Sprague de Camp, author or coauthor of over 80 books, has written fantasy *(The Tritonian Ring)*, science fiction *(The Hostage of Zir* and *The Great Fetish)*, popularizations of science *(The Ancient Engineers* and *Citadels of Mystery)* and the biography of H. P. Lovecraft. He is now at work on the life of Robert E. Howard, the creator of Conan, to whose saga he has contributed many tales. Educated at the California Institute of Technology, he has been a patent expert and served as a lieutenant-commander in the U.S. Naval Reserve before settling down to a career as a free-lance writer. He now makes his home with his wife Catherine in the suburbs of Philadelphia.

Fletcher Pratt (1897–1956) was a connoisseur of heroic fantasy before that term was invented. He read Norse sagas in the original and greatly admired Eddison's *The Worm Ouroboros*. His own efforts in this genre produced *The Well of the Unicorn* and *The Blue Star*. Born on an Indian reservation, he became a prizefighter in the flyweight class before entering Hobart College in Geneva, N.Y. Early in his career he worked for Hugo Gernsback translating European science fiction novels; later, as a writer living in New York City, he collaborated with de Camp on fantasy stories and made his reputation with a popular history of the Civil War, *Ordeal by Fire*.

CONTENTS

PREFACE

In compiling this record of certain of the somewhat dubious episodes centering around Gavagan's, we have enjoyed unusual advantages. In the first place, both of us can take shorthand. To be sure, neither of us has a degree of proficiency that would arouse envy in a court stenographer; and this makes necessary the warning that we cannot vouch for the absolute accuracy of all the quotations. But it is quite possible for either of your reporters—we reject the name of "author"—to sit at one of the back tables with a notebook concealed in his newspaper and surreptitiously set down the remarks of the various guests without any of them being aware that they are talking for posterity.

In the second place, we were fortunate enough to have met Gavagan (rhymes with "pagan") at a comparatively early date—before the unfortunate accident that cost him the use of his left foot and compelled him to abandon his profession as a field oil geologist. He had some money to invest, and the amount was largely increased by his disability insurance. The operation of a beneficent Providence and the fact that Gavagan and Mr. Cohan were fellow parishioners of Father McConaghy led the injured scientist to put his funds into the bar that now bears his name—a business whose details he could handle by remote control, as it were, and without physical activity.

The place was rather run-down at the time, and the clientele was chiefly drawn from the lower orders of society. Gavagan, whose taste is in the direction of the social and intellectual, indeed the refined, redecorated the place in a manner designed to appeal to the carriage trade and solicited the patronage of the better elements in town. It is doubtful whether he would have succeeded but for the influence, talents, and wise acquaintanceship of Mr. Cohan.

This gentleman—Aloysius P. Cohan, to give him his full name and distinguish him from his brother Julius, an officer of the police force—brought with him to Gavagan's a quantity of patronage that immediately established the place in the position it has never lost. Decidedly portly these days, he was at one time a remarkably fine performer at the Irish game of hurling, and is said to have once beaten the champion of Scotland at tossing the caber. His prowess with a bung starter has relieved many difficult situations in Gavagan's. His early biography is somewhat obscure, but the name appears to have been Cohen (pronounced co-*hen*) at one time; he and his brother Julius changed the spelling, not for any reasons rooted in racism, but because they were constantly receiving appeals from both the Jewish and the Catholic charity organizations. Being men of heart, they found it difficult either to refuse the appeals or to support the drain on their resources.

Mr. Cohan had been working in a bar on the far side of town (a city in the northeastern United States) when Gavagan suffered his accident. At about the same time, this place was purchased by a chain bar-and-restaurant organization, which insisted on serving ice cream in all its establishments. This so revolted Mr. Cohan (a fundamentalist on the subject of liquor) that he resigned on the spot. He was on the point of returning to Sligo when Father McConaghy placed him in touch with Gavagan. The former geologist did not hesitate for a moment at the opportunity of simultaneously obtaining a bartender of unrivalled virtuosity and the patronage that would turn his bar into the kind of place he wished to maintain. He not only obtained the refund of his passage money for Mr. Cohan but also paid back to his new factotum the amount that had been expended on passport and visa.

Mr. Cohan's value to Gavagan's will become more apparent in the course of our reports. The material for them has been gathered over a considerable space of time, and we believe that, taken together, they constitute a document of no small social importance. Too little investigation has been given, and too little importance has previously been attached to certain sequences of incident for which Mr. Cohan, both as a bartender and an unlettered philosopher, acts as a catalytic agent.

L. Sprague de Camp
Fletcher Pratt
September 1952

ELEPHAS FRUMENTI

The thin, balding man in tweeds almost tipped over his glass as he set it down with a care that showed care had become necessary. "Think of dogs," he said. "Really, my dear, there is no practical limit to what can be accomplished by selective breeding."

"Except that where I come from, we sometimes think of other things," said the brass-blonde, emphasizing the ancient *New Yorker* joke with a torso-wiggle that was pure *Police Gazette*.

Mr. Witherwax lifted his nose from the second Martini. "Do you know them, Mr. Cohan?" he asked.

Mr. Cohan turned in profile to swab a glass. "That would be Professor Thott, and a very educated gentleman, too. I don't rightly know the name of the lady, though I think he has been calling her Ellie, or something like that. Would you like to be meeting them, now?"

"Sure. I was reading in a book about this selective breeding, but I don't understand it so good, and maybe he could tell me something about it."

Mr. Cohan made his way to the end of the bar and led ponderously toward the table. "Pleased to meet you, Professor Thott," said Witherwax.

"Sir, the pleasure is all mine, all mine. Mrs. Jonas, may I present an old friend of mine, yclept Witherwax? Old in the sense that he is aged in the admirable liquids produced by Gavagan's, while the liquids themselves are aged in wood, ha—ha—a third-premise aging. Sit down, Mr. Witherwax. I call your attention to the remarkable qualities of alcohol, among which *peripeteia* is not the least."

"Yeah, that's right," said Mr. Witherwax, his expression taking on a resemblance to that of the stuffed owl over the bar. "What I was going to ask—"

"Sir, I perceive that I have employed a pedantry more suitable to the classroom, with the result that communication has not been established. *Peripeteia* is the reversal of rôles. While in a state of saintly sobriety, I pursue Mrs. Jonas; I entice her to alcoholic diversions. But after the third Presidente, she pursues me, in accordance with the ancient biological rule that alcohol increases feminine desire while decreasing masculine potency."

From the bar, Mr. Cohan appeared to have caught only a part of this speech. "Rolls we ain't got," he said. "But you can have some pretzel sticks." He reached under the bar for the bowl. "All gone; and I just laid out a new box this morning. That's where Gavagan's profits go. In the old days it was the free lunch, and now it's pretzel sticks."

"What I was going to ask—" said Witherwax.

Professor Thott stood up and bowed, a bow which ended in his sitting down again rather suddenly. "Ah, the mystery of the universe and music of the spheres, as Prospero might have phrased it! Who pursues? Who flies? The wicked. One preserves philosophy by remaining at the Platonian mean, the knife edge between pursuit and flight, wickedness and virtue. Mr. Cohan, a round of Presidentes please, including one for my aged friend."

"Let me buy this one," said Witherwax firmly. "What I was going to ask was about this selective breeding."

The Professor shook himself, blinked twice, leaned back in his chair, and placed one hand on the table. "You wish me to be academic? Very well; but I have witnesses that it was at your own request."

Mrs. Jonas said: "Now look what you've done. You've got him started and he won't run down until he falls asleep."

"What I want to know—" began Witherwax, but Thott beamingly cut across: "I shall present only the briefest and most non-technical of outlines," he said. "Let us suppose that, of sixteen mice, you took the two largest and bred them together. Their children would in turn be mated with those of the largest pair from another group of sixteen. And so on. Given time and material enough, and making it advantageous to the species to produce larger members, it would be easy to produce mice the size of lions."

"Ugh!" said Mrs. Jonas. "You ought to give up drinking. Your imagination gets gruesome."

"I see," said Witherwax, "like in a book I read once where they had rats so big they ate horses and wasps the size of dogs."

"I recall the volume," said Thott, sipping his Presidente. "It was *The Food of the Gods*, by H. G. Wells. I fear, however, that the method he describes was not that of genetics and therefore had no scientific validity."

"But could you make things like that by selective breeding?" asked Witherwax.

"Certainly. You could produce houseflies the size of tigers. It is merely a matter of—"

Mrs. Jonas raised a hand. "Alvin, what an awful thought. I hope you don't ever try it."

"There need be no cause for apprehension, my dear. The square-cube law will forever protect us from such a visitation."

"Huh?" said Witherwax.

"The square-cube law. If you double the dimensions, you quadruple the area and octuple the masses. The result is—well, in a practical non-technical sense, a tiger-sized housefly would have legs too thin and wings too small to support his weight."

Mrs. Jonas said: "Alvin, that's impractical. How could it move?"

The Professor essayed another bow, which was even less successful than the first, since it was made from a sitting position. "Madame, the purpose of such an experiment would not be practical but demonstrative. A tiger-sized fly would be a mass of jelly that would have to be fed from a spoon." He raised a hand. "There is no reason why anyone should produce such a monster; and since nature has no advantages to offer insects of large size, it will decline to produce them. I agree that the thought is repulsive; myself, I should prefer the alternative project of producing elephants the size of flies—or swallows."

Witherwax beckoned to Mr. Cohan. "These are good. Do it again. But wouldn't your square-cube law get you in Dutch there, too?"

"By no means, sir. In the case of size reduction, it works in your favor. The mass is divided by eight, but the muscles remain proportionately the same, capable of supporting a vastly greater weight. The legs and wings of a tiny elephant would not only support him, but give him the agility of a hummingbird. Consider the dwarf elephant of Sicily during the Plish—"

"Alvin," said Mrs. Jonas, "you're drunk. Otherwise you'd remember how to pronounce Pleistocene, and you wouldn't be talking about elephants' wings."

"Not at all, my dear. I should confidently expect such a species to develop flight by means of enlarged ears, like the Dumbo of the movies."

Mrs. Jonas giggled. "Still, I wouldn't want one the size of a housefly. It would be too small for a pet and would get into things. Let's make it the size of a kitten, like this." She held out her index fingers about five inches apart.

"Very well, my dear," said the Professor. "As soon as I can obtain a grant from the Carnegie Foundation, the project will be undertaken."

"Yes, but," said Witherwax, "how would you feed an elephant like that? And could they be housebroke?"

"If you can housebreak a man, an elephant ought to be easy," said Mrs. Jonas. "And you could feed them oats or hay. Much cleaner than keeping cans of dog food around."

The Professor rubbed his chin. "Hmm," he said. "The rate of absorption of nourishment would vary directly as the intestinal area—which would vary as the square of the dimensions—I'm not sure of the results, but I'm afraid we'd have to provide more concentrated and less conventional food. I presume that we could feed our *Elephas micros*, as I propose to call him, on lump sugar. No, not *Elephas micros*,

Elephas microtatus, the 'utmost littlest, tiniest elephant.' "

Mr. Cohan, who had been neglecting his only other customer to lean on the bar in their direction, spoke up: "Mr. Considine, that's the salesman, was telling me that the most concentrated food you can get is good malt whiskey."

"That's it!" The Professor slapped the table. "Not *Elephas microtatus* but *Elephas frumenti,* the whiskey elephant, from what he lives on. We'll breed them for a diet of alcohol. High energy content."

"Oh, but that won't do," protested Mrs. Jonas. "Nobody would want a house pet that had to be fed on whiskey all the time. Especially with children around."

Said Witherwax: "Look, if you really want these animals, why don't you keep them some place where children aren't around and whiskey is—bars, for instance."

"Profound observation," said Professor Thott. "And speaking of rounds, Mr. Cohan, let us have another. We have horses as outdoor pets, cats as house pets, canaries as cage pets. Why not an animal especially designed and developed to be a bar pet? Speaking of which—that stuffed owl you keep for a pet, Mr. Cohan, is getting decidedly mangy."

"They would steal things like that," said Mrs. Jonas dreamily. "They would take things like owls' feathers and pretzel sticks and beer mats to build their nests with, up in the dark corners somewhere near the ceiling. They would come out at night—"

The Professor bent a benignant gaze on her as Mr. Cohan set out the drinks. "My dear," he said, "either this discussion of the future *Elephas frumenti* or the actual *spiritus frumenti* is going to your head. When you become poetical—"

The brass-blonde had leaned back and was looking upward. "I'm not poetical. That thing right up there on top of the pillar is the nest of one of your bar elephants."

"What thing up there?" said Thott.

"That thing up there, where it's so dark."

"I don't see nothing," said Mr. Cohan, "and if you

don't mind my saying so, this is a clean bar, not a rat in the place."

"They wouldn't be quite tame, ever," said Mrs. Jonas, still looking upward, "and if they didn't feel they were fed enough, they'd come and take for themselves when the bartender wasn't looking."

"That does look funny," said Thott, pushing his chair back and beginning to climb on it.

"Don't, Alvin," said Mrs. Jonas. "You'll break your neck. . . . Think of it, they'd feed their children—"

"Stand by me, then, and let me put my hand on your shoulder."

"Hey!" said Witherwax suddenly. "Who drank my drink?"

Mrs. Jonas lowered her eyes. "Didn't you?"

"I didn't even touch it. Mr. Cohan just put it down, didn't you?"

"I did that. But that would be a couple of minutes back, and maybe you could—"

"I could not. I definitely, positively did not drink—hey, you people, look at the table!"

"If I had my other glasses . . ." said Thott, swaying somewhat uncertainly as he peered upward into the shadows.

"Look at the table," repeated Witherwax, pointing.

The glass that had held his drink was empty. Thott's still held about half a cocktail. Mrs. Jonas' glass lay on its side, and from its lip about a thimbleful of Presidente cocktail had flowed pinkly into an irregular patch the size of a child's hand.

As the other two followed Witherwax's finger, they saw that, from this patch, a line of little damp footprints led across the table to the far edge, where they suddenly ceased. They were circular, each about the size of a dime, with a small scalloped front edge, as if made by . . .

THE ANCESTRAL AMETHYST

"We were very good to the Swedes when they ruled over us in Bornholm three hundred years ago," said the stocky man, downing his cherry brandy at a gulp and motioning Mr. Cohan for a refill. "We had to kill all of them one night. While it was being done, some of our people ran into the church and rang the church bells, so that the souls of all the Swedes should rise to heaven on the music. For several hours they continued to pull the ropes, although it was terribly hard work for their arms and they became very tired."

The second cherry brandy followed the first. Professor Thott contemplated the bald cranium, surrounded by a crescent of pale hair, and said thoughtfully: "I can perceive that you Danes are an extremely tenderhearted people."

"That is most true," said the stocky man. His whole face was covered by a network of tiny red lines. "But it is not always for us—how do the English say it?—'beer and skating.' I remember—"

The door opened, and he checked as into Gavagan's came a tall, thin, knobby policeman, accompanied by a small man with sharp eyes, in a neat blue serge suit. The policeman extended a hand across the bar to Mr. Cohan, who shook it fervently.

"How are you, Julius?"

"How are you, my boy?" Then he turned to face the others.

"Hello, Professor," he said to Thott. "Meet my friend, Mr. McClintock."

There was more handshaking. Thott said: "This is Captain Axel Ewaldt, of the Danish merchant marine, Officer Cohan, Mr McClintock. Shall we have a round? He was just telling a story to illustrate how sentimental the Danes are. Make mine a Rye Highball, Mr. Cohan."

"Just a sherry," said McClintock. "A people of high moral standards. They have less crime than any nation in Europe."

Captain Ewaldt beamed; Patrolman Cohan said: "Mr. McClintock gives talks on crime. He's just been over to the Police Boys' Club doing it. He's an expert."

"I have often wondered how one became an expert on crime," said Professor Thott, meditatively.

"By personal association in my case," said McClintock. "I don't in the least mind telling you, not in the least. Until the grace of the Lord came upon me, I was engaged in criminal activity. The title of my talk is 'Crime does not pay,' and I am happy to say my efforts have been rewarding."

Patrolman Cohan said: "This was known as Dippie Louie. He was a left breech hook and could kiss the dog."

Professor Thott gazed at Dippie Louie with polite interest, but Ewaldt said: "Some schnapps, Mr. Cohan. This cherry makes one cold inside, and a man should warm himself." He addressed the officer: "Be so good to explain. I am not understanding."

"A left breech hook can lift a poke—beg pardon, take a wallet out of a man's left breeches pocket. And kissing the dog means he can do it while standing face to face."

"A highly skilled profession," said McClintock. "Ah, my friends, if the effort and training expended on criminal activity were only employed in the service of humanity, we would not—"

Thott said, rather hastily: "You were going to tell us about the Danes being kindhearted, Captain Ewaldt."

"That is correct," said the Captain. "I was yust remembering how I am in the city of Boston one St. Patrick's Day, walking down the dock and minding my own business. Along comes this big Irishman, and anybody can see he has too much to drink, and because I do not have green on for the day, he pushes me. Once is all right, but the second time, I got my little Danish up, and I pushed him in the water—with my fist. But I was really very good to him, because if I have not done this, he would be falling in the water to drown after dark when there is nobody to rescue him."

Mr. Cohan gave an inarticulate sound, but it was McClintock who said: "What makes you so certain?"

"More schnapps, please. Because this is early in the morning, and he would be drinking more all day, and everyone knows that an Irishman cannot drink all day without falling down."

Patrolman Cohan gave an inarticulate sound; Mr. Cohan put both hands on the bar, and said: "And would you be saying, now, that youse Swedes can hold your liquor better than the Irish that's brought up on it? Go on with you."

"I am not Swedish," said Ewaldt, "yust a good Danish man. And I am saying that I am brought up on the island of Bornholm, and I can drink three times as much as any Irishman."

"Would you care to bet five dollars on that, now?" said Mr. Cohan, dangerously.

"It is too little. Five dollars valuta will not even buy the schnapps I am drinking."

"Think pretty well of yourself, don't you?" said Mr. Cohan. "I can see now that you must be a real artist at drinking." Patrolman Cohan snickered at this brilliant sarcasm as Mr. Cohan went on: "Not but what everyone should have something to be proud of. But if you feel that way about it, maybe you'd be liking to have a little contest for twenty-five dollars, and the loser pays the bills?"

Wheels appeared to be revolving in Ewaldt's head. "That I will do," he said. "You are drinking with me?"

"Not me, my fine young felly," said Mr. Cohan. "I have the bar and all to take care of, and it would be worth the best part of me neck if Gavagan come in and found me trying to drink down one of the trade. But Dippie Louie here, he has more than a drop of the right blood in him, and I call to mind many's the time I've seen him lay away his share."

"It was the cause of my ruin and my descent into crime," said McClintock. "But I undeniably possess a special ability to absorb the drink. It's because my ancestors come from Galway, it is, where the wind blows so cold that if a man drinks water and then goes out of doors, he's no better than an icicle in no time at all."

"I am not wanting to ruin you again," said Ewaldt.

Patrolman Cohan spoke up: "You'll not be ruining Louie McClintock, that drank down the Bohemian champion at the truck drivers' picnic. And besides, I'm here meself to see that he gets home all right."

McClintock gravely extended his hand and took Ewaldt's. "For the honor of old Erin," he said. "Twenty-five dollars and the loser pays the bills. What shall we drink?"

"Schnapps some kind. It is no matter to me."

Mr. Cohan set a bottle of Irish whiskey on the bar, produced a couple of Scotch-and-soda glasses and filled them halfway up, adjusting the liquid level with meticulous care. "*Skaal!*" said Ewaldt, and tossed his off as though it were a pony. McClintock went more slowly, rolling the last mouthful around his tongue before he sank it, and said: "That makes you cock your tail, now! Fill them again, Mr. Cohan."

Thott said: "I think that, to be perfectly fair, a slight interval should be allowed for the—ah, dissipation of the shock effect. Mr. McClintock, if I am not too importunate, may I ask what led you to change professions?"

"Education," said McClintock. "Education and the grace of God. I took a correspondence course in writing short stories while I was in Dannemora." He reached for his glass, which Mr. Cohan had loaded again. "Ah, up Erin!" The two Cohans nodded approval, and Thott raised his own glass in salutation. Ewaldt drained his potion off without lifting an eyebrow, tapped the glass with a fingernail, and pushed it toward Mr. Cohan. The bartender reached back for another bottle of Irish and refilled the glasses for a third time.

Ewaldt beamed. "In my country," he said, "we drink not to the country, but to all the pretty girls. Now I have drunk with you to your country, and you are drinking with me to all the pretty girls in Denmark. *Skaal!*"

His third glass of Irish followed the course of the other two with the same easy, fluid motion. McClintock again took a little more time. There was a slight frown in the middle of his forehead, and he appeared to be considering something quite seriously.

"It was the prison chaplain, God bless his soul," he said. "He explained to me that the gains from the profession of crime were b'no means equal to the effort expended. He made me see, he told me that . . ." He turned halfway round and emitted a large burp.

Patrolman Cohan gazed earnestly at him, then turned toward the others and began talking rapidly: "Did I ever tell you now, about the time I found me own wife in the paddy wagon, and her mad enough to have the left leg of me, and saying it was all my fault? It was—" He laid a hand on McClintock's shoulder, but Dippie Louie shook it off.

"I'm okay," he said. "Fill them up again."

"You are not to be drinking so fast," said Ewaldt evenly. "That is how a man is—how do you say it?—be-drunken, unless he is Danish."

"I tell you I'm all right," said McClintock, "and I know how fast I can put it away. Fill them up again, Mr. Cohan."

Mr. Cohan obliged. The last drops came out of the second bottle of Irish as he was filling the glasses, and he had to open a third one.

Professor Thott said: "As a matter of fact, there's something in what the Captain says, though not quite for that reason. It's a question of liquefaction, of the body not being able to absorb any more liquid in any form. Fix me another Manhattan, will you, Mr. Cohan?"

"A Manhattan?" said Ewaldt. "I am remembering them; they are good. You will please to make me one, also." He addressed McClintock with a pleasant smile. "This is not part of the contest, but an extra for pleasure. But you are correct, Mr. Professor; I shall relieve myself."

He started toward the toilet but was detained by a cry from McClintock: "Hey, no you don't! I seen that one pulled the time I drank against the three Stranahans in Chi."

"Why don't you both go?" said Thott, "with Patrolman Cohan to see there's no foul play. After all, he represents the law and can be trusted to be impartial."

As the trio disappeared through the door, he turned to Mr. Cohan: "I hate to say it, but I think your friend Dippie Louie is beginning to come apart along the seams."

"Don't you believe it, now," said Mr. Cohan. "No more than Finn MacCool did when he met the Scotch giant and his wife baked the stove lids in the cakes. That's just the way of him. Would you like to make a side bet now, that he won't have that Swede under the bar rail before he's done?"

"A dollar," said Thott, and they shook hands across the bar, as the three emerged to find the Manhattans and glasses of Irish lined up. Ewaldt disposed of his as rapidly as before, then picked up the Manhattan and began to sip it delicately. He turned to McClintock: "You are the very good drinker for an Irishman. I salute you, as you did. Hop, Eire!"

The Manhattan followed the whiskey. There seemed to be something slightly wrong with McClintock's throat as he accepted the toast. Patrolman Cohan took on an anxious look and Mr. Cohan an inquiring one, but Ewaldt merely indicated with a gesture that he wanted a refill on both glasses. McClintock gazed at his portion of whiskey with a kind of fearful fascination, swallowed once, and then began to sip it, with his Adam's apple moving rapidly. Ewaldt slid his down as before, and picked up the Manhattan. "These I pay for," he said.

McClintock said: "It was him that gave me the office, just like I'm telling you. I was in with a couple of right gees, too, jug-heisters, but . . . mark my words, friends, *crime does not pay.*"

"I never thought I'd live to see the day," said Patrolman Cohan. "A bottle and a half apiece. Louie, you're a credit to the race."

"That is very true," said Ewaldt. "After the Danes, the Poles are the best drinkers. Now we shall change to something else, since you have been making the first choice. Mr. Cohan, you have the Russian vodka?"

"No' for me," said McClintock. "No' for me." He looked at Thott solemnly, blinked his eyes twice, and said, "You're right, Perfessor. Need time for shock effec'. Think I'll sh— sit down for a minute before the next round."

He took four or five long steps to one of the tables and sat down heavily, staring straight before him. Ewaldt, on whom no effect was visible beyond a slight reddening of the nose, said: "Now I have won and it is to pay me."

"Not yet," said Patrolman Cohan. "He isn't out, just resting between rounds. He'll come back." His voice seemed to lack conviction.

"It's the most marvellous thing I've ever seen," said Thott, looking at Ewaldt with an awe tinged with envy. "I wish I had your capacity; it would be useful at class reunions."

"Ah, it's not for me to speak," said Mr. Cohan, pouring the vodka, into an ordinary shot glass this time. "But the way I was brought up, it's not healthy to be mixing your liquor like that."

"Tell me, Captain," said Thott, "how do you do it? Is there a special course of training, or something?"

Ewaldt downed his vodka. "It is only because I am Danish. In my country no one is be-drunken except foolish young men who go down the Herregade and have their shoes shined on Saturday night while they make calls to the girls that pass, but I am too old for that. But some Danes are better drinkers than others. We have in Denmark a story that the best are those who have from their forefathers one of the *ædelstanar* —how do you say it?—amethysts. Observe."

His hand went to the watch chain and the end came out of his vest pocket. Instead of penknife, key ring, or other make-weight, the chain ended in a large purplish stone with an old-fashioned gold setting.

"In the olden times, six hundred years ago," Ewaldt continued, "there were many of them. They were the protection against be-drunkenhood, to place in the bottom of the winecup, and most of them belonged to bishops, from which it is easy to see that the church is very sober."

Thott peered over the top of his glasses. "Interesting. It was a regular medieval idea; the word amethyst itself means antidrunkenness, you know. Did you get yours from a bishop?"

Ewaldt tucked his pocket piece away, and gave a little laugh. "No, this one is descended to me from Tycho Brahe, that was an astronomer and supposed to be a magician. But of course, it is all superstition, like his being a magician, and I do not believe it at all."

He turned to face McClintock, who had come back to the bar and was leaning one elbow on it as he stared at the stuffed owl. "How is it now, my friend? Shall we have one more little bit?"

"Gotta make thish score or I'm a creep," mumbled the collapsing champion of old Eire.

Patrolman Cohan looked at him sharply. "Now, listen, Louie," he said. "You ain't making scores—"

He was interrupted by a kind of strangled sound from Ewaldt, and the others turned to look at the Captain, who seemed in the throes of a revolution. A fine perspiration had broken out on his forehead, and the network of lines had run together into a kind of mottling. *"Bevare!"* he uttered as they watched, and one foot came up to feel for the bar rail. He missed it, and without its support, the leg seemed to have no more stiffness than a rubber band. Captain Ewaldt took a heavy list to starboard, clutched once at the edge of the bar, missed that too, and came down hard on the floor.

As Thott and Patrolman Cohan bent to pick him up, Dippie Louie McClintock suddenly gripped the arm of the latter.

"Julius!" he wailed, and Thott saw a big tear come out on his cheek. "You should have stopped me! You know that when I drink, I just can't resist the temptation! Don't tell anyone that I did it, will you, or I'll lose my job at the fish market and won't be able to give lectures on crime any more. Here, take it, and give it back to him."

He held out the amethyst, detached from its chain, thrust it into Patrolman Cohan's hand, then in his turn swayed, missed a grab at the bar, and joined Ewaldt on the floor.

"I get a dollar," said Mr. Cohan. "The Swede is under the bar rail."

HERE, PUTZI!

The brass-blonde sitting at the table looked up as the muscular young man entered Gavagan's. "Hello, Mr. Jeffers," she said.

The muscular young man said: "Hello, Mrs. Jonas. A brew please, Mr. Cohan." He turned his head and spoke over his shoulder from his place at the bar: "Waiting for the Professor?"

"That's right. He's probably forgotten that he made a date with me and is back in the book stacks at the college library, with half a dozen books spread on the floor around him, chasing references. The way that man behaves!"

Mr. Cohan combed the excess head off the top of Jeffers' beer with a celluloid stick and slid the glass across the counter. The door of the ladies' room opened behind him. From it emerged a massive female of approximately forty-five, both as to age and waistline, with a floppy hat and a gold pince-nez perched in the center of a somewhat belligerent countenance. In one hand she held a suitcase; in the other a lower, fatter bag, with a tarpaulin cover. The woman sat down at the table next to Mrs. Jonas and spoke: "Some Tokay, please. I will see the bottle."

Mr. Cohan came around the bar and set a glass in front of her, and exhibited the bottle, at which she peered after adjusting her pince-nez. "Six *puttonos;* that is good. You shall pour."

As Mr. Cohan extracted the cork with a pop, the Amazon turned to Mrs. Jonas. "Troubles with a man you may have," she said, "but anybody that says mine are not worse is a ignoramus."

"Sssh," said Mrs. Jonas. "You'll frighten Mr. Jeffers off women for life, and he's one of the few eligible bachelors around. I'm keeping him for my second string."

"Oh, I don't know—" began Mr. Jeffers. The large woman swung toward Mr. Cohan with the ponderousness of a drawbridge. "You shall tell her how much trouble I have with my man, my Putzi," she said, firmly.

Mr. Cohan's face took on a firmness equal to her own. "Now look here, Mrs. Vacarescu," he said, "this is a free country, and if you want to talk about your own troubles, I cannot prevent you. But I will not talk about such things in Gavagan's, by God, because in the first place it's bad for business; and in the second, Father McConaghy will be making me do penance. And I'm warning you that your man can come in here and drink his beer like anyone else, but dogs we will not have in Gavagan's."

Mrs. Vacarescu did not appear to be daunted. "I will pay for a bottle of Tokay for him also," she said, drinking heartily. "But it is most strongly important that he does not go out from here while it is still dark. And I know it is here he will come, like always on nights when the Sängerbund is not meeting."

Mr. Jeffers said: "I don't understand all this, but why shouldn't your husband go out of Gavagan's while it's dark? He can't very well stay all night, can he?"

Mrs. Vacarescu favored him with a glance of soul-searing scorn, "Because he is mine Putzi, and this time he is not to spoil my vacation, like always. By night he goes out of here, he is running around with some bitch—"

Mrs. Jonas gave a little gasp; Mr. Jeffers cleared his throat.

"—And next morning I got trouble with him again." Mrs. Vacarescu took another drink of Tokay and looked at her hearers. Mr. Cohan came round the end of the bar with the second bottle of Tokay and set it down beside her. "That will be four dollars and twenty cents," he said.

Mrs. Vacarescu snapped open her purse. "You will also give something to this so-beautiful lady," she said.

"I don't think—" began Mrs. Jonas, in a rather chilly voice.

"Ach, you are thinking I am not a lady," said Mrs. Vacarescu, "because of what I say, not so? But mine friend Mr. Cohan, he will tell you, it is true, and I am not making just bad words."

"We got a good class of trade in Gavagan's," said Mr. Cohan.

Mrs. Jonas said: "I don't believe I quite understand."

Mrs. Vacarescu produced a handkerchief smelling powerfully of patchouli, with which she dabbed at one eye, then the other.

It is mine Putzi [she said]. I will tell you so you understand. Never was such a man as Putzi when I knew him the first time in Budapest; strong and handsome and tall like a tree. We have picnics together on the island by Budapest on Sunday in summer, and we are eating radishes and drinking lager beer, and he is telling me stories and we are picking flowers. He would promise me everything, even a castle in Transylvania, where he comes from, and my mother says he is a good young man and I should marry him. But he will not be married by a priest; he has to have the *Amtmann* for it, like the peace justice here. My mother does not like that, she says a wedding by the *Amtmann* is a no-good, and if Putzi will not marry me by the priest, I should not marry him at all.

But it is love. [Mrs. Vacarescu sighed, pressed one hand to an ample bosom, and drank again.] So one day I run away with Putzi and we get married by the *Amtmann*, like he says. At first everything is fine, only we are not having picnics no more, because he says he has to concentrate on Sunday afternoons. But all he does is drink beer and look out of the window. And at night he is so funny, always walking back and forth in the room, and I cannot get him to go over to my mother's house for a piece of strudel and a cup of coffee.

And that is only the beginning. You know how it is, lady [she gestured to Mrs. Jonas]; those men will promise you everything till they get what they want, and then where are you? It gets to be like that with Putzi. When I ask where is my castle in Transylvania, he takes me by the arm and shoves me into the kitchen and says that is my castle. You got no idea of the things that man does. He don't like the sausages we have for dinner, bang on the floor goes the sausages. He don't like some of my friends that come in for a piece of strudel at night, he says, "Get those dopes out of here before they eat up all the money I make!" Right in front of them, too. When I tell him they are my friends and it is none of his business, he puts on his hat and goes right out the door and that is the last I see of him all night.

In the morning he comes in as sweet like Christmas cake, and he can't do enough for me, so I know something is wrong, like it always is when your man tries to make up to you more than he has to. So I think maybe he is chasing some woman, and the next time some of my friends are there and he walks out like that and stays all night, I start asking people, have they seen what Putzi is up to. The most I can find out is that he goes to Kettler's *Bierstube* and drinks beer there half the night and then he goes away again. And every time in the morning he is still half drunk but trying to make up to me like anything.

He does this once a week for a couple of months till I cannot stand it. So one night I think I will lock the door on him and let the loafer, the bum, stay outside when he gets back.

I went out to lock the door, but when I get by the hall out, here is a dachshund. It is fat and a good dog. Also, even if I have not seen this dachshund before, I can see it likes me, because it climbs up on its hind legs, so, and tries to lick my hand, and when I try to put it out again, it only comes back.

So I said, what can I do if it wants to be my dachshund, maybe it will be better company than Putzi. I found me an old piece of rug for it to sleep on, and gave it some water to drink and a piece of the pig's knuckles that was left over from dinner, and then I went back and locked the door.

But when I wake up in the morning, there is that drunken ninnyhammer of a husband of mine right in the bed, snoring like he was running a steam-engine. This I could not understand because the door is not the kind that just locks, but it has a bolt, and the windows we always close, because the night air is so unhealthy. My mother knew a woman that died of it once, in Szeged.

And when I get out in the kitchen, there is no dachshund. The only thing I can think of is that when my man came home, he kicked it out, so I asked the big lummox about it when he got up. I should have known better, maybe, because Putzi is like that in the morning, he could bite the head off a horse unless he wants to start talking himself. Anyway, all he said to me was I should shut my big mouth.

I don't care who it is, they can't talk to me like that. [Mrs. Vacarescu emitted an audible hiccup and drowned it in more Tokay.] So I told him to shut his goddam trap himself because I'm a lady. Then we had an argument that lasted all day, and Putzi slams the door and says he won't come back till he pleases. Not till he had his supper, though—hah! You can bet he gets his belly full first.

So I sat down with my sewing, and I said to

myself, I'll fix him this time, and when it got real late, I went around to lock all the windows real good and bolt the door, only when I got out in front, here was this dachshund again. Only this time it had another dachshund with it and anyone can see the other dachshund is a bitch. My dachshund tried to bring the other one in with it, but the other one wouldn't come, so I took it in like before and gave it something to eat, and would you believe it? In the morning there was Putzi again and the dachshund was gone.

Then I began to think what must have happened. Like I told you, my man comes from Transylvania. You know, in that part of the old country they got people that turn themselves into wolves at night and run all around. Well, Putzi is one of them, that's why he wouldn't be married by no priest, only he don't turn into no wolf, he turns into a dachshund. And when Putzi is a man, he has lousy bad manners, but when he is a dog, ach, he has manners like an archduke!

It wasn't no use asking him how he done it, because he'd only get mad and start yelling at me. But how he turns from a dog into a man, I do know because of an accident. It is a week after the last time and I was drinking a little schnapps in the evening and I woke up early in the morning, just before sunlight, and here was Putzi the dog scratching at the door to get out. I let him out just as it got light—and right away here was Putzi, my man, red in the eyes and mad enough to chew the paper off the wall. And that other dachshund, the bitch, was just across the street.

So then I know that if sunlight hits him when he is Putzi the dog, he turns back into a man, but also I find out something not so good, that Putzi the dog is chasing around with this bitch. I will not have my man doing that, even if she is not human, but what can you do? I cannot make him stay in every night, he wouldn't do that. So I think maybe if we can get away from Budapest, the change don't work any more. I went to my father, he owns some *Schleppdampfern*—what do you call them?—pugs, on the river, and a little piece of money, and I tell him we have to come to America.

But when we got here, things were the same, only worse. The trouble I have with that man! All he does is eat, eat, eat, and kick when the food doesn't come fast enough, and in the evening he goes out to the Deutscher Sängerbund and drinks beer and sings songs with a lot of Schwobs half the night. He doesn't turn into no dachshund no more, and I am wishing he did until one night somebody from the Sängerbund brings them all over here to Gavagan's after the *Sängerfest*. Then it is just like he used to go to Kettler's *Bierstube*. The first thing I know it is after midnight and I am sitting waiting for my man to come home when something scratches at the door, and it is Putzi the dog, so good, so gentle.

So now I am going on my vacation and I don't want him to spoil it by being like Putzi the man. And always he comes here when the Sängerbund is not meeting and changes into a dog again and goes chasing bitches. But this time, no. I will take him with me in this bag, so the sun does not get at him.

Mrs. Vacarescu poured the last drops from her bottle of Tokay. It tipped over as she set it back on the table and it rolled to the floor with a bump, for at that moment the door swung open as though under the touch of a heavy hand. There appeared to be nobody there, but before Mr. Cohan could come round the bar to close it, a small and very fat dachshund bounded in, wagging his tail so vigorously that his whole rear end was agitated, and hurled himself on Mrs. Vacarescu.

"Here, Putzi!" she called, and stripped back the

tarpaulin on the smaller bag. The little dog jumped in and seated himself contentedly. Mrs. Vacarescu replaced the tarpaulin and strode heavily out of Gavagan's.

MORE THAN SKIN DEEP

Mr. Jeffers turned around. "Hello, Mrs. Jonas," he said. "You're looking so beautiful tonight, I wouldn't mind buying you a drink."

"Thank you," said the brass-blonde, peering into the back of the room. "Isn't Alvin here yet? Then you can. There's absolutely nothing I need more than a drink. A Presidente, please."

She placed one foot on the rail. "Now, now, Mrs. Jonas," said the bartender. "The most beautiful woman in the place you may be, and a Presidente you may have, but you know the rule of Gavagan's. This is a respectable place, and we have tables for ladies."

"Oh, all right," said the brass-blonde. "Come on over and join me, Paul. I feel depressed and need company."

"What's the difficulty?" asked Jeffers, pulling out a chair for her. "The last dregs of a hangover or complications in your love life?"

"Not in mine, but some friends of mine. Do you know the Stewarts? Andy used to come in here a lot. He's that advertising man with Crackerjack and Whiffenpoof or something like that; I can never keep track of those names; and they change them every week, anyway."

Jeffers frowned. "I know him, yes. He's the big, solid chap who looks like a movie star. But I don't think I ever met his wife. What's happened to them?"

"They're getting a divorce," said Mrs. Jonas. "At least Betty-Jo is, and I don't see what else she can do, because he's just walked out on her and is living with a lady wrestler. It's a shame, too, because she was so devoted to him; and Mrs.—the woman who wrote me about it—says she still is and wants him back. But I don't understand it, because he was perfectly crazy about her, too, and would hardly let her out of his sight before he went out there to take over the Chicago office of the agency. I wonder what could have happened. But I guess we never do understand what makes people fall in love with each other, or out of it either. Nobody knew what Andy Stewart saw in Betty-Jo in the first place. She dressed like something that came out of a rag bag; and she can't cook; and though she's quite nice, she's one of the most uninteresting people I ever met. They were married awfully quickly. That's probably why you didn't get to know her."

"If I had, I'd probably have thought she was wonderful, too," said Jeffers philosophically, sipping his beer. "With a low-cut dress and a couple of hours in a beauty parlor, any woman can make herself look like the Queen of Sheba these days."

"It helps," admitted Mrs. Jonas, patting her hairdo complacently. "In preparation for my date with Alvin tonight, I went to a new place, and I must say I think they did a good job on me. Not that it matters to you, but it was Mme. Lavoisin's, over on Arcade Street."

With a tinkling crash, a glass shattered on the floor behind them. Jeffers and Mrs. Jonas looked around to see a smallish girl in a grey dress, with hair pulled straight back from her forehead, just standing up as Mr. Cohan hurried to mop up the debris of a spilled drink.

"I'm dreadfully sorry," said the girl. "But I couldn't help overhearing what you said. About Mme. Lavoisin's. And you mustn't, you really mustn't, go there again. That is, if you're planning on a date with a man. Believe me."

"I really don't see why not," said Mrs. Jonas, with a touch of hauteur.

"Because that's what happened to Betty-Jo Stewart. I knew her, too." The girl laid a hand, which glittered with a diamond-studded wedding ring, on Mrs. Jonas' arm. "And I'm afraid it's going to happen to me."

"If you'll explain," said Mrs. Jonas.

"Yes," said Jeffers. "Won't you sit down and have a drink with us?"

"Can I have another Presidente?" said Mrs. Jonas. "If Alvin gets here late, he deserves to find me fried."

The grey girl drew her coat around her shoulders and sat down. "All right," she said. "A Whiskey Sour."

All right [she continued], I'll tell you. But you must promise never to breathe a word of it to a living soul. Both of you. Because that would be just as bad for me, if people found out and talked about it.

I'm Eloise Grady. I used to know Betty-Jo Stewart well, even before she was married. I even went to college with her, and it was just as you said. She's sweet and easy to get along with, but not very bright, and when looks were being passed around, someone forgot to tell her about it. In fact, the reason I got to know her so well was that we were the two plainest girls in the sorority house and never had any dates. No, [she addressed Jeffers] you needn't tell me how beautiful I really am. I know exactly where I stand. And why.

After we graduated, we both came here, but I didn't see so much of Betty-Jo for a while, and I couldn't have been more surprised when I got an invitation to her wedding. I thought she must have picked up some old widower, who really wanted a nurse to take care of his children. But when I saw the wedding itself I found I could be more surprised than at getting the announcement. It was held at the home of his parents. Everything was dripping with money, and frightfully social. But the big surprise was Andy Stewart himself. He was about the last person in the world you'd expect to fall for an ugly duckling like Betty-Jo. And she hadn't changed into any swan, either. But he used to follow her around with his eyes, as though she were the most beautiful object on earth.

After they were married, she began inviting me to the house quite a bit, for dinner parties, or just to have a cocktail with her. I thought at first she wanted to do a little refined gloating over the catch she had made, but it wasn't that at all. She just wanted to talk, and she often seemed nervous in a way I couldn't understand. There wasn't any reason for it, either. Andy was as devoted to her as ever and gave her everything she wanted.

["Didn't woman's intuition help you out any?" asked Jeffers.]

Not at the time, and just for that crack, you can buy me another Whiskey Sour [said Eloise Grady]. The only time they even had anything approaching a disagreement was during that first winter of their marriage, when he wanted to take her to Florida for a couple of weeks and she wanted to stay home. She won, of course. It seemed to make her more nervous than usual. She had me over for cocktails the next day and made me talk to her for a long time. All about being a business girl. You see, I'd just about made up my mind to live alone and like it then. All the dates I got were from men off the bottom of the deck. But Betty-Jo wouldn't tell me what was bothering her.

And she just stayed home. Andy wanted to go to the ski carnival at Lake Placid, and she let him go alone, finally. And the next summer, when he wanted to take a house at Southport for a couple of months, weekending himself, she wouldn't do that either. It got to be a standing joke about her being such a town mouse. There just wasn't anything else until the October party.

I call it the October party, because it was important to me. It was at it I met Walter—my husband, Walter Grady. Do you believe in love at first sight, Mrs.—did you tell me your name? —Mrs. Jonas? I never did, but the first time I met Walter I knew he was the man I wanted to marry. I also knew I didn't have a chance. He came with that Reinschloss girl, the blonde. Did you ever meet her? She won a beauty contest later and went to Hollywood as "The Society Star." And it was obvious that she wanted him, too.

I may have hinted something about it that night—I don't know. But anyway it couldn't have been more than a day or two later, when I was having lunch with Betty-Jo, that I really let myself go on the subject. We had a couple of cocktails before lunch and a brandy afterward, and I suppose it broke both of us down a little. I know I did tell her I'd given up on live alone and like it. If I could have Walter I wouldn't care for another thing in the world. And it's true—it's true. I still feel that way. Only—

[Eloise Grady drank and looked at the other two.]

I remember her looking at me hard and then saying very quietly, as though she hadn't had anything to drink at all: "Do you really want him enough to go through what I have?"

"What do you mean?" I asked her.

"Oh—missing out on trips, and—a lot of things."

I still didn't quite understand, but I was too wrought up to be curious. I just said: "Yes, I want him that much."

"All right," she said, "the Barnards are giving a dinner party next week, and I know Walter's coming. I'll get them to ask you. But before you go, be sure to go to Mme. Lavoisin's in the afternoon and have a beauty treatment. Tell her I sent you, and it's a date with a man."

I felt let down. You know, as though I'd been expecting to take a tremendous dive, and it turned out to be only a step down to the water. But I did it. I accepted the invitation when it came, and I went to Mme. Lavoisin's. I can't say I was impressed by the place when I went in.

"What was the matter with it?" asked Mrs. Jonas. "It looked all right to me."

"Didn't you get the impression that the place was somewhat shabby? When you look directly at anything, it's clean enough and nice enough, but you always feel that there's something just at the edge of what you're looking at that isn't quite right."

"Well, sort of, when I first went in," admitted Mrs. Jonas. "And I didn't like that receptionist."

"The one with the big black cat sitting on the chair beside her?" said Eloise Grady. She turned to Jeffers. "She's nicely dressed and everything, but she has buck teeth."

"Yes," said Mrs. Jonas, "and the two end ones, right here, kind of pointed. You'd think that a girl working in a beauty parlor like that would get her teeth fixed up. I want another Presidente."

Eloise Grady gave a little sigh.

> Well, I don't have to tell you [she went on]. Or about Mme. Lavoisin herself. She has very black hair and looks as though she were about thirty when you first see her, and then you make up your mind that she's really much older, only just well turned out. The receptionist said she only took people by previous appointment, but I said I wanted a treatment that afternoon, and it was urgent, and Betty-Jo Stewart sent me.
>
> She came out herself. "Is it a question of—meeting a man?" she asked.
>
> I thought that was queer, but I said yes, and and she took me into one of the booths herself. There wasn't anything extraordinary about the treatment, except that right in the middle of it a pin in her dress scratched me on the arm, so it bled a little.
>
> ["Why, that's what happened to me, too!" said Mrs. Jonas. "Only I went there by appointment."]
>
> Yes, I know [said Eloise Grady]. That's why I said—oh, well, after she finished with my hair, she said: "I think you will find that satisfactory. If the treatment gives the results you hope for

and I expect, you had better come back. You will need more treatments."

I will say it gave me results even beyond what I could have hoped. I was a little late at the Barnards. Walter was already there with the Reinschloss girl, and they were talking together over cocktails. He turned around casually to say hello. Then I heard him give a sort of little gasp and do a quick double-take on me, I went on with the introductions, and a couple of minutes later, he dropped whatever he was doing and came and sat by me. It was wonderful. It was like—magic. He hardly looked at anyone else or talked to anyone else all evening long. The Reinschloss girl was furious. Walter called up the next morning and wanted to take me to the ice carnival.

Naturally, I went to Mme. Lavoisin's before going with him. She was very discreet and didn't ask any questions when I said I had another date with the same man. Just gave me a treatment like before, and when she got through, said: "My special customers usually come back." I did keep coming back, too, every time I had a date with Walter, which got to be more and more frequently. About six weeks later, he asked me to marry him.

I told Mme. Lavoisin about it and that I wouldn't be in for a while, because Walter wanted to spend our honeymoon on a six weeks' cruise around the Caribbean. At the same time I said I was sure that her beauty treatments were responsible for everything and thanked her and gave her a rather large tip. Instead of being pleased, she looked worried. "My treatment will last for three weeks, perhaps," she said. "But after that—" and I couldn't get anything more out of her. But then I began to worry, I couldn't tell about what. I understood how Betty-Jo felt, and why she had talked to me so much. But I couldn't tell anybody about it, because there wasn't anything to tell, really. But I did persuade Walter to make it only a two-week honeymoon.

After we got back, I kept telling myself that this was absurd, that nothing could make that much difference. So one time, I didn't go to Mme. Lavoisin's for quite three weeks. Toward the end of it Walter kept asking me if I were ill, and then he'd start looking at me in the strangest way. Till I went back. When I was in the chair, Mme. Lavoisin didn't say anything but: "You mustn't neglect your looks like that, my dear. Men always like to have their wives look as nice as they did before they were married." So I kept going back.

The next thing was Betty-Jo's birthday party. It was a big party. After dinner, over the coffee, Andy got up and made a little speech. He said he'd been saving this as a surprise, but this was a farewell party as well as a birthday party. The agency had placed him in charge of the Chicago office. But before he went out to take over, they had given him four months' leave. And he'd shared his wife with all of us for so long that he was going to have her all to himself for a while. So he had arranged for them to spend the time in a cabin in Tahiti.

He laid the tickets beside Betty-Jo's plate. Everyone applauded, but she looked so white we all thought she was going to faint. I was the only one at the table who understood why. And I'm one of the few people who understands what's happened to them now. And I'm worried myself, because Walter is talking about taking a trip to Europe. You see?

The bus boy came over to the table. "It's Professor Thott on the phone," he said. "He says he's awful sorry he's late, but there was a meeting of the trustees at the college, and he'll be right over, and do you want to talk to him?"

"No," said Mrs. Jonas. "Not now. Tell him I'm very

sorry, too, but I wasn't feeling well and decided to go home this evening. I'll see him later."

She got up. "Thank you," she said to Eloise Grady, and went out.

BEASTS OF BOURBON

Mr. Gross leaned about two hundred of his pounds on the edge of the bar, so that part of him bulged over it, and said: "Mr. Co-*han,* I feel like variety this evening. How about a Yellow Rattler?"

The tall, saturnine-looking man said: "You better be careful. It's the queer drinks like that that end you up with the d.t.'s."

"Not no more than the rest," said the bartender, mixing away. "It's all how you take them. Funny that you would be mentioning d.t.'s along with a Yellow Rattler, now, Mr. Willison. The very last one I mixed in this bar was for that Mr. Van Nest, the poor young felly. The animals was after him, he said, and he needed a drink. But he acted sober when he came in here. As long as a man can stand up and behave himself he can have a drink in Gavagan's."

"Ah, it's a shame when a man has to take so much liquor he gets d.t.'s," said Gross. "I got a nephew knew a man like that once. He cut off one of his own toes with a butcher-knife, saying it was a snake trying to bite him. But he was one of them solitary drinkers."

"Campbell Van Nest wasn't a solitary drinker," said Willison. "Just a solitary guy. Though he had to be after his animals started coming alive on him."

"Yuh?" said Mr. Witherwax, almost choking on the olive from his Martini. "What animals? How did they come alive?"

"The animals out of his d.t.'s," said Willison. "I saw them. So did you, didn't you, Mr. Cohan?"

"Never a one," said Mr. Cohan, swabbing the bar. "That was why he came here, because they would not follow him into Gavagan's. But there's plenty would swear on the blessed sacraments they did see them. Like Patrolman Krevitz, that me brother Julius says is one of the steadiest men on the force, and old man Webster in the tailor shop. Not to be mentioning yourself, Mr. Willison."

"You say the animals from his d.t.'s came alive?" said Witherwax. "I'd like to hear about this. I was just reading in a book about something like that. They call it materialization."

"Well, I don't know," said Willison. "The few of us who knew him have always rather kept it quiet . . ."

"You can tell them," said Mr. Cohan. "No harm to anybody now the poor young felly is dead and gone, and his animals with him."

"Mmm. I suppose you're right," said Willison. "Well—fill me up another rye and water, Mr. Cohan, and let's see. I want to get this straight."

Campbell Van Nest [said Willison] was one of of those natural-born square pegs, I guess. Nice-looking chap, nothing remarkable about him in any way, but it was as though he and the world had made an agreement not to get along together. Everything he tried went wrong somehow. Not in a spectacular way, but a little off the beam, so he was always being disappointed.

He travelled in toys. It will give you an idea of what I mean about the disappointments, when I tell you that although he was good at it and made plenty of money, he didn't like the life, rushing around and meeting people and going to conventions. He liked to stay home and read —a lot of things like astrology and Oriental lore. The part of the toy business that really interested him was designing toy animals—woolly pandas that would walk, and so on. But there isn't much of a full-time job in designing, so they'd only let him do it a week or so at a time, and then send him out on the road again.

He was always falling in love, too; not that he

was a woman-chaser. He'd get into real deep, off-the-end-of-the-dock love with some girl, who always turned him down in the end. You've heard of people being hard-boiled? Well, I would say Campbell Van Nest was too soft-boiled. It broke him all up when one of these girls said no; and because it was the way he learned to do things from other salesmen, he'd go off on a two-day binge.

As near as I can make out, this business started with a day when everything went wrong at once. Van's latest girl threw him down; somebody got into his car and stole all the accessories; and a store to which he had made a big sale went broke, so he lost the commission. He went off on a bender that made the rest of them look like tea parties. It lasted three days; and the worst of it was that it wasn't public, either. He just kept buying bottle after bottle of whiskey and sat there in his room, loading up on it and reading these Oriental books. His landlady called me up on the third day; and I went up there and found the place a shambles, with bottles and books mixed up together all over the floor.

I got him into bed and picked up some of the things, and while I was doing it I noticed that Van hadn't been merely reading while he was on this particular toot. The place was filled with papers on which he had apparently been sketching designs for new animal toys, and some of them would nearly turn your stomach to see.

[Mr. Gross said: "Just like my cousin Louie, the time he stole all them ants." Willison gave him a glance of withering firmness and went on.]

That was all I could do at the time, so I left. The next part of the story comes from Van himself. When he came to, about noon the next day, this thing was sitting on the foot of his bed. I only got a glance at it later, but it looked like some kind of monkey, only bigger, with eyes like saucers and enormously long fingers. I don't know whether it resembled any of the designs

Van had made while he was pie-eyed or not. It had what you might call an evil expression.

A stocky pug-nosed man with glasses, who had been consulting a Daiquiri, spoke up: "I think that would be the spectral tarsier."

"Yes?" said Willison, facing him. "Are they blue?"

"I know of one that was," said the stocky man. "But that . . . Sorry to interrupt your story, old man. There may be a connection. Go on."

Van had never had d.t.'s before [Willison continued], and his first idea was that this was something that had escaped from a zoo. But with his hangover and all, he didn't like the idea of trying to capture it. An animal like that can give you a nasty bite. So he got himself a Bromo-Seltzer and some clothes, figuring that when he was outside, he'd call up the zoo or the S.P.C.A. and have it taken away. This spectral what-is-it just sat there quietly on the foot of the bed, following Van with its eyes.

It was so quiet that he thought he'd slip out for a cup of coffee before phoning. But when he opened the door, with his reflexes not under very good control, the thing leaped down and was through it like a flash. Van expected it to run. It didn't; it came hopping along down the hall and then down the stairs, always keeping about the same distance behind him. Every time he turned around toward it, it would retreat, and then follow him again as soon as he went on. It seemed attached to him.

That made Van think—as well as he could think through the fumes of his hangover—that he might be having a case of heebie-jeebies and not really seeing this thing at all. So he decided to ignore it and started down the street. Then he began to notice other people when he passed them, they'd do a double-take and give a grunt or a squeak or something; and when he looked over his shoulder, there the thing was, coming along behind him; and other people seemed to be seeing it too. He began to walk faster and faster. Pretty soon he passed a girl who was going in the same direction he was; and when the animal hopped past her feet, she looked down at it and let out a good loud shriek. That did for what was left of poor Van's nerves, and he started to run.

You know how it is when anyone runs down the street. People look to see who's chasing who, and with a little encouragement, they'll join in. This time they had lots of encouragment, with that monster coming along behind Van in big jumps. Some yelled: "It's after him!" and, in about half a minute, he had twenty or thirty helpful citizens rolling along behind.

Sheer force of habit, he said later, brought him here to Gavagan's, and he dived in, to get away from all those people and that animal. You remember the day, Mr. Cohan?

"Indeed and I do," said the bartender. "The poor felly came through the door there, like one of them fancy ice-skaters you see in the show, and stood hanging onto the bar. 'It's brandy you need, my lad,' I said, and poured one for him while the rest of them people come milling around, some of them inside and some out, after this animal. But no animal did they see, because none had come in with him. All they saw was Mr. Van Nest having a drink of brandy and his hand shaking. Some of them said it got away over the roofs; but you're telling me that's not true now, aren't you, Mr. Willison?"

Another rye and soda [said Willison]. No, it certainly isn't true. The thing just disappeared. A couple of the people who had followed came in to ask Van about it, and they got to talking. Well, there's only one way you can conduct a conversation in a bar—that is, with a drink in your hand. Presently Van was drinking a Yellow Rattler and feeling better, and then they began treating each other and he felt better still, and the first thing he knew it was evening, and he'd spent the afternoon in here.

Now I won't say he was really drunk, not like he had been the day before; and besides, Mr. Cohan wouldn't permit it. But you can't work all day on brandy and Yellow Rattlers and nothing to eat without getting a little high. What did you say? Oh, he had a roast pork sandwich. So he had a roast pork sandwich and a couple more drinks, and went home and had a couple of nightcaps; and then I guess he was a little more than high. So he tumbled into bed; it was late when he got there.

When he came to, toward noon the next day, this spectral monkey-thing was there again. And this time there was another monster with it, a thing like a lizard with a long tail and thin fingers and something that looked like a big ruff around its neck, as you sometimes see in old ancestor portraits. It was a dark maroon red.

"*Chlemydosaurus kingi*, the frilled lizard," said the pug-nosed man, "in an interesting chromatic variation."

"You know about it?" asked Willison.

"Yes. My name's Tobolka. I'm a biologist." He held out his hand. "May I buy you another?"

Thanks, I will have one [said Willison]. I don't want you to get the idea that Van was stupid. He could put two and two together, even with the bells ringing in his head; and he was perfectly certain that if he got out on the street again those two horrors would be right with him. So he called me up and asked me to come over.

By the time I got there, he was working on a pint he had sent out for to steady his nerves. The animals were there all right, both of them. I saw them. They were about so big. Every time I tried to approach one, it was out of reach like a flash; and then it would settle down and look at Van. He seemed depressed.

"I can't understand what makes this happen," he kept saying.

I told him about putting him to bed a couple of nights before and the shape I'd found the room in, with the books and weird animal drawings scattered around. "What kind of Hindu magic have you got mixed up with?" I asked him.

That made him more depressed than ever. "That's just the trouble," he said. "I haven't any idea. A good many of these books deal with the occult and materialization phenomena in one form or another, but I'm afraid I had rather a lot to drink that day, and I don't know what I tried to do."

We agreed that the only sensible thing to do was to reverse the process, so I went out and got something to eat on a tray; and then we sat down with his books. Those two animals watched us all the time. I couldn't make head or tail of what I was reading, and he couldn't seem to find anything that was of the least use. About five o'clock I gave up and went home, arranging for dinner to be sent up to him. The only thing we were hopeful about was that the animals might go away during the night. He had finished the pint, but that wasn't anything to a fellow of Van's capacity, and you could call him reasonably sober.

But he called up the next morning to say that they were still there on the foot of his bed, staring at him. What was worse, the office was calling. They didn't mind his staying out a couple of days, but this made five now, and he was due for a trip through the Middle West. The idea of going out on a sales trip with those two beasts mixed up with his samples didn't strike him as the way to win friends and influence people.

I went over after dinner, and we talked the whole thing upside and down. Finally, I said: "Look here. There are two parts of this business that may be connected. Aren't those two some of the animals you drew while you were having that toot?"

He dug out the drawings; and although his hand had been pretty unsteady when he made them, this frilled lizard and spectral monkey were recognizable.

"All right," I said. "You remember the first one disappeared when you went into Gavagan's? Now I'll get a taxi and shoot you over there quick; and while you're gone, I'll destroy these drawings."

He said it seemed far-fetched, but couldn't think of anything better; and the second day of consulting his books hadn't turned up anything, so he agreed. I had the cab waiting with its engine running when he came dashing downstairs with the two monsters after him. The lizard one rode on top. I went back up and dug out every one of those drawings he'd made and burned them, for good measure adding some designs he'd made for toys that didn't look like monsters at all.

Then I came over here. It seems quite a few people had seen Van with his monsters—not as many as the first time but enough to make a good deal of conversation—so that practically everybody in the place was buying Van a drink and trying to get him to talk about it. You can imagine what happened. He was as boiled as a fifteen-minute egg by the time I got him out of here, and next morning he had three pets instead of two.

Only it was worse this time. The new one didn't look like anything I remembered seeing in the drawings; it didn't look like anything I ever saw; and Dr. Tobolka, I don't think it looked like anything you ever saw. It looked like an enormous centipede, with the head of a cat. Van called me up and I went over again and saw it. The office had been after him again, and he told them he was sick. I stayed with him a while, trying to work out something more from the books; but while I was out getting something to eat, he got so he couldn't take the stares of the three animals any more, summoned a taxi by telephone, and was off here to Gavagan's again. It was the only place where he felt safe.

["The poor felly said he would clean the cuspidors if he could only stay here in a blanket on the floor," said Mr. Cohan. "I put it up to Gavagan myself, but he wouldn't hear a word of it."]

I hadn't heard from him [continued Willison], but I worked my way into his place on maybe the fifth day after it started. The office had sent around a basket of fruit and then one of flowers by a special messenger. I had to knock four or five times before he let me in and then it was with a suspicious look, peeking around the corner of the door. He hadn't shaved in God knows when; and there was a fifth in his hand, about three-quarters empty. By that time there were six of these animals in the room, all of them but the first two looking as though they had been put together out of spare parts of real animals and beasts from a child's picture book. I couldn't get near any of them; but I was spared the trouble, because Van waved the bottle at me, said: "See?" took a swig, and fell down across the bed, with all those incredible creatures looking at him. They didn't eat; they didn't do anything but just jostle each other and look.

He collapsed across the bed, and I looked at him and thought. He was obviously on the way out in some direction; and if I could do anything to help him, I figured it would be pure gain. There were parts of an evening newspaper strewn around the place, so I picked them up and found in them the ad for a Caribbean cruise. I called the line, the ship was sailing in three-quarters of an hour, and fortunately they had a vacant cabin, since there had been a cancellation. I got him into a cab and took him down to the pier and poured him aboard; and I've always been sorry, because the ship turned out to be the *Trinidad Castle*.

"That's the one that was lost?" inquired Witherwax.

"Correct," said Willison. "Ran on a reef in the Bahamas during a hurricane and went down with everybody on board."

"I doubt it," suddenly said the stocky little man who had described himself as Tobolka.

"I beg your pardon," said Willison, with some disfavor.

"I beg yours. No offense meant, old man. I wasn't questioning your word, merely the accuracy of your data. When you mentioned a blue spectral tarsier, I said there might be a connection with a case I know of; now I'm certain of it. Your friend Van Nest did not go down on the *Trinidad Castle*. If Mr. Cohan will kindly provide me with another Daiquiri, I'll explain."

> [He turned round with a gesture.] Gentlemen, the story has not been broadcast outside the scientific world for much the same reasons that persuaded Mr. Willison to keep it quiet. I am a biologist and have been rather closely associated with several members of the Harvard Marine Life expedition to the Bahamas. You may or may not know that its purpose was to collect specimens of marine life on Jackson Key. This is rather a miserable little sandpit off Great Abaco Island, but it does have peculiarly interesting forms of minor marine fauna.
>
> You may have seen photographs of the expedition at work. If you have, the center of the picture was almost certainly occupied by a young lady clad in shorts and performing some scientific task. She is blonde and extremely photogenic, and her name is Cornelia Hartwig.
>
> The morning after the *Trinidad Castle* disaster, she found a survivor of that ship who had floated into the surf of Jackson Key on a grating. I think there can be very little doubt that it was your friend Van Nest, though he gave his name as Campbell. He was not in good condition when discovered, though not in serious danger. Restor-

atives were applied, but there could be no question of sending him to the mainland at once, because the expedition's supply ship made only periodic visits and neither of the two small motorboats was adequate.

My friend Professor Rousseau says that, when the young man recovered consciousness and was informed of this, he did not appear to object. He was looking at Cornelia Hartwig, and with an almost equal intensity she was looking at him. I should perhaps explain about her. She is a highly competent biologist but, like your friend Van Nest, may be described as always falling in love. On field expeditions like the one to Jackson Key, it is her usual habit to select one of the older and more thoroughly married members of the scientific staff; and this has caused some trouble in the past. In fact, the members of the expedition were waiting with some apprehension to see who would be the victim on this occasion; and it was with relief that they observed her spending the entire day with the castaway. I cannot imagine what they found in common to talk about, but Professor Rousseau says they had no difficulty.

In the evening, when Campbell, or rather Van Nest, was able to be up and about and had eaten something, Cornelia took him to the opposite side of the island from the camp, where there were some palm trees, to look for ghost crabs by the light of the full moon. I don't know whether they discovered any ghost crabs; but as they sat there under the palms, the extraordinary series of animals you describe appeared as if from nowhere and formed a circle around them at a respectful distance, including a blue spectral tarsier and a frilled lizard of a rich maroon color.

There is no doubt that Cornelia was enchanted. At the sight of so many species unknown to science, I would have been myself. The couple did not return to camp until long after all the rest were in bed. When Cornelia told her story in the morning, it was received with a certain amount of skepticism and even of merriment, by the other members of the expedition. I am not surprised. The behavior of Van Nest's animals at Jackson Key was somewhat different than that you describe in the city. Not one of them was visible that morning. They had disappeared with the night.

This reception of her story irritated Cornelia; and, on the following evening, she persuaded Professor Rousseau himself to accompany them to the palm trees. He says the animals appeared to come out of the undergrowth and their description tallied with that you gave, Mr. Willison. He threw a flashlight on them and dispelled any idea that they were hallucinations, for they had solidity; but all his efforts to collect a specimen failed because of their agility.

After this, Cornelia and Van Nest went to the palm grove every evening, often taking along a sketch pad and a flash; and she produced some remarkable drawings. The pair rather rudely discouraged efforts of other members of the expedition to go with them and seemed so much in love with each other that everyone was content to leave them in privacy. However Professor Rousseau observed that after about three weeks Cornelia—whose daytime work suffered severely by the amount of time she spent out at night—appeared to be growing cooler toward the young man.

Seeking the cause, he concealed himself near the palm grove before dark. The moon was now in its second quarter, and he had some difficulty in seeing; but when Campbell and Cornelia arrived and the animals began to come out, it was at once evident that something was wrong. There were only four of them, and these not of the most eccentric character. Moreover, though he was not near enough to hear what was being said, Professor Rousseau declares there was no difficulty in making out the tone of the voices. Cornelia was upbraiding the young man, and he was pleading with her.

Willison put out his glass for another refill. "I think I get it," he said. "That sea air and exercise were getting the booze out of his system. That's what I told him he ought to do."

"Such was evidently Campbell's own conclusion," continued Tobolka. "On the morning after this, while the members of the expedition were at work, Campbell raided the stock of whiskey, drank almost an entire bottle of it, and was found in his cot in a stupor. Professor Rousseau was very much annoyed and reproved Campbell severely. However, the object of his maneuver was attained. Cornelia accompanied him to the palm grove once more and next morning appeared radiant, with sketches of an entirely new and very aberrant form of *Limulus*.

"After this, he persuaded Cornelia to obtain whiskey for him. The process did not last long, for the base ship soon arrived and the work of the expedition was completed. At this point, Professor Rousseau encountered a difficulty, for Cornelia absolutely refused to leave the island until she had seen some more of Campbell's animals. With equal vehemence, he refused to leave her; and they could not come back together because of those same animals.

"Director Rousseau decided that they were both adults, entitled to make their own decisions, so he left them some tents and supplies and arranged for a boat to make periodic calls at Jackson Key. He tells me that, as Cornelia doesn't have a great deal of money and Campbell had none at all when he was cast on the beach, they were finding it difficult to pay for liquor. When last seen, they were trying to ferment coconut milk. Perhaps we may learn some day whether they succeeded."

"Well, thank you, Dr. Tobolka," said Willison. "Maybe I ought to arrange to send his books down there. What do you think?"

THE GIFT OF GOD

"It makes a man sad to see something like that," said Mr. Gross, shaking his head. "In the first place, a Martini is not the drink for an evening, and in the second, a woman that spends her time drinking solitary in bars is on the road to ruination. Who is she, Mr. Co-*han*?"

He motioned with his head toward one of the tables, occupied by a woman who might have been a well-preserved forty. In front of her was a double Martini from which she occasionally sipped, running her tongue around her lips after each sip and staring into the glass as though it were ten feet deep. The bartender glanced, then placed both hands on the bar and leaned over.

"Mr. Gross," he said severely, "it will do you to know that I am the judge of how much people drink in Gavagan's, by God; and I keep it a decent place. Anybody that has to insult the customers can take his business somewheres else."

"I didn't mean nothing," said Mr. Gross, weakly. "I was just thinking of the woman's poor family."

"Family she has none; but if she had, they would not be poor nor ashamed of her neither. That there's Jocelyn Millard, that writes the religious poetry on the radio and all. Father McConaghy says it's as good as a sermon. She's been away for a while now, and this is the first I seen her back."

"The radio, eh?" said Mr. Gross, brightening as he turned to gaze at the poetess again. "Isn't that fine? My wife's cousin knows a man that won a set of dishes on the radio once, but he wasn't married then and had to give them away and the teapot got broke. I'd like to know someone on the radio; maybe with my voice I could get to be one of them announcers."

The object of their conversation approached the bar and pushed her glass across.

"Another," she said in a husky voice.

"Sure, sure," said Cohan. "Miss Millard, do you know Mr. Gross, here? The more people that meet each other, the better it is for all of them."

"Pleased to meet you, ma'am," said Gross. "I was just talking to Mr. Cohan about you being in the radio business."

"How do you do," said Miss Millard. "But I'm not in the radio business."

"Didn't I tell you?" said Mr. Cohan, stirring vigorously. "She only writes the poetry."

"Damn the poetry," said Miss Millard.

"Huh?" said Gross. "Is there something wrong with it, ma'am?"

"Nothing anyone can help."

"Don't say that, ma'am. I call to mind when we were having a party at home on a Saturday night once and the toilet broke down and began flooding the whole place out. You wouldn't think anybody could do anything with all the plumbers closed up, but it turned out that my wife's sister's boyfriend was studying to be a horse doctor, and he just took off his coat and got to work."

Miss Millard sipped gloomily, then appeared to make up her mind with a snap.

> All right, I'll tell you [she said] and you just see what you can do, or Mr. Cohan, either. If you have any sense, you'll run a mile from me. It's worse than being a leper, and I made all the trouble for myself, too.
>
> You know the kind of poems I write? They come over the air on the DIT network at the evening hour, mostly; but I sell some of them to papers, too. Inspirational poems, all about God gimme this and God gimme that. Maybe they're not the best poetry in the world, but they do sell,

and people write me letters saying they're a help. Even preachers and priests sometimes, and there was one woman who said I'd kept her from committing suicide. If people like my poems and get something out of them that makes life pleasanter, why shouldn't I give them what they want? Why shouldn't I?

[Gross shrugged his shoulders to indicate that he was not disposed to argue the point.]

I don't know how it happened, or who did what to me, but now I'm afraid I'll have to go back to schoolteaching. If anyone will give me a job after they find out. You might start mixing me another one, Mr. Cohan; I'll be finished with this by the time you have it ready.

This all started a few weeks back, when I decided it was time for a vacation, so I packed up and got in my car and drove up into the real old French part of Quebec. Rotten roads they have; but the food isn't bad, and I picked up some nice antiques and everything was going the way it should until I got to a place called Pas d'Ange, up on the Benoit River. They have a famous shrine there, run by the Benedictine monks, in a chapel. You know those monks have a choir, too, a real good one.

Now I write poetry that is supposed to have religious aspects, and I try to behave like a good Christian to other people, but I don't usually go into a church from one year's end to another, and I don't suppose I would have gone into the one at Pas d'Ange except that I got there in the afternoon when it was too late to push on to the next town. I'd exhausted all my reading matter, and there wasn't anything else in the place to see.

So I went to the chapel, and sat down in one of the pews. Outside it was a beautiful fall day without a breath of wind. The light came in through stained glass that was really beautiful for so small a place; and as I sat there, I had a wonderful feeling of peace and calm, perhaps the kind of feeling religion is supposed to give you. I sat there a long time, not thinking of anything—in words, that is. After a while, the light began to fade. I got up to go; and at the same time the feeling I spoke of left me, as though a charm had somehow been broken; and I had only the memory instead of the thing itself. I had just begun working with the back of my mind on my poem for the next week, when at the door I met a little priest, just coming in.

He spoke to me in French. I know the language fairly well, but that Canadian French has such a peculiar accent that it was hard to make out what he was saying. I finally made out that he was inviting me to stay for the evening service, with the choir. By this time I was getting hungry and the beginning of my next week's poem was nagging me, so I tried to refuse; but he looked so unhappy that I finally gave in and went back with him. As I did so, he said something I didn't quite catch; something about unexpected blessings, and then left me there.

The choir was all it was said to be; and with the monks chanting and the incense rising in the dusk, the feeling—sort of holy and reverent, if you know what I mean, as though I were lighter than air and could rise right up through the roof—the feeling partly came back, but only in flashes, because all the time I was worrying about my poem. I couldn't seem to get beyond the first two lines:

God give me a child, a tree, a flower;
God give me a bird for just one hour—

After the service was over, I didn't see the little priest again; and after that I was so busy seeing things and finding roads that the poem I hadn't written dropped out of my mind until I got back to town. Then the sight of the streets and stores I knew reminded me that I had a deadline to meet. I started trying to think it out while I was putting the car away, beginning with the same lines as before. As I was going up in the elevator, the two lines reminded me of the scene in the chapel; and I had another flash of the same sense, almost ecstasy you would call it, that I had experienced sitting in the chapel.

The minute I opened the door of the apartment, I knew something was wrong. I heard a squall. I rushed into my living room, and there it was—a newborn baby squirming around on my carpet and yelling its head off. The rest of it was there, too—a young oak tree that seemed to be growing right out of the floor, reaching to the ceiling; a freshly-cut rose lying on my desk; and a yellow oriole in the branches of the tree.

Yes, make me another, Mr. Cohan. You people need to realize that it's one thing to spend years telling God how much you want a child and quite another to find all of a sudden that you have one. In the first place, I'm not married; I never have been; and I had just been away on a long trip. I could see a perfect scandal starting up as soon as it became known that I had come back with a baby. I suppose I ought to be strong-minded and pay no attention, but the people who buy my poems are church-and-home folks, and I have to think of that.

In the second place, the brat had to be taken care of. Excuse me, I suppose it's really a very sweet, lovely baby, just the kind I've been writing about. But I don't know anything about the creatures; when my friends have them, I'm afraid to pick them up. I managed to get this one into my bed and began telephoning for a registered nurse to come and help me, meanwhile trying to figure out a story that would account for the baby. It seemed that all the nurses in town were busy, but I finally did get one. While I was about it, though, the oriole flew out the window and I noticed my clock. It was exactly one hour from the time when I had come in, and I remembered that was the time I had just put in the poem.

When the nurse came, it was worse than ever. I had to spend half the afternoon buying things for the baby—it wet my bed, incidentally—and I couldn't think of any better story than that the child was left on my doorstep. The nurse evidently didn't believe me—she probably thinks I kidnapped it somewhere—and says I'll have to register it. I finally got away, but the apartment is a shambles and Lord knows what I'm going to do now.

"When did this happen?" asked Gross in an awed voice.

"Today. Why do you think I'm here?"

Mr. Cohan, who had been talking with someone down at the end of the bar, interrupted. "Miss Millard, there's a felly here looking for you."

She turned around to face a man in dungarees and a hard hat. "I'm Miss Millard. What is it?"

"Plumber for the building at 415 Henry, Miss Millard. Sorry to come in here and bother you; but it seems like you got some kind of tree in your place; and it must have grown through the bottom of the tub, because the roots are breaking into the gas lines in the ceiling of the floor below; and I had to cut some of them off. They told me—"

Miss Millard gripped the edge of the bar. "God give me strength," she said.

Under her fingers, the small section of wood crumbled as though it were tissue paper; and a shower of little dusty fragments drifted to the floor.

"Them damn termites!" said Mr. Cohan. "I told Gavagan about them a dozen times, and he just won't do nothing till the whole place falls down."

THE BETTER MOUSETRAP

The taxidermist had imparted a drunken wink to the stuffed owl over the bar. Mr. Witherwax returned the wink and kept his gaze fixed resolutely aloft, well aware that if he lowered it, Mr. Gross would burst into anecdote. Considering the quality of the anecdotes, this was something to be avoided at any cost; but there must come the moment when the glass was empty; and Mr. Witherwax must look down to have it refilled. Beside him Mr. Gross cleared his throat ominously. Mr. Witherwax deliberately turned his back to the sound, looked along the mahogany terrain toward the door, and beckoned to the bartender.

"Who's that, drinking by himself down there?" he asked. "Maybe he'd like to join us; a man shouldn't be a solitary drinker. You can leave the cherry out of mine this time, Mr. *Co*-han."

"Co-*han*, by God!" the bartender corrected. "Him? His name is Murdoch, or maybe it's Mud, and I'm thinking he's not a lucky man for you to know. He may be having murder done on him. . . . What'll you be having, Mr. Gross?"

"The usual—a Boilermaker, with a long shot. That reminds me, I knew a man once—"

"What is he, a gangster?" said Mr. Witherwax. "I don't want to get mixed up in nothing, only do him a favor. Bring him down here and give him a drink on me. Tell him the Devil died on Tuesday night, and we're holding the wake."

Mr. Cohan smiled a smile of sly superiority through his folds of fat as he set out the ingredients of the

Boilermaker. "No, he would not be a gangster. It's worse even than that. He lost his dragon."

"A friend of my uncle Pincus was kicked in the belly by a kangaroo once," said Mr. Gross. "He—"

"I don't care whether he lost a dragon or found a mermaid," said Mr. Witherwax, desperately. "Bring him down here and give him a drink."

The bartender, with the shrug of a man who has done his duty and will not be responsible for the consequences, stepped to the end of the bar. As he spoke to Murdoch, the latter turned a thin and melancholy face toward the first comers, then nodded. There was no trace of previous potations in his gait; but he would have a double Zombie, thanks. As he lifted his glass in salute, Mr. Gross gazed at him with fatherly interest.

"Is it true," he asked, "that you lost your dragon?"

Murdoch choked on the last mouthful, set down his glass and looked at Mr. Gross with pain. "If it only was my dragon, I wouldn't care," he said, "but it was borrowed."

"That's right, and I misspoke meself," said Mr. Cohan, heartily. "I remember it was right here at this bar that you loaned it off that magician felly, and him drinking his own special drink."

Murdoch reached for another swallow. He drizzled some of it on his chin as the door opened, then gave a sigh of relief at the sight of a stranger.

Witherwax returned his gaze to the drunken owl, which stared back glassily. "I haven't never seen a dragon, and I don't expect to," he said. "Didn't St. George or somebody get rid of the last one?"

"He did not," said Mr. Cohan, having supplied the new arrival with beer. "This here, now, animal we're talking about I seen it with me own eyes; and it was as dragon as could be; and it belonged to that magician felly Abaris."

"Still does," said Murdoch in a rueful tone. "That is—well, I don't know why I let myself get mixed up—I didn't *like* him—oh, what the hell!" He took a long pull at his double Zombie.

Witherwax turned his gaze to Mr. Cohan. "Who

is this guy that owns a dragon? One of them scientists?"

A magician, I'm telling you [said the bartender]. He gave me his card once; maybe I got it here. Theophrastus V. Abaris [he lined the syllables out slowly]; you would have seen him yourself, Mr. Gross. He used to come in on Thursday nights when you did. A big, greasy tub of lard, not honest fat from the wife's cooking like meself. Pale as a corp he was, with his hair hanging down over his coat collar and a little squeaky voice like a choirboy. It's not easy you could miss him if you seen him once.

One of them real solitary drinkers he was [Cohan continued], that never buy one for the bartender nor get one on the house, neither. Not that he wasn't friendly; he could talk the tail off a brass monkey, only you couldn't understand half of what he said. I ast him once what he done for a living, and all he said was something that sounded like some kind of religion—I misremember the name.

["Pythagorean," said Murdoch, gloomily, and took another drink.]

That could be it, and thanks, Mr. Murdoch. I never heard of it before, but I ast me brother Julius that's on the force about it, and he said it didn't look good, but there's no law against it as long as they don't tell fortunes. It has something to do with books. There's some of them old books that are worth all kinds of money.

That's what he went away for, he said, since the last time I seen him, to get some book, he said, a book by somebody named Nebulous or something like that.

["Zebulon," said Murdoch.]

You should of heard him talk about it. He says it's hundreds of years he's been after the book, which is always the way he talks, so that when you can understand what he's saying, you can't believe a word of it. It seems he had the book once; he says he found it on an island in the pink Arabian Sea, just as though I didn't know seawater ain't pink.

Then he says the holy Saint Peter stole the book off him; and besides being a lot of malarkey, he shouldn't be putting his tongue to the names of the holy saints that way; and I told him so. But now he's going to get it back, he says, because there's going to be a convention of fellies in the same line of business over in Brooklyn, I think he said.

["Brocken," corrected Murdoch.]

Okay, in Brocken. I remember on account of the date being the first of May, and I thought maybe it was some gang of Commies or something like that, but me brother Julius, that's on the force, says no.

Still and all, it's good for business having him in here once in a while, with the tricks he plays, moving his fingers all the time like he's playing a piano that ain't there. Did I ever show you the bottle of private stock he drinks out of, Mr. Gross?

[Cohan ducked down to produce it. "*Vin sable*," read Witherwax from the label. "I know what that means; that's French, and it means 'sand wine.' Have something yourself on this round, will you Mr. Co-*han?*"]

Don't mind if I do; the first today but not the last, and thank you. Well, I guess they must use black sand with it or something, because you can see for yourself how dark it is, like it was mixed with ink. Gavagan gets it for him from Costello's the importer. No, I wouldn't be selling you a drink of it, Mr. Gross; it would be as much as me job was worth. This here Abaris is that particular; and he is a man I wouldn't want to have take a dislike to me, because of the funny things he can do.

[A sound vaguely imitating a rusty hinge emanated from Murdoch.]

Why, you wouldn't believe it yourself sometimes, and I wouldn't either, only I seen them with my own two eyes. You know Mr. Jeffers, don't you, Mr. Witherwax? Well, it's a different man he is today than he was, and all because of this Abaris. A fine young man and a fine young felly he always was, except that in the old days, before you began coming in here, Mr. Witherwax, he maybe had too much money and spent too much of it on girls. Take them alone, either one; the money without the women, or a good girl without the money that can be a help to a young felly, and he's fixed for life. But put them togther; and often as not, the young felly goes on the booze.

No, you needn't laugh, Mr. Gross. I'm not the man to say anything against good liquor, but I wouldn't want anyone to walk out this door that couldn't go on home on his own two feet. Good liquor helps a man to see that after all it's a small thing that disturbs him; but when you take liquor without the trouble, then the liquor becomes the trouble itself, and that's bad.

This was the way it used to be with Mr. Jeffers. He got to taking the liquor with the women, and then without them; and he could be a nasty drunk, too. When I would try to hold him back, he'd go around the corner there to that flashy place, where they don't care what they sell you, and get himself a skinful. Many's the time my brother Julius had to take him home, blind drunk. This evening I'm telling you about, Mr. Jeffers was in here, and so was this Abaris—he used to call himself Doctor Abaris, did I tell you? But when I ast him could he take a wart off her finger for the wife, he said no, so I'll not be giving him the name.

So I said to Abaris, was there any trick he could do to make Mr. Jeffers stop drinking, like maybe the time he borrowed the bottle and poured three different things out of it? So he says: "Yes, my dear Cohan; of course, my dear Cohan. Fill up his glass," in that nancy voice of his, and he begins to make those motions like playing the piano.

I filled up Mr. Jeffers's glass with brandy like

he ordered; and he puts his hand to it; but before he can get the glass to his lips, the brandy is back in the bottle, by God. So after we tried it three times, Mr. Jeffers lets the glass alone; and a funny look comes over his face and he walks out. I thought maybe at the time he was headed for the flashy place again; but he comes back the next night; and you can call me an Orangeman if the same thing don't happen with the first drink Mr. Jeffers orders, while he is cold sober. I don't know how it would be if he come in tonight, but Mr. Jeffers hasn't touched a drop of anything stronger than beer since the day, and you all know it as well as I do. Abaris himself says the trick is simple; it's nothing but a continuing appropriation, he says.

"Apportation," said Murdoch.

"I thank you, Mr. Murdoch. Excuse it, I must see what this gentleman will be having."

"A cousin of mine in Milwaukee once—" began Gross, but Witherwax hastily addressed Murdoch: "What's this business about a dragon? Did he make you think you'd seen one coming out of your drink?"

The young man sipped his Zombie.

No, nothing like that [he said reflectively]. In fact, I thought it was all part of a stock joke, you know, like kidding someone over his luck with the dice or his long ears. I've seen plenty of magicians, like everybody else, at clubs and on the stage; and this Abaris didn't strike me as a particularly prepossessing specimen. In fact, I used to wonder how he made a go of it, because just as Mr. Cohan says, he looked rather greasy and was never well dressed. People like to be fooled; but they want to have it done in the grand manner, by a man with a waxed mustache, wearing a white tie and tails at high noon.

So I was just joking myself when I asked him if he were really a magician. [Murdoch shuddered slightly and took another sip.] He has black eyes, with pupils that have a kind of vertical look that I can't describe; he looked at me out of them and said yes, he was, did I have any objections; and from the way he said it, I knew right off that I'd made a mistake. But there didn't seem anything to do but pretend that I hadn't noticed, so I laughed and said he was just the man I wanted; I needed a magician or a Pied Piper at least, to get the mice out of my apartment.

[Witherwax laid a bill on the counter and made a circular motion over the glasses. Mr. Cohan bent to the task of making refills.]

I have an apartment on Fifth Street [continued Murdoch], on the third floor over one of those Fairfield restaurants. The only thing wrong with it is that it is—or was—simply overrun with mice. I had to keep all my food in metal or glass containers; they chewed the bindings of my books—really an infliction. You haven't any idea of what pests they can be when they get out of hand.

Now, wait a minute [he held up a hand toward Witherwax, whose attitude indicated speech]. I know what you're going to say. You're going to ask why I didn't get an exterminator or a cat. Well, I live alone and do a good deal of travelling, so it would be no use trying to keep a cat. As for the exterminator, I did get one; I got half a dozen, in relays. They came around once a week with traps and mouse seed, which they scattered over the floor until it crunched underfoot, and I suppose they did kill a lot of mice. At least the place smelt like it. But the mice kept coming back.

The trouble was that Fairfield restaurant; it was a regular breeding-ground for them. You know the chain is owned by an old girl named Conybeare, Miss Gwen Conybeare. Like a good many other maiden ladies who have all the money they need and more time than they know what to do with, she fell for one of those Indian sects. You know, with meetings in dimly lighted rooms and a prophet with a towel around his head. I suppose it's her business how she wants to spend her time and money; but this particular religion had a feature that made it my business, too. Her teacher convinced her that it was wrong to take life—not human life, but life of any kind, just as in India, where a man will get rid of a louse by picking it off himself and putting it on someone else.

She gave absolute orders that no death was to occur in a Fairfield restaurant and wouldn't allow an exterminator on the premises. So you see that as fast as I got rid of the mice in my apartment, a new supply came up from below; and I had a real problem.

This Abaris person naturally couldn't know that. When I said I needed a magician to get the mice out of my place, he looked at me with those vertical-appearing pupils and made a kind of noise in his throat that I swear gave me the shivers all through. [Murdoch shivered again and gulped from his Zombie.] I felt as though he were going to hypnotize me, or make my drink jump back into the bottle, like Jeffers's, and so before anything like that could happen, I began to explain that it wasn't a joke. As soon as I got to the part about Miss Conybeare, he smiled all across his face—he has very full, red lips—and made me a kind of bow.

"My dear young man," he said, "if it is a matter of a psychosophist, I should ask nothing better than the opportunity to assist you. They are the most repulsive of existing beings. Let me see—ha, I will provide you with the king of all the cats, and mouse corpses will litter the doorstep of Fairfields."

I explained that the king of the cats wouldn't do me much more good than the crown prince, because of my travelling.

He put a hand up to his mouth and spoke from underneath it. "Hm, hm," he said. "That makes it more difficult, but the project is a worthy one, and I will not willingly abandon it. I will lend you my dragon."

I laughed, thinking that Abaris was a much cleverer man than he looked, to have turned a mild joke around on me in that fashion. But he didn't laugh back.

"It is a very young dragon," he said, "hatched from an egg presented to me by my old friend, Mr. Sylvester. As nearly as I can determine, I am the first person to raise one from the egg, so I must ask you to take particularly good care of it, as I wish to present a report at the next meeting of the Imperial Society."

I thought he was carrying the joke so far that it strained a bit, so I said of course I would take the best of care of his dragon; and if it wearied of a diet of mice, I'd be glad to see that it was provided with a beautiful young maiden tied to a tree, though I wouldn't guarantee the results, which I understood to be usually unfortunate for dragons in such cases.

He gave a giggle at that, but it trailed off in a nasty kind of way and he tapped his fingers two or three times on the bar. "It appears that you treat this with a spirit of levity," he said. "These are high matters. Therefore, and purely as a preventative, I shall accompany the loan of the dragon with an engagement. I shall require you to permit me to put a curse on you when I return from the Brocken if my dragon is not returned in good order." He produced a knife with a small, sharp scalpel blade. "Prick your thumb," he said.

Well, things had gone too far for me to pull out at this point without being ridiculous; and besides I was curious about what kind of charlatanry he was going to produce by way of a dragon, so I stuck myself in the thumb and a drop of blood came out on the bar. Abaris leaned over it and made a little sort of humming song, all in minors, twiddling his fingers in the way Mr. Cohan described. I didn't like the expression on his face. The drop of blood vanished.

[Mr. Cohan had been leaning against the back

of the bar with his arms akimbo. Now he came to life. "Vanished, did it?" he said. "The devil of a time I had trying to get the mark of that drop of blood out, and the best part of it's there yet. If you get the right angle and look close now—see—there it is, like it worked right through the varnish into the wood. Isn't that queer, now?"]

There was nothing queer about the dragon, though [said Murdoch, and for the first time Witherwax noticed that the Zombies were beginning to have some effect on his speech]. It was a real dragon. I knew it was, as soon as Abaris brought it to my place in a metal box, and that was when I really began to worry a little. It hooked its feef—I mean, it cooked its food on the hoof. Wouldn't touch a dead mouse at all, not at all. But when it got near a live one it would go *whooof* and shoot out a flame, and there was the mouse, all cooked.

Witherwax said: "I never thought of that. They must have the flame for something, though. That is, if it was a real dragon."

Murdoch stuck out a finger. "Look here, ol' man, don't you believe me? It's bad enough—"

"Now, now," Mr. Cohan intervened heavily. "There will be no arguments of the kind in Gavagan's Bar. Mr. Murdoch, I am surprised at you. Not a word has Mr. Witherwax said to show he doesn't believe you. And as for the dragon, I seen it with me own two eyes, right here on this bar; and near the end of the bar and all it was."

He brought it in here in a big tomato-juice can [the bartender went on], to show it to me because it was here he heard about it first, and because of the wonderful way it would be cleaning the mice out of his place, so there was hardly one left. I will say it wasn't much to look at, being like one of them alligators about a foot and a half long, with a couple of little stubby wings sticking out of its back.

Maybe it didn't like being out on the bar or

something, because before Mr. Murdoch could get it back into the can, it run down to the end there, and there was a felly sitting drinking a Tom Collins and minding his own business. This dragon let off a puff of flame about a foot long that burned all the hair off the back of the felly's hand, and would you believe it? It boiled the Tom Collins right over the side of the glass so it made a mark on Gavagan's varnish. This felly jumped up and run out of here; and as that sort of thing is bad for business, I told Mr. Murdoch he'd have to keep the dragon out of the place; and that was the beginning of all his troubles.

Now, Mr. Murdoch, it's all right. I was just going to tell them that the reason you brung the dragon in here was thinking it would maybe help with the rats we have in the cellar, bad luck to them; and also because it was getting hungry. The mice were clean eaten out; and Mr. Murdoch had no luck at all when he brought it home a piece of beefsteak or a pork chop, for beef or pork it could not have but must catch its food for itself. The dragon was getting thin, he used to say, and would be saying something like "Kwark, kwark," and even trying to catch flies, that was so burned to pieces with the flame that it had nothing to eat from them at all.

So what does Mr. Murdoch do? He does what any man of good sense would do and tries to take it to the zoo until Mr. Abaris gets home from Brooklyn or whatever it is. He puts it in the tomato-juice can with a cardboard top, but the dragon did not like the trip here to the bar at all, and it burns a hole in the cardboard, and out it comes. Then he puts it in a wooden box and the same thing happens, only it nearly burned up the apartment that time. Then he tries to call the zoo to come get it, but devil a bit would the zoo have to do with that.

"Why not?" asked Witherwax.

"Oh, it's a long story, a long, long story," said Murdoch. "They said they couldn't take it unless I gave it to them, and I said I couldn't do that, and they said I should take it to a pet stop—I mean, pet shop; and I told them it burned a hole in the box. That was bad, because the zoo, it said, what did it say? It said, oh yes, they'd send a wagon right around for the dragon, in charge of a keeper named Napoleon Bonaparte. So I hung up. Maybe the whole thing didn't happen." He drained the last of his Zombie unhappily.

It happened as I'm the living witness [said Mr. Cohan stoutly]. When Mr. Murdoch gave me the word on this, I says to him, if you can't take the dragon to his food, then do the next best thing. Doc Brenner now, he tells me there's places where you can buy rats and mice and things like that for experiments; and if this isn't an experiment, what is? So when I got the address of one of them places from Doc Brenner, Mr. Murdoch goes there right away, and then he remembers he has ordered some wood to make bookshelves out of. So what does he do but leave the key to his place downstairs in the restaurant.

Well, this boy that brought the boards in—he was in here afterward, and young as he was, I wouldn't refuse him a drink, because he was needing it—this lad put the boards down, when all of a sudden a mouse runs out of the corner by the pipes, with the dragon after it. It must of been a new mouse. The dragon was not stalking like a cat, the way it usually did, but hopping across the floor, with its claws scratching the boards and its wings trying to fly, and every third hop it would let out a flame a foot long.

The mouse made a dive for that pile of lumber, with the dragon after him. The lad that brought the boards was hit by a tongue of flame—he had a hole in his pants leg you could shove your fist through—before he got out of there, thinking maybe Gavagan's would be a better place for him. What hapened next I cannot tell you; but the nearest a man can come to it, the mouse crawled in among them boards, and the dragon set them afire while trying to cook the mouse.

However that may be, when Mr. Murdoch got back with a box under his arm and live mice in it, his apartment was in a fine grand blaze, and firemen spraying water through the window and chopping things up with their axes and having themselves a rare old time. That part was all right, because Mr. Murdoch had insurance. But there was no insurance on the dragon, and when he got in afterward, by God, not a trace of the beast could he find. Whether it got burned up, or flushed down with the hoses or run away to the Fairfield restaurant, he has no idea at all. And now here's this Abaris coming back from Brooklyn and Mr. Murdoch with no dragon for him, nothing but the box of mice he has been keeping, hoping the dragon would show up.

So now this Abaris will put the curse on him, and what it will be I don't know and neither does he. No, Mr. Murdoch, you will excuse me from giving you another double Zombie this night.

NO FORWARDING ADDRESS

". . . so this guy Donnelly proves," said Mr. Witherwax, waving his Martini under young Mr. Jeffers's nose, "that the ancient Egyptians and the ancient Mayans must have come from the same place, and this Atlantis is the only place they could have come from."

"What's this?" said Doc Brenner, who had been engaged in contemplating the stuffed owl over the bar. "Don't tell me that you've fallen for Donnelly's ancient maunderings!"

"You mean it ain't a new book?" said Witherwax, with the air of a man about to look crestfallen.

"God, no! It came out in the eighties, and the only people it fools now are those who believe that Bacon wrote Shakespeare." Brenner turned to the bartender. "Mr. Cohan, this puts me in a weakened condition. I need a Sazerac to restore my strength."

"But look here," said Witherwax, "there has to be something to account for all those legends of floods and places that disappeared under the ocean."

"Not any more than there has to be a historical event to account for the Book of Revelation," said Brenner, firmly. "Continents only move at the rate of a fraction of an inch a year. There's no conceivable way you could get the whole Mid-Atlantic ridge down two or three miles below the surface in the ten thousand years allowed by the story, which originally came from Plato. Atlantis just never existed."

"I used to think so, too," said a young man with

blond hair so wavy it looked as if it had received professional attention.

"Don't you any more?" inquired Brenner, thrusting his head forward dangerously.

Witherwax interjected: "Say, mister, ain't I seen you somewhere?"

"If you haven't, it's because you were looking the other way, Mr. Witherwax. I work in the reference department at the public library. My name's Keating," he finished with a touch of self-consciousness.

More names were pronounced, and Mr. Cohan became occupied with another round. Witherwax said: "Do you really know something about there was an Atlantis, Mr. Keating, like this Donnelly says?"

"Not like Donnelly, no. I agree with Dr. Brenner there. But maybe some kind of Atlantis, or something like that. A funny thing happened at the library recently, and it's left me feeling uncertain about a lot of things. Not that I want to contradict you—" he made a propitiatory gesture toward Doc Brenner "—but let me tell you about it. You remember the head of reference, Mr. Mestor?"

"The old guy with the flower in his buttonhole, that knows so much about everything?" said Witherwax.

That's the one. His name was Laban Mestor, but we always called him "Methuselah" around the library. He was the senior member of the staff; been there for thirty-odd years, but was pretty spry and looked as though he were only around fifty-five. I guess he was probably one of the most wonderful reference librarians in the world on anything that touched on history or geography or language or philosophy. The technical reference questions bored him, and he used to pass them on to someone else when he could. But any facts in his field of interest he carried right in his head. Even pretty unimportant facts.

I remember one day somebody wanted to know something about a gang of early American criminals named the Thayers. They took the question up with old Mestor, and without batting an eyelash he came back: "Why, yes; they were hanged in Buffalo, New York, in 1825, while Lafayette was visiting the place." He couldn't find any reference book to prove it, though, and somebody had to write to Buffalo. But he turned out to be perfectly right.

That was the usual way with Mestor. He knew books and what was in them very well, but beyond that he had a whole reference library in his head. I'm in the technical section myself.

There was another funny thing about Mestor, and it has a bearing on what happened—I think. I gather he lived alone; don't believe he had any home life at all. Well, when he was off duty, he didn't go around with a lot of other learned old ducks as you might think. He liked young people. He used to go around with any of us and tip over a few drinks. Whenever he could get the company. And once he got started, he'd take two drinks to your one, and then start telling stories. Perfectly startling ones. I've had him in here a few times and when he got oiled, he even astonished Mr. Cohan.

Mr. Cohan said: "Would that be the tall old felly with the big eyebrows and the joint off the thumb of him, Mr. Keating?"

"That's the one," said Keating. "Kind of wall-eyed, as though he were continually surprised by what he was looking at."

"Sure, he was the one," said Mr. Cohan. "I mind him saying something about Ireland once, and me asking him how he knew, and he says he's been all round the Lakes of Killarney in a jaunting-car."

Yes [continued Keating], that was his method. Especially in his cups. The information he had was always personal. The stories he told happened to someone else, but he learned them on the ground, so to speak. I remember when he was talking about handling a sailing ship on a lee shore in a storm one night. I asked him how he knew. He said that when he was a young man he had spent three years on a whaling voyage to Greenland. I checked up his description afterward by the *Kedge Anchor*, and as nearly as I could make out he was perfectly right, as usual. But it was that whaling voyage and the Babylonian tablet that made us get up the list.

The Babylonian tablet was one of the series the library set out in the lobby in showcases for a "Reading and Writing Through the Ages" exhibit. Polly Rixey had charge of it. You must have seen her around the library, Mr. Witherwax. She's that blonde girl who always wore her hair piled on top of her head.

Mestor liked her pretty well and let her know it. I don't mean he made any obvious passes at her, because he was a gentlemanly old coot. But he was always making opportunities to talk to her, and when she went up the iron grillwork stairs back in the stacks, the chances were that he would be somewhere around the bottom, trying to take a peek at her legs. A lot of girls would have been annoyed—when the others saw him standing there, they used to go around and take another way up—but not Polly. She seemed to take it as a compliment.

She was what you sometimes call a teaser. Not quite on the make, and always perfectly ladylike. But she enjoyed giving the impression things were different. I remember her telling a couple of the other girls how to behave when you go out with an older man—she didn't know I was listening. She said: "You smile at him and listen to everything he says and never interrupt, and if he puts his hand on your knee, go right on eating. He can't really get fresh in a restaurant, and he'll take you out again." There are girls that get a big kick out of that—persuading an older man to make a play for them, especially if he's in a dignified position, and not the kind you'd expect to take an interest in legs. Polly worked on old Mestor that way, and the operation was a success.

Anyway, about the tablet. On this day I had

been out to lunch with Mestor, and as we came in through the lobby, there was Polly Rixey, arranging the reading and writing exhibit. Of course, he had to stop to talk to her, and glanced at the tablet. "My dear," he said, "do you know you're perpetrating a fraud on the public? Your card says that's a hymn to the sun, but it isn't anything of the kind. That's the legend of the childhood of Sargon the Great. Here—"

He picked it up and began to read: "Sharrukin, the mighty king, the king of Agade, am I! Lowly was my mother—" I forget how it all went, but he read it off as though it were in English. He was perfectly right, of course. When Polly took the tablet back to Professor Olmstead at the university, who had furnished the translation, he said he didn't know how such a stupid mistake had been made, probably because the other text had been on his desk at the time.

She went out to dinner with him that night, and let him feel her knee I suppose. The next day I met her in the stacks, and she giggled and said: "Do you know what it is now? I asked him how he could read that Babylonian tablet, and he said he spent two years on an archaeological expedition in Mesopotamia. We ought to keep track."

"Let's," said I. So we did. We not only put down all the places he'd been and times he said he'd been there as he told them to us, but we went around and got lists from the rest, too. I think I still have the general compilation.

[Keating fumbled in his pocket and produced a somewhat worn piece of paper, which he passed to Brenner. It was in tabular form.

Whaling voyage to Greenland	3 years
Living among the Tlingits	1½ years
Studying in Vienna	9 months (?)
In the Argentine	1 year

There were sub-totals as the list went on, and a final "Grand total—228 years, 7 months."]

That's why we called him "Methuselah" Mestor [Keating continued]. You'd say he was just an amiable old liar, and so would I. So did I, and so did Polly. But there were two odd things about the list that didn't impress me till later. One was that there was never anything you could check in these travels of Mestor's. He didn't say what ship he'd been to Greenland in, for instance, and when you tried to press him on a point like that, he'd just talk about something else. You can't come down too roughly on the man you're having a sociable drink with, just to make him out a liar.

The other thing, I've mentioned already. About the information that accompanied the accounts of these imaginary travels being always accurate. I didn't think anyone ever caught him out.

[Brenner coughed: "Mr. Cohan, I'll have another, and so will Mr. Keating here. Are you going to tell me that he said he'd been to Atlantis? Or had some information about it?"]

No [said Keating], I'm not. Thanks for the drink. I'm going to tell you first about what happened one night when we were in here. Mr. Cohan will remember about it. Mestor and I had been having maybe three or four drinks. As we went out, he was saying something to me, looking at me as he did so, and not at the traffic, so he didn't notice a delivery truck that came around the corner on two wheels. I grabbed his arm and yanked him back on his tail on the sidewalk just in time. When we were back here in Gavagan's, getting some tonic for shaken nerves, he said "Roger, I think you have saved my somewhat unworthy life, and I want you to know I'm not ungrateful."

What can you say in a case like that? I was so embarrassed I wanted to paw the floor like a little boy, and he must have seen it, because he let the subject drop. But the next day, as I was sitting in the tower lunchroom, just about to start in on the apple I was having for dessert, old Mestor came poking in with his eyebrows wiggling. He said: "Roger, do you want to come with me a few minutes? I have something to show you."

I followed him, bringing my apple with me. He led the way downstairs to the basement, way in the back, where they keep uncatalogued newspaper files and things like that. He picked around in this wilderness of paper for a few moments and finally hauled out something from a shelf at the back. It looked exactly like one of those scrolls on which ancient manuscripts were written, and it had a rod through it, too. Only the material didn't seem to be paper.

Old Mestor laid it on a pile of newspapers which were in turn on a table. "Knowledge can be a very useful thing," he said, "and I wish to make some small, concrete expression of my gratitude for your kindness last night. This is the *Apodict.*"

I had never heard of the *Apodict,* and when he began to unroll it, I didn't recognize the characters in which it was written, though they looked something like Greek. The most interesting thing, though, was that it was illustrated. The pictures were divided into frames, like in a comic strip. In fact, Mestor remarked on it. "The newspaper comic strip," he said, "is supposed to have begun with Outcalt's *Yellow Kid,* just before the turn of the century, but this is a good deal older. Also it serves a practical purpose. Now look at this series."

They ran from top to bottom on the roll, and there was nothing the least Greeklike about the little human figures pictured in them. In fact, they looked like the conventionalized figures you see in Aztec picture writing, and they had feather headdresses like the Aztecs, too—a whole series of figures going through gestures.

"What is it supposed to be?" I asked.

"That," he said, "is partly a lesson in apportation. Here, put that apple you have on this pile of papers, use your pencil as a wand, and follow through the motions of this figure here."

I was willing. I like parlor tricks. "It won't blow up or anything, will it?" I asked.

"I think not," he said, without smiling. "It will merely be removed elsewhere."

So I began copying the motions of the figure, tapping the apple on top, then once on each side, then making a couple of circles around it with the pencil and so on. The drawing was so stylized that it was hard sometimes to tell what motion was desired. Mestor kept straightening me out, and telling me to do it more smoothly, and to have faith that it would work. I was beginning to get bored and tired in the arm when it happened.

The apple simply disappeared.

One second it was there, and the next it wasn't. I stood there goggling, with old Methuselah Mestor chuckling in the background. "What did I tell you?" he said.

Just then I heard a step and turned around to see Polly Rixey coming down through the piles of newspapers. "My goodness," she said, "I've been all over the building after you. Roger, that Mr. Mandelstammer is here again, wanting you to help find him something about tool design. And there's a visitor for you, too, Mr. Mestor. He said he'd wait, but it wasn't library business and he couldn't talk to anybody else.

"He said to tell you it was Mr. Malek."

"Oh," said Mestor. "I'm afraid I've made a mistake." His voice was so queer that I looked at him, but he only said: "I guess we can't go any further today." He was rolling up the *Apodict* as I went upstairs.

Mandelstammer is one of my particular crosses. He was pushing his paunch against the desk and waiting for me, but on the desk itself was something that interested me a good deal more. It was an apple. I won't swear it was the same one that had disappeared from the pile of papers in the basement, because I hadn't carved my initials on it or anything, but it certainly looked the same. I got Mandelstammer straightened out with his books on tool design and was about to take the next request, when one of the page-girls touched my arm. "Do you know where Mr. Mestor is?" she said. "This gentleman's been waiting for him for quite a while."

She pointed to a man standing at the desk used by the reference librarian. He was even taller than Mestor, and thin, with frizzy white hair all round the edge of his head and very deep-set eyes. I went over to him and told him that I had been with Mr. Mestor in the basement when the message came, and that he should have been up right behind me, but I'd go down and look for him. The old boy pursed his lips and said: "No. You won't find him. He must have learned. Thank you." Then he put on his hat and went out.

Now that was the funny thing I started to tell you about. It was a funny thing to say, and it was perfectly true. We didn't find Mestor. It's almost a month ago, now, and nobody has seen him. He hasn't been home. He's disappeared just as completely as my apple. And so has Polly Rixey. Old Mestor didn't have any relatives listed in the records. But she had a family out in the Middle West somewhere, so the head librarian wrote to them, describing the circumstances, and asking permission to put the Missing Persons Bureau on the case. But the family just answered that if Polly wanted to elope with a man old enough to be her father, that was her business, and to let the girl alone. So there hasn't really been anybody trying to find them. But I doubt if they'll get anywhere if they try.

Brenner said: "Would you mind telling me what all this has to do with Atlantis?"

Keating faced him. "Don't you know? Probably not. I didn't either until about a week ago I was reading a translation of Plato's *Critias*. It contains a lot of very early mythology, the kind in which the scientists are always trying to find some strain of fact. Well, there's a story in that Poseidon once visited Atlantis and fell in love with a mortal maid named Cleito. She bore him ten sons, and one of them was named Mestor."

"Oh, yeah," said Brenner, with a rising inflection. "And I supposed you can do that apportation stunt he taught you."

"Oh, that," said Keating. "You know I had the most frightful headache in the afternoon afterward, and every time I really try to concentrate on it, I get another one. I thought I must be doing something wrong, and went back down there to look up the roll of the *Apodict,* but I couldn't find it either, although I almost turned the place upside down. But maybe I can make it work this time, though."

He took a pencil from his pocket and, with an air of frowning concentration, lightly tapped his glass of rum and water on the top and the two sides.

"No, you don't," said Mr. Cohan. "Magic you may do, but Father McConaghy says this television is witchcraft, and I will not have people trying it in Gavagan's."

THE UNTIMELY TOPER

As the door of the men's room opened, swinging back with a bang, Mr. Cohan started violently, looked over his shoulder, and almost missed Mr. Witherwax's glass with the Martini he was pouring. His expression might almost have been one of relief when he saw that it was little Doc Brenner, who strode importantly to the bar and demanded a Tom Collins.

"What's the matter, Mr. Cohan?" asked Witherwax. "Afraid the hinges were coming off? You ought to be ashamed of yourself for frightening an old friend that way, Doc."

Mr. Cohan, pouring, said: "It's not what's coming off but what's going on that has me counting me fingers, and that's a fact. Me to be short a whole bottle of bourbon in my inventory. Gavagan will never let me hear the end of it."

Mr. Willison said, "Mr. Cohan, you astound me; you even pain me deeply. You who have carried the troubles of so many others, to have difficulties of your own! Give me another Scotch and Soda."

"It's not my trouble," said Mr. Cohan, "though it does be making trouble for me. It's that Mr. Pearce. I never knows when he is at all since it happened."

There was a little chorus of "Huh?" "Since what happened?" out of which rose Witherwax's voice: "I read a book once about a man that didn't know what time he was in and got all mixed up with a lot of Communists in England when he came out of a tin can."

"Yes," said young Mr. Keating from the library.

"That would be Victor Rousseau's *Messiah of the Cylinder.*"

"Could you put a man in a can and bring him out later?" said Witherwax.

"No," said Doc Brenner, eating the cherry from his Collins.

"Hold on a minute," said Mr. Cohan. "You're misunderstanding me. I—"

"Why not?" asked Willison, ignoring Mr. Cohan. "Don't they freeze frogs and—"

"Like the time my cousin Ludwig got locked in the freezer at Greenspan and Walker's," said Mr. Gross, "and ate up all that suet because—"

Doc Brenner said: "Mr. Cohan, I want to hear about this Mr. Pearce. And if you'll lend me your bung starter, I'll see that you're not interrupted before the end of it. What do you mean by that curious statement: 'You don't know *when* he is'?"

"Mr. Pearce," said Mr. Cohan, "is that young felly that comes in here mostly on Thursdays, the one with the little mustache and the big ears. And what I should have said is that I wish I knew *where* he is and *when's* he coming back from wherever that may be because he—"

Willison emitted a sound. "I remember. If he had ten times as much brains as he has and cheated on the entrance examination, he might be able to get into a home for the feeble-minded."

I would not be saying that [said Mr. Cohan]. It's bad for the trade to run down your customers, and Gavagan wouldn't like it. But as long as you have put your tongue to it, I won't be denying what you say, neither, and what's more I will tell you that he's always driving around in one of these hot rods with some girl beside him, and she not the kind you'd want to be meeting your mother. Me brother Julius, that's on the force, says he'll be cutting somebody's throat one of these days just to prove he can do it, and that's a hard thing to say of a man, but it was the man that made it to be said.

Most of the time he's in that Italian place

around the corner, where they have a juke box and will let him get as drunk as he pleases, but every now and then he has an unholy row with his friends or they have one with him, and he comes to Gavagan's. Always talking about his troubles he is, as though honest liquor wasn't enough to get for his money, not that I mind helping a young felly along when he needs some advice, but I'm not the man to be spending my time telling anyone how to make the waitress at Rosenthal's.

Well, this night when it started, Mr. Pearce was in here getting the beginnings of a load on, and so was this Doctor Abaris. D'ye know him?—Theophrastus V. Abaris, that calls himself a magician though he ain't never been on the stage, and a doctor, though when Mrs. Moon had a seizure in here one night he could do nothing about it whatever.

Witherwax interjected, "Say, whatever happened to that guy Murdoch, that this Abaris was going to put a curse on or something because he lost the dragon?"

Brenner and Gross shrugged, and the former said, "I don't know. He just stopped coming in, I guess."

That's right [continued Mr. Cohan], he just stopped. That's the way it is running a bar; sometimes they stop coming and you never know why till you read in the paper that they've taken a ride in a hearse or married a woman with a million dollars. It's a sad business, it is, and I'm looking forward to the day when Gavagan will let me retire. You're always losing your best friends.

Not that I would call this Doctor Abaris one of my best friends, with his hair hanging down to his collar and his pasty face, but he's always the gentleman and always stands there quietly drinking that wine that Gavagan imports for him special. Mr. Pearce was drinking—let's see now, it was Lonacoming whiskey, and talking about some change he was going to make in his hot rod, when all of a sudden there's a bat flying back and forth at the top of the room. Doctor Tobolka, when I asked him about it, said it had probably been asleep up there at the top of the pillars and just woke up, though how it got in in the first place I don't know.

Now, me, I don't care about bats one way or another, but this Pearce, he got all excited and ran back there and grabbed the broom and begun chasing this way and that through the bar, trying to hit it. He was climbing up on chairs and even on one of the tables, yelling like a wild man, and I was just thinking I better cut down on his Lonacoming when Doctor Abaris says to him, "Take your time, young man, take your time!" Not real loud, but you couldn't miss hearing him.

He might as well have been talking to a deaf man, for this Pearce made one swipe with the broom and then another, and whop! the dead corp of the creature dropped down on the bar right in front of Doctor Abaris.

Mr. Pearce put the broom away and you would have said he thought he was a hero. But Doctor Abaris he picked up the dead bat with a sorrowful expression on the round fat face of him, and took out a handkerchief and wrapped the bat in it and put it in his pocket. Then he turned to Mr. Pearce with a look on his face that I'd not be wanting to take to bed with me at night, and he says: "Now, young man, you *shall* take your time."

"Huh?" says Mr. Pearce. "You didn't want that thing flying around here, did you? They're dirty."

Never a word says Doctor Abaris. He just gets down off his stool and pays for his drink and walks out, and I'm thinking it will be a cold day in July before we see him again. I said to Mr. Pearce, "Look here, young felly," I said, "maybe they'll let you throw things around and break up the place in that Italian joint around the corner, but we will not stand for it in Gavagan's."

With that he gets red in the face and says may he drop dead if he's ever found in this crummy dump again—that's the way he talks—and drinks off the rest of his Lonacoming and starts for the door, then changes his mind and goes toward the men's room instead. We might have had a couple more words on the subject, but just then in came Mr. Jeffers with a couple of his friends and I had to wait on them and gave no more attention than to think that, if young Pearce never did come back, it would be good riddance of bad rubbish, even though it was one less customer for Gavagan's. I didn't see him come out of the men's room, and when I went there later myself, he wasn't inside, so I thought he must have slipped past the bar while I was bending over for cracked ice or something.

The very next night, that would be a Friday, I was waiting on the trade as usual, about 9 o'clock and not many people in here, when the door of the men's room opens and out comes this Pearce with a kind of funny look on the face of him. I could of swore I hadn't seen him come into the bar, and especially after what happened the night before, I thought he had his nerve with him.

He comes right up to the bar and says: "I want a double Lonacoming."

Now I'm a man that is willing to let bygones be bygones or I wouldn't be behind the bar at Gavagan's, so I poured it for him and said nothing. He takes a drink of it and says, "What kind of trick are you trying to put over?"

His voice was that nasty I started reaching for the bung starter, but all I said was: "That's as good whiskey as you'll find in this town."

"Oh, that," he says. "I don't mean that," and points to the calendar there on the wall, where I mark off each day as it comes up to keep things straight. "Today's the twenty-seventh."

"It is not," says I, and I got the evening paper to show him it was the twenty-eighth.

He acted like somebody had pushed him in

the face. "Something's cockeyed," he said, and went over to make a telephone call.

After a couple of minutes he was back. "I've lost a whole day out of my life," he said, "and my girl has given me the air because I stood her up." With that he orders another double Lonacoming and starts in on it.

I'd heard enough of his girl stories not to want to hear another, so I went down the bar to wait on some of the trade, just keeping the corner of me eye on him. I'll say this much: something seemed to have knocked all the fight out of him; he was as quiet and decent as you'd expect a man to be in Gavagan's and, for all the effect the whiskey had on him, it might have been soda pop. After a while he went to the men's room again.

The place was filling up by this time and I didn't have a chance to folly him right away, but as soon as I got everyone taken care of, I went in there. And it was empty; there was neither hide nor hair of Pearce anywhere in Gavagan's. And he didn't slip out the door, neither; I was watching it.

The next time he showed up was two days later, on the thirtieth, in the afternoon. The day man told me about it when I came on that night. I hadn't said nothing to him about the way this Pearce disappeared, because Gavagan likes to keep a very orderly place and doesn't want things like this to be happening, so it was him told me about it, warning me about a felly that had four, five drinks of Lonacoming whiskey and slipped out without paying for them. He descripted this felly and it sounded like Pearce.

"Did you see him come out of the men's room?" I asked.

"I did that," says he, "and with his eye all the time on the clock and the calendar while he was drinking. And the last I saw of him, he went back in again."

"And did he look like a man well gone in drink?" says I.

"If he had, I would not have served him in Gavagan's. He walked like a judge and stood like a traffic cop."

"Then he'll be back," says I.

"He had better be," said the day man. "Nobody is going to get away with owing Gavagan $3.15, plus tax."

Well, we fixed it up that whichever one of us was on the next time this Pearce came round would get the $3.15 from him and tell him that since he'd said he didn't like this place, he could take his feet out of it and never come back. But he fooled us. He did indeed.

The very next morning when the day man opened the place, there was an empty fifth of bourbon on the bar, lying on its side and a glass beside it and the bar all spotted and stained in a way I would never leave it. There was only one thing it could mean, and that is that this Pearce came back after the place was closed and helped himself. The worst of it is that now he was changing drinks, from Lonacoming to bourbon. A man that switches like that has no control of himself. And I'm short a bottle of bourbon on me inventory, a thing that's never happened before.

There was a little silence. Then Willison said, "I'm afraid I don't quite see. . . ."

"Why, it's as clear as a bottle of good gin!" exclaimed Mr. Gross. "You see, this Pearce—"

"It's the business of the men's room, isn't it?" Doc Brenner asked shrewdly.

"It is that," Mr. Cohan nodded. "I have never seen the felly come in or go out through the front door of Gavagan's. It's always to the men's room he's going, or coming from there—"

"That's just it!" cried Mr. Gross. "There's no other—"

"Like you said," Mr. Witherwax broke in, "you must have been bending down behind the bar—"

"Listen to me!" Mr. Gross screamed. A sudden

silence fell. Mr. Cohan stared hard at Mr. Gross and said: "Now, Mr. Gross, Gavagan's is a quiet—"

"Listen to me," Mr. Gross repeated in a calmer tone. "It's as plain as the nose on your face. On my face, rather." They grinned. "You were right the first time, Mr. Cohan. When you said '*when* he was.' Because that's just what it is. When Pearce killed that bat, Dr. Abaris put a hex on him or something so that, instead of losing his legs when he starts to walk across the room—like a guy does when he's had too much—this guy Pearce loses his feet in *time*."

"By golly," whispered Willison.

"Shut up," said Doc Brenner. "Go on, Mr. Gross."

Mr. Gross beamed. "Now, the first time I don't guess Pearce was very tight. So he only lost a single day, like he said. But then he got a lot drunker—on double Lonacomings, remember—and it was two days gone. Next three days and now, on this whole fifth of bourbon, it's four days he's missed. He'd oughta be back pretty soon now, Mr. Cohan, although I don't know just how much liquor causes him to lose how much time, if you see what I mean."

"By golly," said Mr. Willison again.

"I do indeed see what you mean, Mr. Gross," said Mr. Cohan. "And as you have so kindly solved my problem, you will have your usual Boilermaker on the house."

The rest of them stared with awe, first at Mr. Gross, then at Mr. Cohan as the latter reached down under the bar, then came up with a dusty bottle of what was obviously very old bourbon. From this bottle he meticulously filled a double shot glass to its brim and carefully, not spilling a drop, he placed it before Mr. Gross. After returning the ancient bourbon to its lair, he drew a glass of beer (without collar) and placed that alongside the shot glass.

Finally, Doc Brenner cleared his throat. "I—ah—don't wish to stain Mr. Gross's triumph," he said, "but as I see it, Mr. Cohan, your problem is only half-solved. How are you going to untangle Pearce's feet?"

"By God, that's right!" exclaimed Witherwax. "How are you going to get him back from where—*when*ever he is and keep him here—now?"

"Otherwise he'll probably steal a whole case of liquor from you," said Willison.

Mr. Gross sipped his venerable bourbon.

Mr. Cohan slapped the bar with a heavy palm. "I have it. Look now, the young felly is staggering every which way through time because he's drunk. Right?"

There was a chorus of nods.

"Well, then, we'll sober him up." Once again Mr. Cohan rummaged beneath the bar, but this time he produced a bottle filled with a thick brownish liquid. "I'll be waiting here for that young felly day and night until he shows up, and there's the tipple he'll be getting!"

"What in heaven's name is that?" asked Mr. Witherwax.

"A Prairie Oyster, with Worcestershire in it, and tomato juice, and some bitters to give his stomach a kick in the pants, and red pepper for the good of his soul."

The door of the men's room was flung back with a bang, and the habitués of Gavagan's turned as a unit to face what was indubitably the missing Pearce. Except for a certain disarrangement of the hair, he had not the appearance of a man deeply under the influence of liquor, but the lines at the base of his mustache were twitching and his eyes seemed to be popping out of his head as he stared at the calendar.

"I need—a drink," he said, clutching the bar with one hand, and with his eyes still on the calendar, fumbled for the dose Mr. Cohan poured. A long swig of it went down before he restrained himself, gasping, and dropped the glass on the bar.

"My God!" he said. "What was that? Are you trying to poison me?"

"I am not," said Mr. Cohan, firmly, but was spared any addition to this statement by the appearance Pearce gave of being in the throes of a revolution as violent as any that ever afflicted a Latin American republic. His mouth came open and little sounds emerged from it, he clutched the bar-edge with watering eyes, and then, emitting a series of gigantic burps, he released his grip and dived for the security of the men's room.

Willison gazed at the closed door behind him and addressed Mr. Cohan. "Your treatment was certainly drastic," he said. "But I don't quite understand."

"You do not?" said Mr. Cohan placidly. "Then go look in that men's room. You'll be finding it empty. The man is stone sober by now, his feet are on the right time track, he's back where and when he belongs, and thank the Lord this is one place he'll not be coming to again. It's not that I like to be discouraging the trade, but there are a few things we cannot have in Gavagan's."

THE EVE OF ST. JOHN

Mr. Witherwax, in very good voice that evening, was explaining to little Doc Brenner something he had been reading in a book.

"It's like this," he said. "All you gotta do is find out whether something is progressive or not. Then you don't have to worry about whether it's right or wrong. It says in the book that when you say something is right, you only really mean it helps make progress, see?"

A massive young man on the other side of Brenner turned around and said: "Phooey!" with great emphasis.

Mr. Cohan, from farther down the bar, dropped a discussion of the Brooklyn Dodgers and sidled along to extend a placatory hand toward the massive young man. "Now, now, Jerry—"

"I didn't mean phooey on these people here," said the young man, amiably. "As a matter of fact, I like the way they look, and while you're mixing another Angel's Tit for me, give them a drink, too, Mr. Co-*han*. But I say phooey on progress."

"Let me make you 'quainted," said the bartender. "Mr. Witherwax, Doc Brenner, this is Mr. Shute."

"How do you do?" said the young man, formally, compressing Mr. Witherwax's hand to the consistency of an octopus's tentacle. "I say there isn't any such thing as progress."

"Don't bite the hand that feeds you," said Doc Brenner. "If it weren't for progress, you'd probably have died of diphtheria while you were a kid."

"Like this book says," said Witherwax, "you might as well help progress along, on account of you can't stop it."

"Inescapable law of nature," said Brenner.

"No, it isn't," said Shute, downing his Angel's Tit at a gulp and munching on the cherry. "I escaped it. Or else I made progress backward. Fill it up again, Mr. Cohan." He laid a bill on the bar; so did Witherwax.

"Here, here," said Brenner, "this round is on me. Rye and plain water."

"All right," said Witherwax, "let's roll for it. That box of yours, Mr. Cohan. Want to come in?" He addressed Shute.

"Not I," said the massive young man. "Sorry, and no disrespect to you, but I just don't dare gamble on anything. That's how I got mixed up with what you call progress, and I almost died of it."

He stared gloomily at Mr. Cohan, who was busy with a Martini for Witherwax. "Right you are, Mr. Shute," said the bartender. He turned to the others: "He has his reasons."

"Doesn't sound reasonable to me," said Brenner.

"Well, I'll tell you," said Shute. "I'll tell you the story, though you probably won't believe it. That's the trouble; nobody does. They think I'm a prehistoric survival or a plain nut." He sipped from his Angel's Tit and continued:

My father was Francis Shute. You probably never heard of him, but he wrote a lot of books on folklore and early magic, sort of picking up where Frazer left off in *The Golden Bough,* if you know what I mean.

I understand I can't ever be president of the United States. I wasn't born in the country. At the time they brought me into the world—I think that's the right phrase, isn't it?—my parents were living in the Harz Mountains in central Germany. That's the greatest folklore country there is, the place where the Brothers Grimm got their start. They were trying to collect tales that the Grimms might have overlooked, or new and altered versions of the stories the Grimms already had. My father worked on the theory that folklore is an explanation of something and contains a basic stratum of truth of some kind, but when the exterior events are different, then a new folklore story comes around, getting a little closer to the underlying truth of what makes the world tick. It's really very interesting. That was 'way back before the First World War, you know, but he found stories growing up that the Grimms never heard of—not about individuals, but the Germans as a race of heroes who were going to save the world from a lot of dirty monsters with long beards, and that sort of thing.

[Brenner cleared his throat.]

Yes, I know, what's all this got to do with progress. Wait. My parents lived in a German peasant cottage with a straw thatch, that might have been an illustration for one of the fairy-tales. I used to see pictures of it when I was a boy.

I was born on the night of June 24th, and they tell me it was one of the stormiest nights ever seen in the Harz, with the wind howling outside. Just as I was born—so they say—there was a big puff from the fireplace, the logs turned over, sparks flew out into the room and people began coughing! I daresay I bawled.

The local midwife and her assistant had come in to help the local doctor. They began muttering and one of them crossed herself. My father knew what that meant. You see, the 24th of June is St. John's Eve, when the fairies are supposed to be especially active, particularly in that part of Germany. According to their ideas, the puff of wind and the sparks and smoke were evidence of a fairy coming down the chimney to bestow a gift on the newborn baby. They didn't know whether it was a good fairy and a good gift, or one of the other kind. They rather thought it might be bad because it was such a foul night out, but said I'd have to find out for myself, and exactly what the gift was, when I grew up.

My parents told me the story, and while I was quite small, there was the kind of family joking you'd expect about my fairy gift and what it was. This became less and less as I grew up, just as the talk about Santa Claus becomes less. You can't assign any definite date when you stopped believing in the real existence of the old guy with the whiskers and reindeer, but you gradually get the idea.

Well, I got the idea about my fairy gift, or thought I did, until I was well along in college. The frat house there was the first place I ever really played cards for money. We played at home, for chips and things, of course, but my father was such a rationalist that there never seemed much sense in risking money on the game because, as he pointed out, it all came out of his pocket anyway.

I don't mean to say that we did any serious gambling at the frat house. It was the usual college idea of a big evening: penny ante with a nickel limit and a couple bottles of beer, that left us all unprepared for recitation the next morning, but feeling like very gay dogs. I enjoyed the association and I liked the game, but it wasn't very long before I found out I couldn't afford it—financially, even at penny ante, and because I got bad-tempered. You see, I couldn't seem to win a single pot unless everybody dropped out before the betting began. We'd play about once a week. I kept track over a period of six weeks, and I went that long without winning once, not one single pot.

All right, I know you're going to say that's the complaint of a man who doesn't play his cards well. It just isn't true. I was a good card-player. In fact, I made the college bridge team in my sophomore year, and we won the team-of-four championship tournament from five other colleges during the Christmas vacation. After that happened, I told myself that this failure to win at poker was silly, so I got a copy of that book that has the percentage chances of winning on various types of hands, and studied it harder than I did my lessons, until I had committed it to memory. If you hold a flush in a five-man game, for instance, the chances are 508 to 1 that nobody will hold anything better.

After I had memorized the whole business, I got into the weekly poker game again. I didn't win a pot; I had a full house beaten once, and once a set of fours. So I gave up poker.

[Shute paused in his narration, motioning Mr. Cohan to fill his glass again.]

At the time, I didn't connect it with the fairy's gift, or anything of the kind. I thought it was some mannerism of my own, by which I unconsciously announced the strength of my hand. Of course, that wouldn't account for my being beaten with a full house, but that angle of it didn't occur to me—at least till after the Ellington football game.

You know, that was the year we had the wonder team, with Prewalski, Mack, Cassaday, and Loomis in the backfield; the team that hadn't been scored on the year before, and that had run up at least four touchdowns on every opponent down to the Ellington game. The day before the game, some of the Ellington brothers came over to stay at our frat house, and when one of them became patriotic enough to offer five dollars on his team, which had won two games and lost four, I naturally obliged him.

Maybe you remember reading about that game in the papers. There was never anything like it. On the very first play, Cassaday broke his leg; and that was already pretty bad, because he was the only really good line-plunger we had, and with him gone, Ellington could open out for pass defence. That didn't make too much difference with Mack doing the passing, because he could have thrown a football through the eye of a needle, if he found one big enough. It was one that had worked all season; Prewalski was in the clear, ready to take the pass, Mack got it away like a machine—and when the ball was about a yard out of his hands, the lacing on it burst open, the air squirted out, and the ball dropped to the ground. I know that sort of thing doesn't happen in college football, but it did this time.

The game was all like that. It wasn't that our team did anything wrong, but that everything they did went wrong through sheer bad luck. A substitute ran off the bench to pick up a piece of paper that had blown on the field, and the referee called back a touchdown run and penalized us for twelve men on the field—that sort of thing. They beat us, nine to seven, and nobody's been able to explain it since.

It was after that game that I really began to put things together. I remembered then that it wasn't just football and poker. As far back as I could go, I never could remember winning a bet. Even when I was a kid in high school, I'd say: "Bet you a nickel," and have to pay the nickel.

I mentioned this quirk to Johnny Bell Griscom, who was my roommate and a psychology major—the whole business, including the queer idea that maybe my birth in the Harz Mountains had something to do with it. That the fairy gift had been one of not being able to win a bet, that is.

He laughed at that, and then turned serious. "I don't doubt that you have trouble winning a bet," he said, "but you mustn't attribute it to anything like fairies. It's a perfectly good case of psychology—perhaps with some parapsychological influence added, you know, a certain amount of ESP which, in a manner we don't understand as yet, warns you that something is not going to happen, so you bet on it. It's analogous to the death wish."

I told him that I didn't wish for any death: I just wanted to win a bet once or twice to prove that I could and then forget the whole business.

Johnny Bell got very serious and professional about it. He said, yes, this whole business was giving me a neurosis, and I better get rid of it before it became serious. Otherwise, I couldn't make any progress. The way to do it, he said, would be to make a bet on something that was an absolute certainty. He'd help me.

So we went out for a walk. I remember it was in October: a windy day. As we came down the street toward the Hotel Bristol, I noticed they had a new awning out over the street, a big blue one. "That's the first awning the Bristol has put up in five years," I said. "I'll bet you a quarter it lasts all winter."

"Done for a quarter," said he. The next minute a gust of wind caught that awning and ripped it from hell to breakfast.

I paid him the quarter and we went back, with me feeling pretty low. Johnny Bell said that when a neurosis like that hit you, the thing to do was progress through it and out, and if it couldn't be done one way, it could in another. So we talked it over some more, and he thought of a plan that might work out, in view of the fact that was an election year. We were all of us pretty liberal there at college, but we knew Truman didn't have a chance. So Johnny Bell and I went down to a betting room, and I put ten dollars on Dewey. If he won, I'd be money ahead, and be rid of that jinx, or neurosis, or whatever it was; if he didn't, why then, I'd be happy anyway.

Election night I didn't even bother to sit up hearing the returns. Don't tell me it was the unions getting out the labor vote or the Republicans all staying home, or the farmers, or anything like that. I know better. It was my fairy godmother keeping me from winning a bet.

Johnny Bell said it was the most interesting case of parapsychology he'd ever studied. He talked to me about my father's work and made a lot of notes. At the same time, he said that if I had a neurosis like that, it was something like having one leg or being allergic to lobsters. The right thing was not to submit to it as a handicap, but to capitalize on it and make use of it as a source of progress.

He asked me what I was worried about aside from this betting matter, and I told him he knew as well as I did, that I was a good deal upset about my mid-term examinations in physics and chem. I wasn't lying down on the job. I just couldn't seem to get those two subjects through my head. It was serious, because my father had died by that time, and my mother was making some sacrifice to put me through college. If I flunked those two, I would be set back a year.

"All right," said Johnny Bell, when I told him. "We'll make an experiment. I'll bet you fifty cents, even money, that you pass both exams. You bet that you flunk. I know you want to pass badly enough so you'll try."

We wrote it out. As soon as I got into the examination room for physics, I knew I had it worked. The only questions on the paper were exactly the few to which I knew the answers. It was so easy I was tempted to turn in a couple of blank sheets to see what would happen, but I decided there was no sense in crowding things too far. As it was, I got an A on the examination, the first one I had had in physics all year.

All I had to do, then, was bet against getting anything I really wanted. That gave me an idea. The thing I wanted most right at the moment was Mary. She was the daughter of the Latin prof and more or less the belle of the campus. I had dated her a few times, but so had nearly everyone else, and especially Loomis, one of the halfbacks on the football team. It looked as though he had the inside track, because in addition to being an athletic hero, he came from a family that was pretty well fixed. So I hunted up Loomis one night and led the conversation around to Mary by asking him if he was going to take her to the New Year's Eve party.

"I haven't asked her," he said, "and I don't think I will."

"Why not?" said I.

He laughed in a rather embarrassed way. "Well," he said, "she's a perfectly nice girl, and good fun and all that, but confound it—I want to look around before I put on the ball and chain."

"What do you mean?" I said.

"Not that I blame her," he said. "Things aren't too good there at home. But she's pretty frankly on a husband-hunt. I'll bet she gets married within six months. She'd even grab you if you asked her in a nice way."

You can imagine the opening that gave me. I said: "Oh, phooey. Girls that try that hard never make it. I'll bet you five dollars that she doesn't marry anyone within three years—least of all, me."

"You're on," said he, and we shook hands on it. I figured that if the prohibition against my winnings bets worked this time, it would be cheap at the price.

I didn't tell Johnny Bell Griscom about that bet; I don't know why. But I took Mary to the New Year's Eve party. Rather late in the evening we were sitting out a dance, and I was trying to work up enough courage to ask her what I wanted to, when she suddenly turned to me and put one hand on mine. "Jerry," she said, "let's be modern. As long as leap year isn't quite over yet, I can ask you—I want you to marry me."

There it was, you see. I went around in a kind of purple swoon all through the spring term. If I hadn't been thoughtful enough to bet Johnny Bell Griscom on the result of the finals, I doubt whether I would have passed. We were married right afterward. Loomis was the best man, and I gave him five dollars for his services.

That brought up another problem, though. I didn't have any money and neither did she, and the jobs for young college graduates weren't very wonderful. But figuring it out carefully, I thought I saw a way to make progress through the very thing that had been dogging me—

whether it was a fairy gift, or parapsychology, as Johnny Bell Griscom called it.

So, without saying anything to Mary, I took nearly all the money we had and went out to the race track. I don't know anything about racing, but I could tell easily enough from a newspaper that in one race there was a favorite named Lanceolate, on whom the odds were 3 to 2. I went to the window where they place the bets, and waited till I saw a likely-looking customer who made a bet on this horse. As soon as he got away from the window, I struck up a conversation with him. I told him he was crazy to bet on Lanceolate; that the horse had fallen arches or something. I forget what reason I gave. Of course, since he had just placed his money on the horse, that made him angry enough to argue, which is what I had counted on. I pretended to get argumentative, too, and ended by offering to bet him five dollars to one that Lanceolate didn't win.

He offered to take all the money I wanted to bet at that figure, but I wouldn't give him any more. You see, all I wanted to do was get it recorded that I had made a bet against Lanceolate. Now I knew that Lanceolate would win. He couldn't help it; I had bet that he wouldn't. So then I went up to the window and spent everything I had—it was about five hundred dollars—on tickets for Lanceolate to win.

I guess I was so busy with my scheme and figuring out how I was nearly going to double my money that I hadn't noticed the clouds gathering overhead. But just as the man at the window shoved my tickets across to me, the clouds cut loose with a tremendous lightning-flash. It made a crack like a cannon-shot. The lightning hit the flagpole not fifty feet from where I was standing and blew it all to splinters. The shock knocked several people down, and upset all the horses so that the next race had to be held up nearly half an hour.

There wasn't any rain. After the panic had

settled down a little, I pulled myself together and went up into the stands with the rest of the people to watch the race.

Of course, Lanceolate didn't win. Instead of nearly doubling my money, I was just out nearly every cent I had. When Mary found out what I had done, you can believe she let me know what she thought of it, too. It wouldn't have been the least use to talk to her about parapsychology or the fairy curse, either. She just didn't believe in that sort of thing. As far as she was concerned, I had just thrown the money away.

I don't know how much of it I believe myself, but I believe enough of it to be scared. I was never so scared in my life. I'm convinced that flash of lightning was aimed at me, and the next time I make a bet, there'll be another one, and this time it won't miss. That's just what I get for trying to progress. I say phooey on it. In fact, I say phooey on everything. I want another drink.

. . . He brought his fist down hard on the bar. Mr. Cohan smiled amiably. "Now, Jerry," he said. "The little woman will be expecting you soon."

The massive young man looked at the clock. "My God!" he said. "You're right." He scooped up the change from his bill and dived for the door.

Mr. Cohan said: "There's a fine lad that has had some bad luck. That woman he married now would sour the temper of the blessed saints, so she would. Ah, well, it ain't all of us can marry happy."

THE LOVE NEST

"It's like this," said Doc Brenner, drinking from his Scotch and Soda as he sought for the proper phrase. "Like this: this Lysenko claims that if you change the environment, like the soil a plant grows in, for instance, a change is produced in the germ plasm, and future generations will have new and different characteristics."

Mr. Jeffers produced a handkerchief with which he mopped his brow, either as an antidote to the heat of the day or to the flood of Brenner's words. "But isn't that sometimes true?" he asked. "I read once where, if you take seeds of the best Turkish tobacco and plant them in Kentucky, you get Kentucky tobacco."

"It works the other way, too," said Brenner. "There isn't any real change in the tobacco plant in such a case. It only takes up certain flavors from the soil it grows in. What this Lysenko means is that by changing the soil or the water or something, you could get a tobacco plant to produce apples and to keep on producing them."

"But look here," said Jeffers. "How does this germ plasm get changed, then? If it didn't change somehow, we'd all still be monkeys, wouldn't we?"

"We would not," said Mr. Cohan, severely, setting a fresh glass of beer before Jeffers. "I mind the day me brother Julius, that's on the force now, came home with words like that on his lips. The priest gave him fifteen Ave Marias and me own father, God bless him, washed the boy's mouth out with soap and water."

"How do the changes happen?" persisted Jeffers.

"Mutation," said Doc Brenner. "There isn't any one simple answer—or rather, we don't know what the real answer is. All we know is that in each generation a few individuals show some variation from the normal, and if the change helps them get along better, there are more and more who have it."

"Like breeds of dogs, you mean?" said Jeffers.

"That's the trouble with things the way they are now," said Mr. Gross, putting down the chaser of his Boilermaker. "Dogs everywhere. If we had a decent administration in Washington, now—"

"Approximately," said Brenner. "The breeds aren't yet separate species. But they illustrate the point that something which begins as a more or less accidental mutation can become fixed through careful breeding together of individuals that have the most of it. Most changes in species are pretty gradual. I wouldn't expect you, for instance, to have a child with leopard-colored spots."

"I would," said Mr. Gross. "My wife's got a second cousin that—"

"Doesn't it ever work the other way?" said Jeffers. "Quick, I mean."

"Yes," said Brenner. "I know of a case, or think I know of a case—I can't be certain, because the records disappeared along with the girl. A real major mutation in human anatomy. Perhaps a view of the coming race, if she could have married the right man."

Jeffers looked at his watch. "Fill up the glasses again, will you, Mr. Cohan?" he said. "I want to hear about this. Was it something like having six fingers?"

"A good deal more than that," said Brenner. "I admit that the whole thing was unsatisfactory. It could be that one of her parents had been around a nuclear fission laboratory, so that the germ plasm became violently altered and she was just a freak. That sometimes happens. It could be that she was a genuine mutant; it could even be that I was too quick about putting things together and imagining the result. It all happened long ago, when I was young and charming, and I haven't heard anything of it since; while, if the thing had been real, I'd have expected to.

"At that time I was interning in St. Matthew's, and they brought this girl in with a case of polio and put her in an iron lung. Her name was Avis Fowler, and both I and Ozzie Stroud, who was interning along with me at the time, were much interested in her."

Gross leaned his bulk on the bar and behind a hamlike hand addressed Mr. Cohan: "Who is that toward the end of the bar that is so interested in what the old crowd is saying?"

The bartender glanced in the direction of a neat gentleman with shell-rimmed glasses and a beard of the type affected by the late Admiral William Sowden Sims. "I wouldn't know him from Brian Boru, that I wouldn't," he replied in a stage whisper. "But any man is free to stay in Gavagan's so long as he behaves himself."

"I don't like it," said Gross.

"Excuse me," said Doc Brenner.

"Don't mention it," said Gross.

This Avis Fowler's chart [Brenner continued] said she was eighteen; she was dark-haired and had one of those thin, triangular faces that can be so very pretty when you get used to them. When she could speak, which wasn't very much at first, but got to be a good deal more, because she made a perfectly wonderful recovery—when she could speak, it was evident that she was just as bright as she was beautiful. For a girl of her age she had read a lot; she knew about music, and she had a kind of elfish humor when we discussed the kind of philosophy young people talk about.

Only—there was something queer about her. You know how it is with most young girls that age. Social contacts are very important to them, they're interested in personalities and emotions, particularly their own. Avis Fowler was different. As far as I could make out, she had no social contacts outside her family. She never mentioned another person or doing anything except by herself. The only personalities and emotions she would discuss were those of people in books; and when, as young men do, I hinted that I might be falling in love with her, she didn't react at all normally. She acted frightened, not in the coy way girls usually behave, but perfectly terrified, as though I had suggested something dreadful, like pushing the head nurse out the window.

"You mustn't ever talk like that again," she said, and when I asked why not, she began to cry.

Her parents were apparently pretty well fixed, because she had a private room and day and night nurses while her case was serious. I asked Ozzie Stroud one night about the patient in 303, mentioning that she was rather mysterious.

"Oh, Avis Fowler," he said. "Yes, that's a fascinating case, isn't it? Have you seen the X rays?"

As a matter of fact, I hadn't. I told him I wasn't interested in her anatomy, except as a work of art, but in her background and personality. "She doesn't seem to have been to school since she was about thirteen," I said, "and she isn't going to college."

"The family has done quite a lot of travelling," he said, and just then something interrupted.

It didn't occur to me at the time that his remark showed a considerable degree of intimacy with Avis Fowler. In the egotistical fashion of young men, I was assuming I had the inside track with her because she seemed always glad to see me, and I could talk about books and music, while Ozzie was a pretty solemn character, interested in very little outside his profession. In fact, I didn't even wake up when I noticed some flowers in her room one day, and she said Dr. Stroud had sent them, he was very much interested in her case; and then went right ahead talking about *Northanger Abbey*, which we had been discussing.

You see, Ozzie naturally would be interested

in her as a case. She was making one of the most rapid recoveries from polio on record, and I heard Doc Tayloe, the resident, one day bemoaning the fact that she wasn't a clinical patient, so we could keep her there under observation and find out what it was in her bodily chemistry had produced this result. Ozzie was in the room at the time. He said: "Doctor, may I suggest that it could be a by-product of the other mutation?"

Mr. Cohan, will you fill the glasses again?

You see, I'm recalling all these things now, because they seem to fit together. At the time, that remark about "the other mutation" blew right past me. Avis Fowler didn't look like a mutant of any kind to me. She had the usual number of arms and legs, and very shapely ones, too, and that was what I was mainly interested in with regard to her. I was intending to specialize in surgery in those days, and a recovery from polio, however wonderful, was outside my orbit.

It was a month, and I'd swear a month almost to the day, after I saw Stroud's flowers in her room, that the incident of the egg came up. By this time, Avis Fowler could move around the room a little, though not quite enough to leave it. On the afternoon of the egg incident, I dropped in on Avis. She was in bed and looked rather pale. When I spoke to her, she seemed cross and out of sorts, didn't want to talk about anything. When I tried to find out what was wrong, she began to act afraid, like the time before, and asked for Ozzie. I told her, which was the truth, that he was out on an emergency case over on the West Side and probably wouldn't be back till after dark. She said: "Oh," and turned her head in the other direction. I thought for a moment she was going to cry again, but she only gave a little sigh and then turned back to me.

"Come back and see me tomorrow, will you, Bill?" she said. "It's all right, anyway."

A man is reduced to a pretty helpless condition when women behave like that. I went away, wondering what gives, and the next thing was that the nurse who had just taken Avis her supper and prepared her for sleeping called me into the hall.

She had a wastebasket in her hand, and she looked puzzled. "Dr. Brenner," she said, "you were visiting the patient in 303 this afternoon, weren't you?"

I said yes, but only as a friend, not because she was my patient.

"Well, it's the oddest thing," she said. "Whatever in the world is this?"

She reached into the wastebasket, came up with a handful of cleansing tissue, and then held it out to show me what was left. It was an egg; quite definitely an egg, about so big. [Doc Brenner held out his hands to indicate an object the size of a child's football.] It didn't seem to have a shell, only a kind of tough, leathery skin that gave a little when I touched it.

You can imagine the kind of wild surmises that leaped into my head. This would explain everything; why Avis had left school at thirteen, why she had stayed away from other people, why she had been frightened, the business about mutations, Ozzie's interest in her. But I wasn't going to tell the nurse any of that. Naturally; nurses talk too much. The poor girl would have been badgered to death, and just when she was getting over a case of polio. Thinking fast, I said: "Oh, that's just something Dr. Stroud was experimenting with. It's all right."

I would have given anything to get possession of that egg, but I didn't dare ask for it after it had been found in the wastebasket. Even that would have roused too much curiosity. But I went to see Doc Tayloe.

Unfortunately, he was busy at the time, and it was nearly an hour before I could get to him. I told him about the nurse with the egg in the basket. "I've been waiting for this!" he said, tremendously excited. "Where is it?"

We ran down together to waste disposal, but it was too late; the egg was gone. After we were back in his office, he swore me to secrecy and told me that he had suspected from Avis Fowler's X rays that she was a genuine human mutant, an egg-laying woman. Of course, the hospital's first duty was to cure her of polio, so he hadn't done anything about it at the time. But this was pretty conclusive; not conclusive enough to write a paper about till we had an actual egg, but enough to make us watch for the next one. [Doc Brenner stopped and drank from his Scotch and Soda with an expression of unhappiness.]

["Didn't you get it?" said Jeffers. "Another round, Mr. Cohan."]

No. We forgot Ozzie Stroud. When I came to the hospital the next day, almost the first thing I found out was that Avis Fowler was gone. She had left word with the night floor nurse to have Ozzie come and see her as soon as he got in, and as soon as he did so, he did a lot of telephoning. About midnight, Avis's parents showed up with a wheel-chair and a hired ambulance and took her away. Ozzie countersigned the release papers and went with them. I haven't heard from him or of him since. He never came back to the hospital and he isn't a member of any of the medical societies. He just disappeared, and so did the Fowlers. Doc Tayloe couldn't get any information at the last address given for them on the records. Not that I blame them. They probably wanted Avis to lead a reasonably normal life.

"You ought to hire a detective," said Gross. "Some of them private detectives can find out anything, like the time old man Webster wanted to know who put the clam chowder in the bass drum."

The bus boy emerged from the phone booth and said something to the man in the Admiral Sims beard, who got off his stool.

"Huh?" said Gross. "It sounded like he said his wife wanted him to come home and keep the egg warm."

The bearded man paused in his exit. "He did," he said. "Avis wants to go to the movies. Hello, Bill; long time no see."

Dr. Stroud briefly shook Brenner's hand and went on out.

THE STONE OF THE SAGES

". . . so," said Doc Brenner, "the radioactive sulphur is in chemical combination with something in the animal's food. Then you can use a Geiger counter every so often to check what part of the animal's body the stuff is in."

"But doesn't it kill the animal?" asked Mr. Willison. "I thought all the radioactive elements were dangerous."

"Oh, no," said Brenner. "Mr. Cohan, another Scotch and Soda. You can get almost any element in radioactive form now, and some of them are quite harmless. Even gold."

"Make mine a Martini," said Mr. Witherwax. "But if they can make gold out of lead or iron or something, why don't they instead of storing it all away at Fort Knox?"

"Because it doesn't pay," said Brenner. "It takes a million-dollar machine a week to turn out ten cents' worth of gold. Let's see, then the machine would pay for itself in ten million weeks—"

"Over a hundred and ninety thousand years," said Willison gloomily. "There ought to be an easier way to get rich."

"I read in a book where there used to be an easier way," said Witherwax. "You get something they called the Philosopher's Stone, see? And you put it on a piece of lead or mercury, and boom! it turns to gold."

"That's just a story from the Middle Ages," said Brenner.

"Mister, I bet you it was mo' than a story," said a

new voice. The others turned to look at a stocky, solidly-built man, deeply tanned, with close-cut hair and a nose that had been broken. He had the remains of a Rum and Coke before him.

"I just naturally bet you-all it was mo' than a story," he repeated, with the slight slurring of sibilants that suggested he was nearing Mr. Cohan's limit.

Brenner frowned. "I'd take that bet if there were any way of proving a negative," he said. "All I know is that no one ever has been able to prove that there was any such thing as a Philosopher's Stone."

"You think so, mister?" said the tanned man. "All right, you-all smarty pants just tell me what this is."

He thrust a hand into a pocket and brought out something yellow, which passed from hand to hand.

Brenner said: "It looks like a half-dollar made of gold."

"Mister, you are one hundred per cent absitively right," said the tanned man. "That's just what it is."

"Is it gold clear through?" asked Willison, "or just a regular silver fifty-cent piece, gold-plated?"

"Heft it," said the tanned man.

Willison produced a normal half-dollar and balanced the two against each other, first in one hand, then in the other. "That's gold, or at least it's heavier than the other one," he admitted. "But what's the story on it, Mr. Uh?"

The tanned man smiled a smile of crafty inebriation. "No, suh," he said. "You ain't goin' catch me that way. First thing you find out who my folks are, where I'm from, and then she's gone. No, sir."

Brenner said: "Mr. Cohan, refill the gentleman's glass with my compliments. Sir, we have no intention of pumping you, and even if we had, I do not believe it would be permitted in Gavagan's Bar. To us, you shall remain a nameless Mr. Uh or Mr. Wuk if you choose. But sir, you made the statement that the medieval legend of the Philosopher's Stone was something more than a story, and in proof you offer a modern American half-dollar which appears to be made of gold. We would appreciate having the connection established, sir. I need another Scotch and Soda."

The tanned man gasped a trifle and drowned the gasp in a pull at his renewed Rum and Coke. He looked at the stuffed owl and appeared to ruminate, his forehead wrinkling in concentration. Finally:

I guess you got me there, mister [he said]. Maybe I ought to have kept my big fat mouth shut, but I'll tell you. I'll tell you everything except what will let you find it. Le's see.

[He closed one eye, then opened it again.] I'm from Fla'da. I live down there; a little piece north from St. Augustine, never you mind just where. I was out there early in the morning a few weeks ago having a swim all by myself, when the surf began to rough up some, so I come in. Besides, Marybelle, that's my wife, was waiting for me with breakfast, up back a way. We often eat breakfast outdoors like that.

Just as I got into shallow water, my foot came down on something sharp. The beach along there is mostly ground-up shell, so fine it's plenty good to walk, but once in a while you get a piece of angel wing or razor clam worn down to a sharp point, and I thought maybe I'd stepped on one of them, so I bent down to see what it was.

Well, sir, it was something like I never seen on that beach before, a kind of crystal a little bit like they have on some of those old chandeliers, about so-so size, only it was a pinky color, and all worn round the edges. I thought maybe Marybelle might like it, so when I walked up the beach I took it along with me. A little farther along I found Bob—a friend of mine that had come down in his car to have a swim for himself, and there she was stalled.

He asked me to help give her a push to get her going, and I did. But when I did I tried to put that old crystal in the little pocket I have on my swimming trunks, where I keep the car keys and fo' bits for to pay my beach fee with. They got a cop on that section of beach that don't do nothing but walk up and down collecting beach fees for the town. Well, the crystal wouldn't fit in my pocket along with the car keys and the money, so I said to hell with it, and I th'ew the stone away. Mister, that must of been the dumbest mistake I ever made.

We was too early for the cop that morning, so he never did come 'round for the fo' bits, or else I might have caught up with myself even then. Marybelle and me, we had our breakfast and packed up and went back home, and I plumb forgot all about that business on the beach and the crystal for maybe three-fo' days more. Then one day when I came home from work, here was Marybelle waiting for me, 'most as excited as if her kin-folk come to call.

"Where did you get this?" she said, and showed me that little old piece of money right there.

I said I didn't know nothing 'bout it and what was it, and she said I have to know on account of it came out of the pocket of my swimming trunks that she was going to put a new elastic in. Then I remembered the morning I went swimming before breakfast and didn't pay no beach fee, and I said that must be the same fo' bits, but I couldn't figure out how it got that way, the trunks just lying in the closet.

Marybelle used to be a schoolteacher before she got round to marrying me, and she's smarter than a mule in a pea-patch. Right away she begun asking me about everything that happened that morning, and when I told her about that crystal she said that must of been what done the job, that it was probably all hotted up with stuff like in one of them atom bombs. So we took that fifty-cent piece down to the drug store, and they tested it and said no, it wasn't nothing like that, it was just plain old gold all the way through.

The druggist, he wanted to buy that thing, but we wouldn't sell it to him, and we wouldn't tell him where we got it neither. I guess maybe that was kind of dumb, too, on account of his brother, name of—well, never mind his name—is chief of po-lice, and you know how it is in Fla'da, if you got friends on the po-lice, you can get anyone pinched you want to. But we wasn't thinking anything about that then, on account of Marybelle was all excited and said I ought to go back to that beach and try to find the crystal, and she wanted to go up to Washington and look up something about it in the Library of Congress.

We fixed it up for her to go to Washington all right, but that there chief of po-lice come round and said he heard I had some gold coin, and it was the law I have to turn it in to the gov'ment. I had this piece pretty well hid, so I told him to go chase himself for a while, and he run me in. 'Course he couldn't keep me mor'n a couple of days on account of I hadn't done nothing, but I couldn't get down to that beach to look for the crystal, and by the time I got out, Marybelle was back from Washington, and she didn't want me to go looking for it. Right way, that is.

She said that Clem—that there druggist was smart enough to have an idea what I got and to have someone watching me when I went back for it. And what I got was that Philosopher's Stone you was talking about, and that it would turn any other kind of metal into gold. When I tried to stick it in my pocket, I must of just hit that fo' bit piece without touching the car keys, or they'd have been gold, too. She got it all wrote down real nice up there in the library.

[The tanned man fumbled in his pocket and produced a slip of paper, slightly dirty along the folded edge.]

Here it is. It seems that some guy named Para—Paracelsus found it first, way back in fifteen hundred and forty. It tells all about it in one of them old books. Here's the name of it.

[He handed the paper to Brenner, who read: "*Liber de Salute per Sanguinem Leonis*, Prague, 1671. That means Book of Salvation Through the Blood of the Lion."]

That's what Marybelle said [continued the

tanned man.] She says this Paracelsus died the next year after he found the stone and left it to the Archbishop of—of Salzburg, and that the Archbishop sold it to a Jew named Moses of Orleans. I dunno why the Archbishop didn't use it; against his religion I guess. Well, this Moses of Orleans was the guy that backed the expedition that come over to Fla'da and founded a colony there in fifteen and sixty-two, and then the Spaniards come along a couple-three years later and killed them all off. I figure maybe this Moses was along on the expedition, or maybe these Frenchmen stole the stone from him, and that's how it got there.

Anyhoo, Marybelle's got a kind of kissing-cousin that's a lawyer up here, and we came up to see if he can't maybe get a lease or something on that beach, and then we're just naturally going to take it apart till we find that there stone. No thanks; I've had about all I can carry now, and if I don't get back to the hotel, Marybelle will be mad enough to find out how red I am inside. G'night.

They watched him weave his way to the door and vanish into the night.

Willison said slowly: "He needn't have been quite so secretive. That would have been Jean Ribaut's Huguenot colony, and its location is pretty well known. But I'm afraid his lawyer friend isn't going to do him much good."

"What do you mean?" said Brenner. "Or do you think there was some trick about that gold half-dollar?"

"Look here," said Willison, dragging a newspaper from his overcoat pocket and pointing to an item. Witherwax and Brenner leaned over opposite shoulders to read:

SEAPLANE BASE TO RISE

JACKSONVILLE, FLA. MAR 8 (U.P.)—THE U.S. NAVY ANNOUNCED TODAY THAT A NEW NAVAL AIR

STATION WILL BE SET UP ON THE FIVE-MILE STRETCH OF OCEAN FRONT BETWEEN MAYPORT, AT THE MOUTH OF THE JOHNS RIVER, AND JACKSONVILLE BEACH. THE GROUND HAS ALREADY BEEN ACQUIRED, AND WORK WILL BEGIN IMMEDIATELY. WHEN COMPLETE, THE STATION WILL HOUSE . . .

"They'll dredge the hell out of the place," said Willison, with an air of melancholy satisfaction, "and our anonymous friend's pebble will end up as fill for some dock."

"Yes," said Brenner. "But won't the navy look silly when the blade of one of its bulldozers turns to pure gold?"

CORPUS DELECTABLE

"The light doesn't have the power of a regular flashbulb, but it can be used over and over," said young Mr. Jeffers. He aimed his camera at the stuffed owl over the bar. There was a bright, noiseless flash, which caused the owl's eyes to light up yellowly for an instant. A shutter clicked; Jeffers pressed a button, and there was a faint whirr as the little clockwork motor wound the film through the next frame. "No double exposure," said Jeffers.

Mr. Gross looked up from his Boilermaker. "I got a cousin by marriage that got run in for that once," he said.

"What, making pictures of stuffed owls?" asked Mr. Keating from the library.

"No, taking off his clothes in the theatre. He done it twice, and the second time—"

Mr. Witherwax slid his glass across the bar and indicated his desire for another Martini by sign language. "Mr. Jeffers," he said in a firm voice, "I noticed that when you was taking the picture of that owl, it almost looked alive. Did you ever take a picture of someone and almost make them look dead?"

"Yeah," said Jeffers, and indicated a man down the bar, one with a rather handsome but time-worn face under a mop of white hair, who was drinking a double Scotch. "This one, now—I'll bet when the picture is developed, he'll look as though he just came out of a coffin." He lifted his camera and the flash went off again.

The white-haired man started so violently that he

only recovered his drink with an effort. "What did you say?" he almost shouted, taking two steps toward Jeffers.

"I'm sorry," said Jeffers. "I didn't mean to be offensive. I only thought you'd make a good subject—"

The white-haired man gripped him fiercely by the arm. "What business are you in?" he demanded.

"Now, now," said Mr. Cohan, from behind the bar. "In Gavagan's it's against the rule to have fights. When a man is drinking good liquor, he should have no grudges against anyone."

"It was my fault, really," said Jeffers, laying down his camera, and turning back to the white-haired man. "If it makes any difference to you, I work in a law office." He produced a card case. "May I buy you a drink and ask why?"

"Oh," said the other, with a gasp that might have been relief. "I beg your pardon. Mr. Cohan, will you put both drinks on my check? I thought—" He produced a card case of his own.

"That's me, Frederick Moutier. Chevrolet agency; that is, I work for it. I used to have my own business until I had to give it up because of what you just did. In Indianapolis." He smiled glassily.

"Do you mean taking pictures of you?" asked Jeffers, incredulously.

"Just about. Don't you want something that has a little more taste than that beer? Let me ask you this, my friend; how would you like it if—oh, hell, you just won't get it. Nobody does, not even the damn looney-doctor my wife sent me to."

He buried his nose in his Highball. Jeffers, whose low opinion of the psychiatric profession was frequently and forcefully expressed at Gavagan's, encouraged him by remarking that the only time a psychiatrist got anything was when he got it out of somebody's pocket.

> Ha, ha, ha, that's rich! [said Moutier]. Do you mind if I use it some time when I'm speaking before Rotary? That is, if I ever do again. [His face assumed its former melancholy.] My friend, they've got me on the skids; yes, sir, royally on

the skids. It shouldn't happen to a dog, and certainly not to old Freddie Moutier.

Look, it all started with a man named Smith, Leroy Burlingame Smith. I wish I'd never met him. I did, though; we both bought houses in one of those new developments outside Indianapolis, and there we were, next-door neighbors. Well, of course the first thing that happened was the little woman got acquainted with Mrs. Smith, and the next was that we were going over there to play bridge. I'd rather have a little five-ten poker game myself, but you know how it is with women, and I never saw one anyway that had sense enough to lay off inside straights.

Well, right away it developed that Smith was an undertaker. Now I know some people feel funny about undertakers, but I always say it's un-American to be prejudiced against a man because of his profession if he's a good citizen. Why, we even have some undertakers in Rotary. So we went over and played bridge, and when we got through they put out some beer and pretzels, and we sat around chatting for a while and getting acquainted. They seemed like a real nice, wholesome couple. He had his own business and I could tell from the way he talked that he probably had an A-1 credit rating. In my business you get so you can spot them every time.

Well, the women liked each other all right, too, and it wasn't long before we got to be pretty good friends. If we didn't have anything else on, we'd get together in the evening and have some bridge, or maybe take in a movie and sit around a little afterward. But about the time I began to sort of measure him for a new Olds—ha, ha, I had the Oldsmobile agency out there—Leroy began acting kind of funny. I don't mean he was any less friendly. In fact, he was more so, and when I hinted that he might want to make his next car an Olds, he took me up so quick that I never even had a chance to explain the selling points.

But when we were playing bridge, he'd sit

there with the cards in his hand, and all of a sudden he'd be staring at me, kind of half-asleep, until his wife had to remind him that it was his turn to play. Then one evening he said he didn't feel like bridge at all, just wanted to listen to the radio. Well, golly, I could have understood it if there had been something special on, like Fred Allen or the Hit Parade, but he just tuned in on some classical music for a whole hour and sat there all through it, staring at me like I was some kind of Frankenstein.

["You mean Frankenstein's monster," said Keating.]

Do I? I thought Dracula was the monster. Give me another drink, Mr. Cohan. Well, anyway, that's what he did. I remember talking to the little woman about it when we got home, asking her if she heard anything from Elise Smith about Leroy maybe being sick or things not going right in his business. But she said no, she didn't know of anything, and she was pretty sure she would, because Elise was always over there or they were going out together.

Well, it was the next morning after he was so funny about the radio that old Leroy called me up at the agency. He said he was ready for his demonstration on the Olds, and would I bring it around and stop in at his shop. I got out the demonstrator and went. The place was a big one with a couple of those potted palms in front and more inside, very dignified. It made a good presentation, you might say. I asked for Leroy and while I was waiting for him, I stood talking to one of the other men in his shop. He kept staring at me real hard, something like Leroy had the night before, and I was just going to ask him what was the matter with me when Leroy came in.

He introduced me to his staff and showed me all around the place. I thought it was an awful lot of trouble to take with someone who was just there to demonstrate a car, but you don't catch Fred Moutier telling another man how to run his business, no, sir. So I thanked him, and we were just leaving when, bingo! a big flashlight went off right in my face. I jumped about three feet and said "What the hell!" but Leroy just said: "Sorry I startled you, old man. I thought I'd like a picture of you some time, so I got Hulberd to take one. He's pretty good with a camera."

Well, you can't get sore at someone that likes you so much he wants your picture, especially when you're trying to sell him a car, so I just laughed it off, and to make certain Leroy knew I was taking it the right way, asked him to be my guest at Rotary on Wednesday. I was giving a speech I had worked out on "Salesmanship and American Ideals"; maybe you've heard of it. I've given it at a lot of Rotaries and places around the country, about how America is built on the ideal of salesmanship service, and when the government spends a lot of money to give things away, we're getting to be like those Socialistic Communists.

Anyway, Leroy bought the car, and the little woman and me began playing bridge again with the Smiths, and even if he did keep up that funny habit of staring at me, it wasn't as bad as before. I forgot all about that picture until one evening we were over at his house, and he got up to go to the can or something, and the two women started gabbing about clothes, so I picked up a magazine that was lying there.

It was an undertaker's trade journal, and when I opened it, right there smack in the middle of the book was a great big picture of myself, lying in a coffin with flowers piled all around me. Underneath it said: "Arrangements by Leroy B. Smith, Funerary Director of Indianapolis."

Well, I got kind of sore. When Leroy came back, I told him what a hell of a trick I thought he'd pulled, and the little woman and I went home. Elise Smith tried to fix it up the next day by coming over and telling the little wife that it was intended as a compliment, and that Leroy thought I was the most perfect subject for an undertaker he had ever seen, but as far as I was concerned that only made it worse, if you get me. We cut out going over there for a while, but the two women kept on being friends, and you know how women are, I guess they might have fixed things up except for something else that happened.

I went over to Columbus to give my speech about "Salesmanship and American Ideals" to Rotary there, and afterward I was in a bar with a couple of the boys from Columbus Rotary having a little drink before I had to hit the road again, when this fellow stepped up to me. He had on a blue serge suit and a white shirt with a polka-dot tie and he said: "Pardon me, but I'm sure I've seen you before."

I said maybe he had at that, and told him who I was, and he said his name was Francis X. McKenna and bought a round of drinks. All the time he kept giving me one look and then another, as though he had my name all right, but wondered who the hell Fred Moutier was. Finally it seemed to hit him; he pulled me off a little to one side and said: "I remember now. You're the one who posed for that wonderful presentation by Leroy Brown in the *Living Mortician*. Look here, Mr. Moutier," he said, "I know you have your own business and you're not a professional, but if you'll spare half an hour of your time letting me build a presentation around you, I'll make it well worth your while."

The white-haired man gloomily finished his drink and motioned for another.

"What did you do?" asked Witherwax.

Do? I was so sore I could have let him have it right in the puss, but I thought, no, that wouldn't be good for Rotary, so I just walked away. Well, that was only the beginning of it. It seemed I couldn't go anywhere or do anything without having one of them show up, handing me his card and asking me to call on him, or just sitting there staring at me. They used to come to the agency sometimes, and I got so I could tell when a prospect wasn't listening to me at all, just standing there on the floor looking at me; he wasn't interested in the Olds, he was just another damn undertaker. I've even had them follow me on the street. You know how you get a little prickly feeling in the back of the neck when somebody's looking at you behind your back like that? I know there are some people say it's a superstition, but I'm telling you it happened to me. Anyone from Indianapolis will tell you that my reputation for telling the truth about things like this is A-1. Absolutely A-1.

Well, the worst of it was when I got an invitation to give my speech at the Queen of Heaven Association in Chicago. I thought it was some sort of religious group, so I went, but when I got there, it was a whole roomful of these undertakers, sitting around the lunch tables and staring at me, some of them taking notes. It was so bad I couldn't even give the old speech. I had to fake I had a bellyache and get the hell out of there.

"Wait a minute," said Keating. "It seems to me that you could save yourself a lot of trouble with a thing like that by just relaxing. If you're so valuable to undertakers that they'll want to use you as a model all the time, why don't you just have some pictures taken and sell them to them? That's all they want, isn't it?"

Yeah [said Moutier] that's what the looney-doctor said when the little woman sent me to him. My friend, let me tell you there are a couple of difficulties about that program. In the first place, it wouldn't look good for a member of Rotary to have his picture plastered all over every undertaker's shop in the country, looking as if he was dead and all laid out in a casket.

The little woman wouldn't stand for it, and I wouldn't blame her.

And in the second place, it's a lot more serious being a—uh—subject for an undertaker than you might think. I told you I wasn't seeing Leroy B. Smith any more; but the little woman, she kind of kept up the connection with Elise Smith, and they used to gab at each other in the back yard. You know how women are. Well, about a month after this Queen of Heaven Association luncheon in Chicago, the little woman tells me at dinner one night that Elise has some news. She says Tony Passone has bought out the Weizmann undertaking shop over on Third Street.

I said: "What the hell do I care? The less I hear about undertakers the better."

She said: "You needn't be rude. Elise was just trying to do you a favor."

I said I didn't want any favors from undertakers or their families, and maybe we had a little argument, but after she quieted down, she told me that this Tony Passone had been one of these gangsters in Chicago, but decided to go into the undertaking business—burying the stiffs other people made instead of making them himself, ha, ha. Only it wasn't very funny when I got to thinking that maybe this Tony Passone had been in the audience at the Queen of Heaven Association, if you get it.

Well, I was right. This Passone hadn't been in town for more than a week before I got a circular from him, you know the kind undertakers put out, with photographs of tombs and stone angels. I didn't pay any attention to it. There was nobody dead in the family and I didn't want anybody to be. But about a week after that I got a phone call. The voice at the other end said this was Passone's Sympathetic Service, and Mr. Passone would like to have me call. I said I didn't want any service from Mr. Passone and hung up; but after I hung up, I got to worrying about it, so I went around to the police station and asked them for protection.

When they asked me who I wanted to be protected against, and I told them, they just laughed and said that Tony was a legitimate businessman now and the only way to be protected against an undertaker was to stay alive. That's the way things are with this Raw Deal administration they have in Washington, and the next thing I knew, there was another call from this Passone, saying I better come around and see him.

Well, I didn't go, but about three days after that, when I had finished demonstrating the Olds for a man who lived about twelve miles out and was coming back alone in the car, another car pulled up alongside me at a red light, with a couple of guys that had hats down over their faces, and somebody took a shot at me. If I hadn't been nervous about this undertaker business and seen his hand coming up, and if the Olds didn't have such wonderful pick-up, he might have hit me, too.

Well, it didn't take me long to figure out that I'd be just as good to Tony Passone dead as I would be alive, and the police still wouldn't believe that he was after me, so I just said to myself, Fred Moutier, you're getting out of here, so I gave up the agency and sold my house and came here. And you can see why I get nervous when somebody says I'm a perfect subject . . .

Moutier had been showing a tendency to run his sentences together. Now his words went down to a mumble, and as though the bones in his legs were melting, he folded gradually and gently to the floor.

"Ah, the poor felly, now," said Mr. Cohan. "I never should of given him that last one. But with him talking along and all, I thought he was all right."

Jeffers and Keating bent to help the prostrate figure but, before they could get him upright, a voice said: "Let me assist him. I assure you I will take very good care of him, very good."

They looked up and saw a man in a sober blue

serge suit, with a white shirt and a polka-dot tie. He wore an expression in which eagerness combined with melancholy, and his fingers were twitching slightly.

THE PALIMPSEST OF ST. AUGUSTINE

Mr. Cohan brought a roll of currency out of his pocket, peeled off the topmost bill, and handed it to the priest. Then he drew a glass of beer and slid it across the bar to Jeffers.

"It's like this Spinoza says," said Witherwax, "when I read it in a book. You ain't got no right to say something is bad just because you don't like it personally. You gotta consider other people. If there wasn't no ocean there, how could you get to Europe?"

The priest had turned toward them and appeared to be listening. He had sharp blue eyes behind rimless glasses, and there was an air of easy-going competence around his mouth.

"That hasn't got anything—" began Jeffers, and broke off to stare at a man who came trotting through the double doors and up to the bar with:

"Whiskey. I don't care what kind. A shot."

Mr. Cohan's eyebrows went up, but he poured out the dose. The man, a burly fellow in a shabby suit, slightly in need of a shave, tossed it off, set down the glass and tapped it with a forefinger to indicate a refill, then gripped the edge of the bar in large hands, breathing a little hard and contemplating his reflection in the mirror as though it might have been that of a stranger.

Witherwax took a drink of his Martini. " 'Smatter, brother, see a ghost?" he asked.

The burly man was dealing more slowly with his second shot. "I dunno, mister, but I'm afraid that's just what I seen. In church, too." He shuddered.

"Huh? Tell us about it."

The priest's foot tapped and the burly man appeared to become aware of his presence. "No offence meant, Father, but I seen something."

"You may have seen the appearance of something. To the uninstructed eye, the world has the appearance of being flat."

"Look, Father, maybe you can help me out on it. I'm over at St. Joseph's, see? And the priest there, he's a little, dark priest I ain't seen before. He was starting to go round the church lighting the candles. Only he don't light them, see? They start lighting themselves up before he gets to them. Well, I'm up toward the front of the church, and I seen him go past, and he's praying in Latin when he goes out and his hands are shaking."

Mr. Cohan said; "That'll be Father Palladino, now, won't it? At St. Joseph's? I did hear he was just back from retreat."

"I'm afraid you're right." The priest's blue eyes held an expression that was less displeasure than unhappiness. He held out a hand to the burly man. "My name's McConaghy. It is not our place to question the means God uses to effect His purposes, but this is a rather dark business."

The burly man said; "My name's Czikowsky. Pleased to meetcha, Father."

"What goes on here?" said Witherwax. "Spooks in a Catholic church? That don't seem right."

"It isn't," said Father McConaghy.

"I think we should be telling them about it, Father," said Mr. Cohan. "It's better they be hearing it from us than from anyone else."

As the priest hesitated, Witherwax said: "How about a drink, Father? Indulge?"

Father McConaghy shook his head. "No, thank you. I appreciate the offer, and don't let me restrain you; I don't mind in the least. But a little wine with a meal is as far as I go."

"Another Martini, Mr. Cohan. How about the story, then?"

"Well," said Father McConaghy, thoughtfully. "I should like to set you right, to be sure. On the other hand, my time is rather taken up just now, collecting for the repair fund, and I am due at—"

Jeffers said: "May I make a little contribution to your repair fund? I'm sure the Church won't object to Protestant money." He suited the action to the word, and Witherwax also produced his wallet.

Father McConaghy produced a bankroll held together by a rubber band and added the contributions to it. "Let me see—I believe the first manifestation occurred here in Gavagan's, so that Mr. Cohan is rather better qualified than I am to describe it. But before he does, I should like you to understand that Father Palladino is a serious-minded man, very studious, and with at least the appearance of piety. If he has any fault at all, it's the lack of a sense of humor. This can hardly be considered a sin; but on the human side, a sense of humor does lighten the load at times. Mr. Cohan, what was your observation?"

"Right you are when you say he's serious," said Mr. Cohan. "Never a man more so, and it was on a serious errand he come into Gavagan's that night, for that Tony Grasso was in here, drunk so he could hardly stand. I had refused to sell him anything earlier, knowing about his wife and children and how he sucks up the money that should be feeding them, so he went elsewhere and when he come back, here's a bottle of whiskey in his hand with the cap off and maybe one drink out of it. He sets it on the bar, he does, and says this is a public place, and bedamned to me, but I can't prevent him drinking his own whiskey. I says bedamned to him but we'll see about that, and I'm just looking around for the bung starter when in comes Father Palladino.

" 'Tony,' he says, 'I want you to come home with me now. Your wife is waiting.'

" 'Not till I finish my whiskey,' says Tony, and points to the bottle, then turns to face Father Palladino.

" 'You aren't going to drink that whiskey,' says the Father, and just as he says it, the bottle on the bar, with Tony's back to it and meself three feet away, falls over flat on the bar and all the whiskey runs out before anyone can lift a hand.

"Father Palladino turns as pale as any man you ever saw, but he just stands there looking at Tony, and Tony looks at the spilled whiskey and then at him and goes out with him, and I do not have to use the bung starter after all. Have I told it right, Father?"

[Father McConaghy nodded.] I believe that to be correct, as you have told it before. Naturally, I did not learn about it from Father Palladino, as I am not his confessor, but I know he was gravely disturbed and for some time devoted himself to prayer and penance. But this was followed by the incident of the palimpsest.

["Excuse me," said Witherwax, "but what's a palimpsest?"]

A palimpsest [continued the priest] is a piece of parchment, usually ancient, that has been used twice. When parchment was the normal writing material, a piece that had been used was not thrown away after the utility of the first writing had passed. The material was too expensive to be wasted. So an effort, usually not very effective, was made to erase the first writing with pumice stone, and the parchment was used for a new piece of communication. It was customary to write the second message with lines at right angles to the first to make it a little more legible.

This was the case with the palimpsest that Father Evans, a very able man, was dealing with. The second message was quite legible, but nothing very important, something about some titles to land somewhere in North Africa. But the parchment itself and the few words of the underlying writing that he could make out, indicated that it was very early, possibly from the fifth or sixth century, and that it was some kind of tract, or treatise on theology. This was very exciting and important, because so many points with regard to the Faith came up at that time, and some doctrinal questions haven't been settled yet

—not with regard to the Faith itself, but the human vessels through whom it was expressed.

Now this evening at supper, while Father Evans was going along about his palimpsest and his troubles with the under-writing, some of us noticed that a curious change had come over Father Palladino. He had stopped eating and was sitting upright, with his eyes closed, breathing hard, and making peculiar gasps and groans. We spoke to him, and even slapped him on the back and offered water, but he answered none of us.

We thought he must be ill and were about to take him away from the table, when he began to speak, in a loud and clear voice. The language he spoke was not English. It took us two or three minutes to recognize that it was Latin, which you might think peculiar, since we all study Latin in training for the priesthood. But on this occasion Father Palladino's Latin had a very peculiar accent.

Father Evans was the first one to understand. He asked us not to take Father Palladino away, but to let him go on, and began taking notes like mad. Presently the talking stopped. None of us had gathered very much of it, but we were all sure we had recognized one phrase—"*Aurelio Augustino,*" which is, of course, late Latin for Aurelius Augustinus, or St. Augustine. I don't need to tell you who St. Augustine was, but perhaps you don't know that he lived in North Africa, at Carthage. And Father Evans said that this Latin had a strong Carthaginian accent, that he had understood nearly all of it, then asked to be excused and left the table with his notes.

Naturally, that left all of us very excited, and as Father Palladino began rubbing his eyes and looking around, perfectly recovered, we began to discuss it. Father Muller, who has studied some medicine, said Father Palladino must have what the psychologists call a personality dissociation. But our good bishop, who happened to be present, took another and more serious view.

He quieted the talk and asked Father Palladino whether he understood the Carthaginian dialect of Latin.

Father Palladino had just said he did not, when Father Evans came bursting into the room again, carrying his palimpsest, and almost shouting that he had found the key at last. The few sentences he transcribed from Father Palladino's speech in his trance corresponded almost word for word with some of those in the document. As for the document itself, it was nothing less than St. Augustine's treatise on the Trinity, which was known to have been written, but of which no other copy has survived into modern times. He added that he couldn't be sure as yet, but it looked very much as though the tract would establish St. Augustine once and for all as having been doctrinally sound on the subject of the Trinity. St. Augustine, you know, was converted from Manicheism to the true doctrine, and it has always been suspected that he retained some of his former beliefs. But this would make it clear he was orthodox.

As soon as Father Evans had finished, we all looked at Father Palladino. He groaned, and burying his face in his hands, leaned forward on the table, saying: "God forgive me if this be true." We—

Witherwax said: "Excuse, Father, but would you mind telling us why?"

"Why, it would mean a visitation of evil spirits."

"But if it was really St. Augustine speaking, with Father Palladino as the voice, would that be an evil spirit?"

I'm afraid you don't understand [continued the priest]. The incident did have all the appearances associated with psychic manifestations, as they are called. The teachings of the Church are quite definite in this respect. We hold that the greater part of such manifestations are simply fakery; but there is a small residue that cannot be accounted for by material means. It can be shown on sound theological grounds that the entities responsible for this residue are and must be evil spirits—devils.

Now in Father Palladino's case, there could be no question of fakery, of course. He is a sincere man. But that left us with an extremely serious question. For either we had witnessed something approaching a miracle, which cleared the name of a great father of the Church from an unjust accusation, or we had to assume that Father Palladino had been visibly possessed by a demon. The evidence of the palimpsest itself favored the former theory; but the palimpsest may have been faked at an early date, and in any case it could hardly outweigh the question of this mediumistic practice itself. This was the view our bishop took.

He imposed heavy penances on Father Palladino, though no heavier than those Father Palladino imposed upon himself in addition to those awarded to him. The fact that this malevolent entity appeared to be actuated by a kind of genuine affection for Father Palladino, that everything it did could be regarded as a favor to him, something to make his lot easier or more gracious, was not allowed to weigh in the matter. It was arranged for him to go into a long retreat, where by fasting, meditation, and prayer, he hoped to free himself from his difficulties. Yesterday he returned, and I fear it has not been altogether successful.

Thank you for your generosity, my friends. I'm afraid I must be off on my fund-raising.

WHERE TO, PLEASE?

". . . So that elevator fell down the shaft and everyone in it was killed," said Mr. Witherwax, reaching out as Mr. Cohan slid his third Martini across the bar.

"It probably didn't make any difference," said Mr. Willison, sadly. "He probably would have slipped on the bathroom floor next week and cut his throat on an old razor blade."

"Oh, listen," said Mr. Jeffers, "if everyone felt that way—"

He was interrupted by the entrance of a character who plunged through the door so hard as to bang it back on its hinges, almost feverishly clutched at the bar, and said hoarsely: "Brandy. A double."

The bartender's eyes opened wide, pushing a couple of rolls of fat aside in the process. "Good evening to you, Mr. Titus," he said, pouring.

The man he addressed took a gulp, coughed, looked at the stuffed owl and around as though he were seeing the place for the first time. His clothes had spots of dust and mud, and he was badly in need of a shave. "It's still here," he said, as though talking to himself. "It's all right." He sipped, and seemed to pull himself together. "Mr. Cohan," he said, "have you seen Morrie Rath?"

"Not this week now," said the bartender. "Would you be knowing these gentlemen? This is Mr. Gilbert Titus; Mr. Jeffers, Mr. Willison, and Mr. Witherwax, and isn't that a fine name to give a man?"

Hands were shaken. Titus said: "Sorry if my hand

feels moist. I've been through an experience. Better give me another, Mr. Cohan. But make it a Brandy Smash this time."

"What kind of an experience?" asked Jeffers. "More beer, while you're about it, Mr. Cohan."

"I don't know. I wish I did. That's why I want to find Morrie Rath in a hurry and check with him. Do you know him? Real-estate man."

"I've heard of him," said Jeffers. "Isn't he the one who promoted that big Belleview development?"

"That's the one. With every house furnished complete, down to and including a TV set and a lot of chromium-pipe furniture in the living room. I think they're horrors myself, and they're certainly no good for my business. I'm a junk dealer—antiques, you know."

He dug his nose into the Brandy Smash. "He wanted to show me how convenient those modern houses really are when they're lived in, so he took me out to a cocktail party at Joe Cox's. Do you know Joe? Well, anyway, that's where we went; Morrie picked me up right here at Gavagan's. You remember, maybe, Mr. Cohan?"

"That would be the last I seen of him," said the bartender.

"Indeed? Well, since you don't know Joe, I'll tell you that he's a good man with a cocktail shaker. He kept plying everybody with his concoctions, and since there was a big enough mob present to keep the ball rolling and a big table loaded with snacks, nobody worried much about doing any more formal eating, least of all Morrie and myself. I don't mean we drank our dinner, but we came pretty close to it, and the first thing we knew, we were the last guests present and Ethel Cox was saying something about trotting off to bed and leaving us to continue the conversation."

So we phoned for a taxi [Titus continued] and, as it was a fine night, went outside to wait for it at the street. Joe Cox's place stands at the top of that big Belleview hill. We could look down through the trees and see the lights of the city in the distance, long strings in irregular patterns. I seem to remember that they put me in a slightly sentimental mood. I said: "I'd give anything I owned to see that view as it was a hundred years ago, and go down into the city and find it as it was then. They lived a more comfortable life."

This was more or less a continuation of an argument we'd had inside. Morrie said: "That's just because you don't know what it is to live without conveniences. I'd give anything I owned, including my soul, to see the place as it will be a hundred years from now."

It was a silly argument, but we were still at it when the cab drove up. It was an independent, not one of those yellows. I always like to look at the driver's name, and I noticed that the little card that has it was missing. But it sometimes is. The driver turned around till he was almost facing us—he had the most flexible neck I ever saw on a man, but the cap covered all his face except a long nose—and said: "Where to, please?"

I was full of my argument for the good old days, and still fuller of Joe Cox's booze. So I said: "The Barclay Hotel, please!"

"You mean Bedbug Palace?" said Morrie. "That old joint was crummy when they tore it down, six years ago."

"Crummy, my left foot," I said. "It was a monument. Abraham Lincoln stopped there on the way to—"

"Okay," said Morrie. "Have your joke, and I'll have mine." He tapped on the glass. "Make that the first stop, driver, and then take me on to the Lonergan Building. That's as far in one direction as yours is in the other. They won't get it finished for five years. Let's see, you paid on the way out, didn't you? I'll take care of this end of the trip."

I said no, he had paid for the trip out, and I thought so, too; so we argued about that for a while, and then got onto something else, neither one of us noticing that the driver had started out, just as though he knew exactly where he was taking us. In fact, I didn't notice anything until the cab pulled up, the driver turned his head around on that prehensile neck and said: "Here you are, sir."

I got out without thinking and found that although the air up at Belleview was clear, there was a good deal of fog down here in the valley. I heard Morrie call "Good night, Gil!" Then the cab door slammed, and there I was, alone on the sidewalk. Then I noticed that the street was cobbled and the sidewalk was flagstones.

You see, as I said, I'd had quite a few drinks, and it wasn't until that minute that it occurred to me to wonder where the hell the driver had dumped me out. I turned around, and there right in front of me was the big familiar-looking porte cochère, all ornamented with iron curlycues, with the letters reading "Hotel Barclay." Through the glass of the doors, I could see a little light inside, enough to show that somebody was about, though there didn't seem to be as much activity as you'd expect at a big hotel.

I hesitated about going in. I knew as well as anybody that there wasn't any Hotel Barclay any more, and there must be something fishy about this deal. But I looked up and down the street, and couldn't make out anything but a couple of street lights, dim in the fog, and there wasn't a sound anywhere. Besides, with the liquor, I was so groggy that all I wanted was to get into bed somewhere and solve any questions later.

So I put on my fighting face, as they say, walked up to the door of the non-existent Barclay, and pulled it open. Inside, by what little light there was, I could make out that I was in an ordinary hotel lobby, with chairs and tables standing around. The furniture was Early Victorian—mahogany, with heavy lines—thick legs and lots of curves, but without the carved foliage that came in during the Late Victorian.

Across the lobby was the usual hotel desk, with a space for the room clerk and a wicket. On the desk stood an oil lamp, but turned down way low, so that it only lit up the place very faintly. It stank, and I recognized the type of lamp; it was one of the kind they used to use for burning whale oil. The only sound was a faint gurgle-gurgle, as though someone had had his throat freshly cut.

It gave me a chill until I realized that it was only the night clerk snoring, curled up in the farthest corner behind the desk, back of the cashier's wicket. I couldn't reach the clerk to shake him, but there was a little bell beside the lamp, and I jangled it.

The clerk shook his head a couple of times, stood up and said: "You wish something, sir?" He was a young chap, with his hair full of grease and little sideburns growing clear down the sides of his face. He was wearing an old-fashioned hard-boiled shirt, and a vest over it, but no coat, collar or tie.

I said: "I want a room for the night."

He looked me from top to bottom sort of wonderingly—it wasn't until later that I realized my clothes must have affected him the same way his did me—but he shoved the register at me, with an inkwell which had a wooden penholder attached to it. He said: "I can let you have Number 207 for seventy-five cents, or Number 311 for a dollar. That has a sitting room."

It was too late to pull out now, and I was feeling so sleepy I didn't care what kind of a flea bag this was, so I said: "I'll take 311."

The clerk looked over the desk to see if I had any baggage. "In advance, if you please," he said.

That was to be expected. I pulled a bill out of my wallet and handed it to him. He had already started to open the till for change, when he stopped, turned up the lamp and took another look at the bill.

"What under the canopy is this, eh?" he said.

"A five-dollar bill. What did you think it was?" I said.

"Never saw the like," he said, and squinted hard at the picture of Lincoln. "Who's this?" He scowled over the fine lettering. "Uh—Lincoln. Oh, that Whig Congressman. Series of 1934. Say, this wouldn't fool—Oh, I twig! A campaign dodger, ha, ha, ha, pretty cute!"

I didn't want to start an argument, so I said: "They're going to run him for president," and fished in my pocket. Fortunately, I've been in the habit for years of carrying around an old silver dollar as a luck piece. It was my grandfather's estate, the only thing he left. The clerk bounced it on the counter to see if it rang right, looked at it a little suspiciously and picked up the lamp.

"Follow me," he said and led me down the corridor, where we climbed up two stories to No. 311. He showed me in, handed me the key, lit a match that went off with a great flare and sputter, and applied it to a gas jet. It gave off a little yellow unshielded flame.

"You know about that rule, don't you, sir?" he said, jerking his thumb toward a sign tacked to the inside of the door. In big letters it warned: DON'T BLOW OUT THE GAS!

"Sure," I told him.

He explained anyway. "A lot of rubes come in here that have never seen gaslights before and don't know that you turn it out like this." He demonstrated.

"I know about it," I said, yawning, and handed him a quarter for a tip.

He looked at it and said: "Haven't you made a mistake, sir?"

"I don't think so," I told him. "Why?"

"But this is a quarter of a dollar."

"I know," I said. "It's for you."

"Oh, thank *you*, sir," he said, and went out.

I got rid of my clothes and climbed into bed; and the next thing I knew I was being wakened by a loose shutter somewhere banging in the breeze. The room was still dark, because the shutters at the window had been left closed. I had the usual hangover thirst, and the only water I could locate had stood all night in a pitcher on the washstand. But I took a swig of that and went over and pushed open the shutters. It was broad daylight—somewhere near noon, I would judge. As I looked over the city, I could see that something was undoubtedly fishy; no tall buildings, no autos, no nothing. Just like a damned set for a Dickens movie; and the actors in it were wandering around with the women in big long skirts and the men in long coats and straw stovepipe hats.

This was somewhere else; or rather, some time else. While I was dressing, I tried to do a little figuring. I know all about those stories where a man gets thrown backward in time and settles down to make his fortune by inventing the multiplication table or something like that. But they're fiction, and written by people it never happened to. That demon taxi-driver had taken me at my word and delivered me to the Barclay in its heyday; and here I was, in outlandish clothes, with a pocketful of money dated far in the future, and no prospects. I wouldn't know how to put an electric light together if I had the pieces, and a telephone is a mysterious act of God; the only thing I understand is antiques. Besides, I have a family and I like them. I wanted home.

In the meantime, I thought it would be worth while finding out what date I was in; I was hungry and didn't think a shot would do me any harm. Going out didn't appeal, but a rope came through the wall with a tassel on the end of it and the legend PULL beneath. I pulled; and then sat down to count my resources. None of the bills was any good, of course, and the Lincoln pennies and Roosevelt dimes were just as bad. That left me with one more half-dollar, three quarters, a couple of Liberty dimes, and six of the Jefferson nickels.

It wasn't very much. When my ring was answered by a chap about the same age as the night clerk, with a thin fringe of red whisker around his chin, I told him I wanted a newspaper and asked what the hotel charged for lunch.

He said: "Oh, we have the American plan here. You'll find it quite a bit different than in England, Mr. Titus."

I said: "England?" rather stupidly.

He smiled. "You musn't think we Americans are rubes, Mr. Titus. Mr. Baker, the night clerk, told me you were an English millionaire."

I said: "Oh, all right. Bring me a bottle of whiskey along with the food," and recklessly handed him one of my remaining quarters. My spirits took a jump. I had noticed what seemed to me a slight accent in the voice of the night clerk, and now in this chap's. They had apparently caught the difference in my speech, and between the clothes and the quarter tips, it caused them to set me down as an eccentric and wealthy Britisher. If I didn't push matters too far, this would be a big help.

The bellboy was back in a few minutes with a tray that held enough food to give a lion indigestion—a cut of roast beef, a cold chicken, a big slab of cheese, bread, and a whole pie, beside a pot of chocolate and my bottle of whiskey. I sat down in front of them with my newspaper. The date was 1859, and the headlines spoke of things like ATTACK ON COLONEL HOFFMAN'S ESCORT BY THE INDIANS, and the Sickles trial with ARGUMENT ON ADMITTING EVIDENCE OF ADULTERY. I also remember something about a DISTRESSING CALAMITY AT HOBOKEN.

After I had eaten as much as my stomach would stand for, I got the whiskey open and tried a snort. Man, that was strong stuff! Nothing like your modern blends, but pure corn that went down my throat like a torchlight procession. I sat there with it all afternoon, nursing it along, reading my newspaper, and occasionally taking a bite to eat. But I still wanted to get back, and, though it didn't seem quite so important any more, from time to time I'd give a thought to that problem, too.

By and by it began to get twilight outside, and from the window I saw a lamplighter coming along the street. He had to stop once for one of those queer, high-seated cabs, and I had an inspiration. I rang for the bellboy and told him I wanted a cab—not any cab, but one that would take me to Gavagan's Bar. He trotted off and must have been gone half an hour. When he came back, he looked a little anxious.

He said: "There's only one driver who says he thinks he knows where it is, sir. But he says it's over on the East Side."

"What of it?" I said.

"There are a good many blood-tubs around that section of town at night, Mr. Titus."

"Oh, I don't think they'll bother me," I said, principally because anything was better than sitting there, and picked up what was left of my bottle of whiskey.

The cab driver was certainly a character to make one think twice, and not in the least like my driver of the night before, as I had hoped. As he leaned down from that little seat in the back, I saw he had a broad, heavy face with red blotches on it. He said: "So you're the English lord that wants a place called Gavagan's?"

I said I was and got in. It had begun to rain by this time, and it was very dark. There was no one on the street, and as we went along, it got still darker, because my driver was taking me into a section where the street lights were farther apart. We were in a tough section of town, all right; I heard a scream come out of one house, and we kept passing saloons.

Finally, he pulled up at one of these places. "Here we are, lord," he said. "That will be twenty-five cents."

It didn't look the least like Gavagan's to me; but I got out, handed him the quarter, and stepped up to the door, thinking that if one transformation scene had been worked on me, this might be the occasion for another. As soon as I opened the door I saw my mistake.

There were three or four roughs drinking at the bar, who looked around as I came in. "Here he is, boys," said one of them, "Come on." He picked up some kind of cudgel that had been lying on the bar and started for me.

I slammed the door and ran, with them bursting out behind me. I don't know where I was and didn't know in what direction I was going. But I cut around corners a couple of times, gained on them, and after a while lost the sound of feet in the rear. The sidewalks were made of wood planks when there were any, and they were in bad condition. I stumbled several times, and I don't know how long I walked that way before I saw another cab standing at a corner under a street light. The driver's face was muffled up to his plug hat.

When I said: "Is this cab taken?" he merely shook his head. I got in. "Where to, sir?" he said.

I said: "Hotel—no, take me to Gavagan's Bar." And that's all the story. Here I am.

Titus finished his Brandy Smash and his eyes suddenly focussed on the leaf-a-day calendar behind the bar. "Holy smoke!" he said. "Is that the right date?"

"It certainly is," said Mr. Cohan.

"Then I've spent over a week on that day back in 1859. I've got to do some telephoning quick."

He was back from the booths in a couple of minutes. "My family's all right," he said, "though they did have Missing Persons looking for me. But Morrie Rath hasn't been home. I guess he hasn't got back from the Lonergan Building in the future yet."

Willison said: "I don't think he'll be back. Did you see this?"

He produced from his pocket a newspaper and pointed to a headline. It read:

LONERGAN BUILDING NOT TO RISE

COMMISSIONER REVOKES PERMIT;
CALLS IT TRAFFIC HAZARD

PROMOTERS ABANDON PROJECT

METHOUGHT I HEARD A VOICE

Doc Brenner came in just as Mr. Jeffers was delivering himself explosively.

"Psychiatry, phooey!" he said. "Psychology, phooey! Psychoanalysis, phooey! They're a bunch of witch-doctors. All they do is substitute one phony belief for another. It wouldn't do him any good."

"What wouldn't do whom any good?" said Doc Brenner. "I will start the evening with a double Manhattan, Mr. Cohan."

"Dr. Bronck here," said the stoop-shouldered and tweedy Professor Thott. "Dr. Bronck, meet Doc Brenner. He's a medical man and may be able to put you on to the person you want."

Brenner shook hands with a tall man who had a glittering smile, greying hair worn a little longer than normal, a vest edged with white piping, and a pince-nez on a black ribbon. "How do you do?" said this individual in a low tone, and glanced apprehensively over his shoulder toward the back of the room, where two other customers were playing pinochle at a table. In a still lower tone he said: "I fear this young man is right. I doubt whether a psychiatrist would be the right person for my case."

"What seems to be the trouble?" asked Brenner, downing his double Manhattan and putting the cherry into his mouth.

He addressed Dr. Bronck, but it was Thott who answered. "He has a bad case of zombies."

"Zombies?" said Brenner.

"Zombies!" said Jeffers.

"Only one to a customer," said the bartender, firmly. "I am not forgetting the night that poor young felly, Mr. Murdoch, come in here and I let him have three of them. Him and his dragons!"

"It's all right, Mr. Cohan," said Thott. "As a matter of fact, I'll have a Scotch and Soda, myself. We weren't ordering, just discussing real zombies—the un-dead, as they call them in *Dracula*."

"Is that what they call zombies after, now?" said Mr. Cohan. "Sure, it's a disgraceful thing, putting the name of a corp to good liquor."

Brenner cleared his throat, and looked at Dr. Bronck. "Do you see them?" he asked.

"No, they see him," said Thott, once more speaking for his acquaintance and, as the latter again looked over his shoulder at the pinochle players: "I suppose I had better tell him about it, Fabian. It might be something that could be cured by a throat operation."

Dr. Bronck shuddered; Thott turned to Brenner:

He's really in a cruel dilemma, since he's a professional lecturer and things have become so bad that he hardly dares raise his voice above a whisper these days. We thought perhaps a psychiatrist—[Jeffers snorted audibly into his beer] —might be able to resolve the problem by reference to something in his past; but it is equally possible that the question is purely medical. We would value your opinion.

I'm sure you must have heard of Dr. Bronck, even if you haven't met him before. No? That's because you're too exclusively a city mouse, Brenner. You should get out into the heart of America sometime, around among the ladies' clubs, and places adult education is conducted on the basis of attending one lecture a week all winter. You will find Dr. Bronck better known there than Albert Einstein, and considerably more intimately. Dr. Bronck is a travel lecturer. Especially with regard to Egypt and the Holy Land, a subject on which he is uniquely qualified to speak, by reason of having studied for the pastorate of the Dutch Reformed Church in his native Netherlands. Why didn't you go on with it, Fabian?

[Dr. Bronck whispered something behind his hand to Thott.]

Oh, yes, I remember you telling me now. He felt he could carry a more meaningful message to his audiences, and they would be more interested, if he did it in a secular way. It is his view that when people pay to hear a thing, they will accept it more readily and give it more thought, than when it comes to them, so to speak, as a gift. In fact, one might call Dr. Bronck a secular religious teacher. He is very successful at it, and has been heard by many thousands; I believe that they have frequently been forced to turn people away from his famous *Breakfast in Bethlehem* and the equally praised *Sailing in the Steps of St. Paul.*

Both these lectures, like others in Dr. Bronck's repertoire, have been given so many times in the course of the thirty years he has been on the platform that his delivery of them has become practically automatic. It is his custom, I understand, not to alter so much as a word. When he returns from one of his summer trips he works up an entirely new lecture for the delectation of those audiences who have already heard his previous list but will not willingly forgo the privilege of having Dr. Bronck with them again.

It is thus apparent that the text of what he has to say can in no way be responsible for the extraordinary affliction that has come upon him. Neither can it be his voice alone. Many years ago, at the very outset of his distinguished career, Dr. Bronck underwent a course of instruction at the Della Crusca Institute of Polyrhythmic Vocal Culture to improve both his speaking voice and his knowledge of English. The tonal habits he acquired at that time have changed only so much as advancing years would allow; when he delivers a lecture, it is identical with the last previous reading of the same text, not only in the words used, but as to gestures, intonations, and pauses. Do I exaggerate, Fabian?

[Dr. Bronck shook his head, beckoned to Mr. Cohan, and pointed to the glasses. "More libations, good Boniface," he said in a stage whisper.]

It is possible that his voice alone might have a hypnotic effect on certain individuals under the right conditions. It is also possible that the subject matter may in some way combine with the voice, but I am at a loss to account for the—spreading of the contagion.

However—Dr. Bronck spent his summer in the Holy Land that year, retracing the footsteps of Saul and David. It was something he had done before, but on this occasion he was putting the whole thing on to color film, including the famous cave of the Witch of Endor, for his lecture entitled *Sorcerers and Spiritual Leaders of the Old Testament,* which is so much appreciated throughout the South.

The lecture is one that he had delivered in previous years without provoking untoward incidents and then dropped for some time, because he had only slides to illustrate it. He revised it somewhat for reappearance on the list, and it made the sensational success that is usual with Dr. Bronck's lectures. [Dr. Bronck smiled his ample, tooth-displaying smile, ducked his head slightly as though acknowledging applause, and said: "Thank you" in a small voice.]

I do not believe he noticed the change in the reception of this lecture at first, although if he had, it is difficult to see how he could have avoided the trouble that later arose. The change came about as gradually as the emergence of a forest fire from a single dropped cigarette, and its origin is as hard to trace as the point where the cigarette was dropped.

Looking back over it, Dr. Bronck is inclined to believe that the first manifestation which forced itself upon his attention was when he gave

Sorcerers and Spiritual Leaders in Birmingham. Am I right about its being Birmingham, Fabian? At the end of a lecture, it is his custom to have a question period, since a part of his popularity is due to the feeling of personal acquaintanceship he leaves with his audiences. Many people, of course, do not wish to stay for this period, so when the lights are turned on and he says ". . . and so, my friends, we take leave of the Holy Land and return to our workaday world," there is a certain amount of movement toward the exits. This was true at the Birmingham lecture; but two men in the audience, instead of leaving in the ordinary way by the doors at the back of the hall, marched straight up and out the emergency exit at the side of the speaker's platform.

At the time Dr. Bronck was extremely busy with his questions and the incident only flicked at his attention as a minor discourtesy, which he noted out of the corner of his eye. It was only later, when the matter became more important and he was trying to remember details, that he realized that something odd about the appearance of the pair had registered on his subconscious memory. They were staring straight before them and lifting their feet very high as they walked; and Dr. Bronck recalls the thought flashing across his mind in the fraction of a second that both men must be drunk.

What is it, Fabian? . . . Oh, yes, he says it is not unusual to prepare for a religious lecture in the South by the liberal ingestion of corn liquor. People seem to feel that it enables them to attain more readily the emotional state desirable for receiving a revelation. Which reminds me, Mr. Cohan, our emotional states require a little bolstering. Will you see to it?

On that circuit, a lecture at Birmingham is usually followed by others at Tuscaloosa, Selma, Montgomery and Mobile. Dr. Bronck recalls nothing of special interest about the first three; but at Mobile, where the lecture was held in the open air under a tent, the Birmingham incident was repeated—that is, men shouldered out straight past the speaker's platform when the lights came up. Only this time there were four of them instead of two, all walking in the same peculiar dazed manner. Again Dr. Bronck was too busy with his questions to notice the incident except as one makes a mental remark upon a repeated peculiarity. It was not until he had covered Pensacola and Tallahassee and swung up to Waycross, Georgia, that the matter really forced itself upon his attention.

At Waycross, seven or eight people, men and women alike, nearly half a row, stood up and marched out when the lights came on. They used the normal exit at the rear of the hall this time, but Dr. Bronck was looking directly at them, and he could not miss the fact that the whole group, who had been sitting together, left with the same high step and fixity of vision he had remarked at Birmingham and Mobile.

After he had finished the usual post-lecture reception at the home of one of the social leaders of Waycross and was in his hotel room, restoring his emotional state, he connected the occurrence with the two previous incidents. As he did so, something struck him with prodigious force. Two of the four men of Mobile had also been present at Waycross, and as nearly as he could recall, the same two were the pair that had pushed past the speaker's platform at Birmingham. Then he remembered also that in all three places he had given the same lecture—*Sorcerers and Spiritual Leaders.* At Selma and Pensacola, where the audience exhibited their admiration of Dr. Bronck in the normal manner, he had given *Breakfast in Bethlehem;* and at Tuscaloosa, Montgomery, and Tallahassee, it was *Sailing in the Steps of St. Paul.*

You may judge that it was with some trepidation that he approached the next reading of the unfortunate *Sorcerers and Spiritual Leaders* lecture, which was scheduled for Columbia, South

Carolina. As soon as he reached the platform and began looking over the audience in the few minutes while being introduced, his fears were justified. The same two men were there, now sitting in the middle of a row of people, all of whom seemed to bear a family resemblance, in that their faces had a curious colorless character. They were perfectly well behaved, merely sat there with their hands in their laps, waiting for him to begin; did not even applaud when the chairman finished his introduction and Dr. Bronck stepped to the podium. And when he had finished, they marched out in single file, the whole row of them, moving as though they had been hypnotized or stunned.

However flattering it is to a lecturer when part of his audience follows him from place to place, it is a somewhat unnerving experience to be a focus of attraction for a growing group of people who look as though they had just come from a graveyard, and who are not really there to listen to the lecture but to be thrown into a state of ecstatic catalepsy by the lecturer's voice. Not to mention that Dr. Bronck felt that his position as a religious teacher might be compromised by such events, which, although not altering the value of his teaching, might be taken in the wrong spirit by the unthinking.

By the time he reached Asheville and there were twenty of these persons in the audience, Dr. Bronck was more than a little disturbed. It was evident that the people who are normally his listeners had begun to notice the intrusion of these peculiar characters, and were not taking it too well. And it was also apparent that the effect of the lecture on these individuals was impermanent; they reached their period of exaltation after hearing Dr. Bronck for an hour. Then the effect apparently gradually wore off, so that they had to have the dosage renewed. He was thus being pursued about the country by a retinue that was growing embarrassingly.

Upon consideration, he decided that in a manner which he could by no means explain, the zombie effect was produced by the lecture *Sorcerers and Spiritual Leaders of the Old Testament.* By telegraphing ahead, he managed to persuade his sponsors at Lynchburg, Virginia, to accept *Breakfast in Bethlehem* instead. His special group was present, larger than ever, not having been advised of the change, but he was relieved to see that only one of them—one of the original two from Mobile—left with the typical high step and fixed stare. The rest shambled out, looking at the floor, with their hands in their pockets.

This particular tour ended at Richmond, and Dr. Bronck enjoyed a week of rest before taking a swing through New England and central New York. In the interval he waited on his agents, McPherson and Kantor, and told them firmly that he declined to deliver *Sorcerers and Spiritual Leaders* again. They are notorious slave-drivers—I have been under their management myself—but they were not too averse, as audiences in the northern states require a somewhat more sophisticated and more sentimental approach, and Dr. Bronck's habit of not modifying his lectures was well established.

He did Connecticut and Rhode Island easily, though at Bristol, where he gave *Characters of the Crusades,* he thought he recognized one of his southern friends in the audience. At Worcester, however, he was shocked. The lecture was *Sailing in the Steps of St. Paul* and his eye, now attuned to looking for it, caught the zombie effect in at least two of those present. One of them was definitely a person who had attended one of the *Sorcerers and Spiritual Leaders* lectures in the south.

You will understand that Dr. Bronck has little opportunity to make personal observations of the thousands of people who come to hear him, except as they are unusual in some way. But the Worcester experience was shocking because at that point he realized that his peculiar clientele had not deserted him when he ceased to give *Sorcerers and Spiritual Leaders*. They had merely been following him and accustoming themselves to the accent of his voice until anything he said in any lecture would produce the effect they desired.

At Albany, he felt himself on safe ground again, having given *Breakfast in Bethlehem;* but at Utica, where he gave *Sailing in the Steps of St. Paul,* there were four who left with the cataleptic march; and by the time he reached Binghamton and *Characters in the Crusades,* the number had become eight.

He managed to finish this tour, which terminated at Buffalo, without having his private audience attract too much attention from the others and, after another brief rest, went out for a trip along the Pacific Coast. This had no incidents, except for the simultaneous exhibition of the zombie effect on almost a third of his audience in Los Angeles. It was fortunately the last lecture of the year; he believed that he had conquered whatever influence was at work—at least on audiences above the Los Angeles level—and happily embarked for Rome, where he spent the summer in working up a new lecture.

[Dr. Bronck abruptly emitted a loud burp and motioned for the refilling of his glass.]

Yes, Fabian, I know. Mr. Cohan will take care of the matter. In the fall, the first tour arranged for him was through Ohio, Kentucky, and Tennessee. I believe it opened at Columbus, did it not, Fabian? Dr. Bronck had just arrived in the city and was seated in his hotel room, restoring his emotional state, when he received a telephone call. It was a man's voice, with the sugary accent of the Deep South. He said that he had heard Dr. Bronck lecture during the previous year and wished to discuss a theory with him. The theory was that the world had really been created in 1932, complete with records and people whose memories indicated an earlier existence. Now this sort of thing happens rather frequently to lecturers, as good God, I know, and Dr. Bronck put up the standard defense, which was to say that he was engaged, with somebody in the room. But the man was persistent, and Dr. Bronck was forced to enter upon explanations. After a minute or two he asked some semi-rhetorical question, ending with "Wouldn't it?" or something like that, and was rather surprised to get no answer. He called "Hello!" two or three times, still without drawing any reply. There was no click of the phone hanging up; just nobody answering at the other end. That night—

["That night was bloody awful," said Dr. Bronck. "I need a drink when I think of it."]

Indeed, it must have been awful, Fabian. There were at least twenty of the grey-faced people in the audience; and, although the lecture was the new one he had made up in Rome, *Children of the Catacombs*, every single one of them got up and went out with the sleepwalker gait. They had apparently been increasing their sensitivity by practicing with transcriptions of Dr. Bronck's voice. Or perhaps, during the summer in Rome, the voice itself had acquired the additional richness and timbre necessary to the easy production of the zombie effect, regardless of the words spoken.

At Dayton, Dr. Bronck found the numbers of his special audience tragically increased; and at Cincinnati, where he gave *Breakfast in Bethlehem* in an effort to dismiss them for one night at least, he found that they had attuned themselves even to this lecture. He gave but one more public lecture—at Lexington, after which he wired to McPherson and Kantor that he was suffering from a severe nervous breakdown, and would have to cancel the rest of the trip. He—

"That isn't the worst, my friend," said Dr. Bronck, his voice showing evident traces of the improvement in his emotional state. "That isn't the worst at all. They try to telephone me; at all hours of the day and night they try to telephone me. They ash—ask questions—where is the Mount of Gibeon? Wha' line of march did the Israelites take under Joshua? My friends, it is a conspiracy to keep me talking until the wire goes dead. They meet me on the public streets in their cerements of a forgotten world. They are ruining my profession; they are depriving me of the privilege of carrying joy to many souls in spiritual need. They form associations and besiege my agents with requests that I speak before them—calling themselves the Arcane Adepts of St. Louis, or the Blavatsky Circle of Los Angeles—they offer me fabulous sums to pander to—"

His voice had risen, and as he flung out one arm in an oratorical gesture, "Look!" said Doc Brenner, suddenly, and pointed.

The two pinochle players at the back had dropped their cards. With arms at their sides and heads held back, staring straight before them with unwinking eyes, they were marching toward the door, each foot carefully lifted and placed before the other.

ONE MAN'S MEAT

It was a very quiet night at Gavagan's, with the wavy-haired young Mr. Keating from the library and Dr. Tobolka slowly exchanging views on some subject of interest only to them, over a Rye and Soda and a glass of Slivovitz respectively, when the middle-aged man came in with a package under his arm.

He was dressed in a neat blue serge and wore glasses, and he reached across the bar with: "Mr. Cohan? Name of Smith. I'm told you can probably help me with a problem of some importance."

Mr. Cohan dried his hands on his apron and shook hands. "Pleased to meet you. And what would you be wanting?"

"I want to find a Czechoslovak magician, and I'm informed that if one can be located, you're the man to do it."

Mr. Cohan put one hand to the side of his face, frowned, and said, "Dr. Tobolka here now would be the kind of man you want if he was a magician, which he is not."

The snub-nosed Tobolka turned. "He means me. Will you have a drink and explain to me why you need a Czech? Won't rabbits come out of hats just as rapidly for a Swede or an Argentine?"

"It's strictly a Czech magician I had in mind," said Smith. "And I don't think I will have a drink just now —no discourtesy intended."

"Oh, you mean like that fellow Theophrastus V. Abaris," said Mr. Cohan. "More like a Greek he was, and I'm thinking not too healthy a man for you to know. Now what would you be wanting another one like him for?"

Smith glanced around. "That's something I'm afraid I'm not in a position to state right now," he said. "That is, unless I find my man."

"Perhaps you've found him as a team operation," said Keating. "I've done a good deal of study of magic back in the stacks, and Dr. Tobolka is a Czech."

Smith stared at him for a minute. "It has to be here or nowhere," he said. "May I ask you gentlemen your first names?"

"Roger," said Keating, while Tobolka produced a neat cardcase and handed Smith an item from its contents.

"Excuse me a moment," said the man with the package, and stepped to the phone booth.

"Looks like a man with a mission," commented Keating, as the door closed behind the newcomer.

"If you're asking me, he acts like a fellow with a hole in his head," said Mr. Cohan. "Can you imagine it now, refusing good liquor in Gavagan's? What does he think this is, that Italian place around the corner?"

"Some people have to be careful," said Tobolka. "On the Committee for Czechoslovak Freedom, now, we—"

The phone booth door swung open and Mr. Smith emerged, looking relieved. He stepped across to the bar and laid his package on it. "The FBI says you're both all right," he said, "so I can tell you about the problem. Now I will not only have a drink with you, I will buy a round for everyone, including you, of course, Mr. Cohan. Make mine a Tom Collins, not too sweet." He turned, faced the others, and took the wrapping from the package. "This," he said, "is the essence of the matter."

Keating said, "It looks like a kind of sausage, with a heavy coating of wax."

"That's what it is," said Tobolka, prodding it with one finger. "It's called a Bismarck sausage, and they make them in Saxony and Sudetenland. The wax is to keep it from becoming unendurable as human company."

"Ah!" said Smith, drinking deeply from his Tom Collins. "I'm a salesman for Singer sewing machines."

Neither of the others appeared to be able to follow the connection, but: "Isn't that fine, now?" said Mr. Cohan from behind the bar.

Not so fine as you might think [said Smith]. What I'm going to tell you, you mustn't breathe to a living soul, and I wouldn't tell it even then but for the emergency. I sold Singer sewing machines in Czechoslovakia up to a little time ago. Travelling through the country in a car, one of those little German Volkswagens. And while I was travelling, I was picking up certain—uh, documents of interest to our government from people opposed to the Communist regime.

["Spies?" said Tobolka.]

People on our side [said Smith]. I had a portable Singer special made with a false bottom to carry the documents in, and as my profession allowed me to travel all through the countryside, it made an ideal arrangement. Well, last—uh, you will pardon me if I don't give the date, it might involve other people—a short time ago there was given to me a document of most unusual importance. It was a map of the big new arsenal and munitions depot at Prodnice, with all the tank traps, antiaircraft positions, and guard stations indicated, the biggest thing in Czech armament and the most secret.

["I was born near there," said Tobolka, "only it was Austrian and called Wörsten then."]

I don't think you'd recognize it now. Shortly after I got the map, I heard that the Russians had become dissatisfied with the way things were going in Czechoslovakia and had decided to tighten up by installing their own people in key positions in the more important ministries—Agriculture, the Interior, Education—with Russian a required course in the schools, and so on.

Now, that meant trouble for me. In Czechoslovakia, the police and border guards are under the Interior Ministry, and wherever I had to show my papers, I would be running into Russian MVD men, who are a lot tougher than the Czechs I had been dealing with. I had impressive evidence of just how difficult it was going to be when I got to Pilsen. My contact there was a man we called Aleš. He was a journalist, which gave him an excuse for running around a lot and asking questions. We used to meet at an inn on the Ludmilla Gasse, pretend a kind of nodding acquaintance, and after a drink or two—by the way, Mr. Cohan, there seem to be empty glasses on the bar. Will you do something about it? After a drink or two, he'd get up to go, leaving behind a newspaper with the reports folded into it.

On this particular day I knew there was something wrong the minute I stepped into the place. We always met at the same table. There was a man at it, sipping beer, and he had a newspaper, but it wasn't Aleš. Of course, it might be someone working for him, but I thought it safer to sit down at another table and size things up. After a while, one of the waiters shuffled over to take my order. He bent over as though he were a little hard of hearing when I spoke, and then said under his breath, "Go! Russky."

Well, you can believe I finished my beer in a hurry and got out of there. If they had Aleš, they probably had a warning out for me, with some kind of a description, and it was going to be touch and go to get across the frontier. So I headed in the direction of Prestice, Klattau, and Eisenstein. That would be the quickest route to Bavaria, which is in the American zone of Germany.

Dr. Tobolka here knows that this took me right into the heart of the Böhmerwald, which is just about the biggest and oldest forest in Europe, all full of legends. It's supposed to be where the kobolds lived—beautiful country, rather wild, and not many people.

I got through Klattau where, as I had hoped, there was only an ordinary Czech police post, which made no trouble about my papers, and was on my way to Eisenstein, when I saw an old man with a long white beard sitting on a bank beside the road. He was a big man and looked as though he might have been powerful at one time. The thing that caught my especial attention was that he was crying—just sitting there all alone in the forest with the tears running silently down his face.

I pulled the car up and asked him what was the matter. He said: "There is no place in Bohemia for me any more. The Russians have taken all."

They usually refer to Czechoslovakia instead of Bohemia, so that was a little odd, but I said: "Lots of people get across the border."

"How can I reach the border?" said he. "They will have it closed."

"Look here," I told him. "I'm an American businessman, and my peddler's passport allows me an assistant, so you're appointed to the job. Hop in."

He climbed to his feet rather heavily, carrying a bandanna with something wrapped in it. I opened up the luggage compartment, which is in the front in a Volkswagen, told him to put his package in, and went round to the back to look at my motor, which I suspected of overheating. When we started, I said: "My name's Smith. I'd better know yours if you're working for me." He shook his head a little, said: "Veles," and—

Tobolka said: "That is not a modern name. Nobody is named that now."

"It's good Czech, isn't it?" asked Smith, a trifle belligerently.

"Mr. Cohan," said Tobolka, "you will give the gentleman some Slivovitz to drink to the honor of Bohemia. Most assuredly, sir," he said to Smith, "Veles is good Czech!"

Well, I thought so [said Smith, lifting his glass in acknowledgement to Tobolka].

Anyway, as soon as I saw the border guard station at Eisenstein, I thought the jig was up. It's a square white building at one end of a barrier like those they have for grade crossings over here, and there was a big, blond lad in a Russian uniform out in front, with one of those machine-pistols cradled in his arm. I held out my papers to him, but he never looked at them, just motioned with the machine-pistol for me to get out, and said something in Russian to the two Czech border guards with him. And gentlemen, all I could think of was the disappearance of my contact, Aleš! One of them told the two of us to stand in front of the building, while the other one opened up my luggage compartment and began to get the stuff out. It was then that the old fellow spoke for the first time since he got in the car. He said: "Be not troubled. You will be rewarded."

All the same, that big bruiser started going through my stuff in a way that made me plenty troubled. Pretty soon they hit my portable Singer. On most inspections, they'd pass it up. The Russian prodded it, and the border guard said: "Come here. He wants you to open it."

I don't know how I managed to walk over and open up the machine. The Russian looked at it, frowned, and then pointed his gun at my stomach and said something else. The guard translated it for me. "He says it has a secret compartment and you are to open that, too."

I knew they had me then, but there wasn't any chance of making a break with that gun on me, so I pressed the stud that opened up the compartment. I was never more surprised in my life, and I guess they weren't either. Instead of the documents I had put in there, the compartment was full of neatly wrapped Czech cream cakes, together with this sausage I have here.

That puzzled the hell out of my Russian friend. He wanted to know why I was carrying sausage and cream cakes out of the country in this secret way, and I couldn't think of any very good answer, except that I sometimes got hungry along the road. He turned around to yell at the other guard, the one with the old fellow. And then he got another shock, and so did I. The old guy was gone.

Well, they had a big yak about it. I don't understand more than a few words of Russian, but between what I do know and the guard's pantomime, I could get it that he was pretending he had only turned his head to watch me open up the compartment and the old fellow had vanished.

After a while the Russian gave it up and snapped something that the border guard translated for me as: "You are obviously carrying more food than you are entitled to under the rationing program of the People's Republic, and therefore your cream cakes are confiscated. But you may keep the sausage, which is named for the fascist monster Bismarck, and is no longer permitted."

The Russky apparently just didn't want sausage that day. I had to put my luggage back in the compartment, and when I crossed the border, the last thing I saw was the three of them licking their fingers as they wolfed down cream cakes.

Smith mopped his hand across his brow at the memory of a harrowing experience, and said: "I will return Dr. Tobolka's compliment with the Slivovitz, Mr. Cohan. Now, there's the story. I saved my skin, but I didn't save the reports, which doesn't matter in the case of most of them. But that one on the Prodnice installations was pretty vital. It's perfectly obvious that this old fellow Veles pulled some kind of sleight of hand performance and exchanged the sausage and cream cakes for my documents, but the question is how did he do it and where are they now? I haven't been able to trace him, but I know professional magicians have associations and that sort of thing, and he must be in touch somewhere with other Czech magicians. That's why I want one, and I think the sausage is intended as a clue."

"Of course it was," said Dr. Tobolka. "Obviously."

"What do you mean?" asked Smith.

"Simply this: Veles is one of the oldest of our legends, far back before the time of King Krok. He watches over the forests, flocks, and foods of the Bohemian people. *Foods*, Mr. Smith."

Smith choked over his Slivovitz. "Come now, Dr. Tobolka!" he snorted. "You mean I was driving a hitchhiking kobold?"

"Not kobold. A god."

"Could be," Keating said. "He sure vanished into thin air, didn't he? And how about that switcheroo on the documents!"

Smith said, "Misdirection."

Suddenly, both Mr. Keating and Dr. Tobolka opened their eyes and their mouths and began to talk, alternately, like a smooth-working crosstalk team.

Keating said, "What was the Austrian name of that place where you said the map came from—"

And Tobolka said, "Wörsten. The German word for—"

"Sausages! And Veles was the god of—"

"Food!"

They both turned to Smith, and Dr. Tobolka said: "Mr. Smith, the sausage is more than a clue. I'll bet anything the map is inside it—or it has some note that tells where the map is."

Smith sipped and considered. "All right. All right. It's worth trying. Got a knife, Mr. Cohan?"

Mr. Cohan rummaged under the bar and came up with an all-purpose piece of cutlery, which Smith poised over the sausage.

"Not that way," said Keating. "If the map or a note is in there, you'll cut it in half. Cut it open lengthwise."

Smith grasped the handle firmly and drew the knife through the sausage in a long, firm longitudinal cut.

The sausage separated into halves, revealing two cross-sections of pure meat, brownish-red with numerous white patches and a network of little white lines connecting them. Just what would be expected in a sausage of this kind. There was no note or piece of paper. Keating's face fell, Tobolka looked disappointed, but Smith goggled at the spectacle. "My God!" he said.

"What's the matter?" asked Tobolka.

"It's the map! In sausage meat! See, here are the antiaircraft positions, and the bunkers holding ammunition, and the shell-loading plant, and there's the outer guard post. Those little white lines have it all."

Tobolka said: "In the Böhmerwald, it is not good to be a skeptic."

Smith picked up the paper that he had earlier unwrapped from the sausage and began to assemble it again. Halfway through this task, he stared at his companions and once more mopped his brow with his hand, as though to get rid of some pressure within. He said: "But how in God's name am I going to convince Army Intelligence that this damn thing is *it?*"

MY BROTHER'S KEEPER

"Would you be sure about needing another, Mr. Walsh?" said Mr. Cohan in a tone that caused the regular customers to look around in the expectation of seeing someone placed on the Indian list.

"'Course," said the stoutish, palish, baldish young man. "Wouldn' say so urrwise. Need 'nother whiskey. Whiskey chaser. Gotta get two men drunk."

Mr. Cohan placed both hands on the bar. "Mr. Walsh," he said severely, "in Gavagan's we will sell a man a drink to wet his whistle, or even because his old woman has pasted him with a dornick, but a drink to get drunk with I do not sell. Now I'm telling you you've had enough for tonight, and in the morning you'll be thanking me."

Walsh solemnly closed one eye, then the other, assumed an expression of intense foxiness, and placed a finger beside his nose. "Aw ri'," he said. "Take my business to a wholesaler." He almost missed the door going out.

"I've seen him somewhere before," said Doc Brenner. "Only, I thought it was at that conference on raising money for the community chest, and he was a delegate for one of the churches."

Mr. Gross said: "My Uncle Pincus knew a pair of twins like that once, where one of them was a cop and pinched the other one for stealing food from the animals at the zoo. But that was because he couldn't speak the language."

Mr. Witherwax shook his head, clucking. "I read in a book once that the harder a man works, the harder he has to relax. Maybe this Walsh just got to working too hard for his church. I'll have another Manhattan, Mr. Cohan."

"Him work for a church?" said the bartender, stirring. "It would take the holy angels to get him near one. You would be thinking of the other brother. This one now is Lester Walsh, and his own mother would be ashamed of some of the things he does."

"You mean they're identical twins?" said Doc Brenner.

"It's like I told you," said Gross. "He was out there the day that bath house burned down, trying to hide in a blanket, and I seen the scar where the doctor cut them apart."

"Huh?" said Doc Brenner. "Do you mean the two Walshes were Siamese twins and separated by surgery?"

Witherwax said: "But they can't do that. I read it somewhere, and it says they always die."

"They didn't this time," said Gross firmly. "Mr. Cohan, I want another Boilermaker, and you should tell Mr. Witherwax here that something he seen in a book ain't as good as something he seen with his own two eyes. Not that I see it myself when he wrecks the church sociable. Or the time he tried to hold a prayer meeting right here in Gavagan's, either. Ask Mr. Cohan; he'll remember that if you don't believe me."

"Indeed, and I do," said the bartender, heartily. "Gavagan himself was in here that night when Mr. Walsh comes in. And before he can even order a drink, a funny look comes over the face of him, and he says he's going to pray and will anyone join him."

Brenner looked at Witherwax and Witherwax looked at Brenner. The latter said: "Look here, maybe you better give us the story from the beginning. I don't quite understand."

Like I said [said Gross]. Him and his brother Leslie was born connected together. My Aunt Sophie knew the family, and went around to see Mrs. Walsh in the hospital. She was one of them women suffragists or something, and she said she wasn't going to be the mother of no circus freaks, so she told the doctors to cut them apart.

Don't ask me how they done it. All I knew about is what my Aunt Sophie told me, the one that had the delicatessen and got into all that trouble with the inspectors on account of the green snake. She used to say them two Walshes was that healthy you'd never know they were one person, sort of, and I know nobody thought there was anything nutsy about them till they was in school.

With twins like that, their people get a kick out of them; dressing them the same way and bringing them up to do the same things, so they're as much alike as possible. Old Mrs. Walsh used to do that with her kids. I remember I went over once to my Aunt Sophie's place to play with my cousin Pershing, and the Walshes was right down the street, so we went there. One of them, I forget which, you couldn't tell them apart even then, was out in the yard playing something with us. All of a sudden, he twisted up his face and began to bawl. We couldn't figure out why; neither one of us laid a hand on him.

Well, we got in the house and there was the other twin, and he had fell downstairs and had a big bang on his head. Old Mrs. Walsh thought that was wonderful and gave us the business about how sympathetic Lester and Leslie were, and how if one of them got hurt you couldn't hardly tell which one it was, because they'd both be yelling their heads off.

My cousin Pershing went to high school with them. He says it was the same way there. The two of them was together all the time, and if one got into a fight or anything, the other one would get mad and make out to help him. You ought to expect that with twin brothers, only it was more like they was still connected. Like one time Leslie got locked up in the cellar at home, and my cousin Pershing says Lester sat there all day in school like a stupe and wouldn't say nothing. And with girls—oh boy!

Gross finished his Boilermaker in an appreciative swig and signaled to Mr. Cohan.

"What about girls?" asked Witherwax "Did they chase them?"

They didn't have to [said Gross]. Only it was always the same girl they was making time with. No matter whether it was Leslie or Lester that picked her up first, they would go out with her together, maybe with another babe along. But they wouldn't pay no more attention to her than if she was a rag doll. Dames don't like that. They don't even like to have two guys after them, not unless they can take them one at a time. But if they made any kick to the two Walshes, they'd give her the air both together, the way that belly-dancer over on Monroe Street got accused of doing with her husbands, the one with the ears that didn't match.

Doc Brenner opened his mouth to say something, but before he could achieve more than an inarticulate beginning of speech, a voice pronounced: "Pardon me, but can you tell me if Mr. Lester Walsh is about? I was told that I might find him here."

The group looked around at a tall man wearing striped trousers, a carnation in his buttonhole, and a worried expression. "He was here, sure enough," said Mr. Cohan, "but he left."

"You might find him in that Italian place around the corner," said Witherwax, "but you ain't going to like what you find."

"I was afraid of that," said the tall man. "This is most inconvenient, most embarrassing, for a number of people." He glanced around the bar, elevated his nose disdainfully, and left.

See? [said Gross]. Them things are always happening with the two Walshes. Anyway, by the time they was getting out of high school, the old woman figured maybe she was going too good on this racket of making the kids alike. It didn't work every time, only when one of them got real excited, or sore, or gloomy, but then the other one had to be like that, too, or nearly bust his britches.

["I see," said Doc Brenner. "The *rapport* was related to the intensity of the emotion."]

What do you know? [said Gross]. And I always thought a report was one of them things a spiritual medium kept in a closet. So old Mrs. Walsh thought it would be good for them to get to be different. So she sends Leslie to a college run by the Methodists up in New England, and Lester off to one of them colleges in Texas where they don't do nothing but play football. In a way, it worked all right. When they come back from college, they was quite a lot different. Lester is big as a beef trust compared to Leslie right now, and besides they was different in other ways.

Maybe the report didn't work from New England to Texas or something. Leslie Walsh no sooner come out of college and got a job than he began teaching in Sunday School and going to prayer meeting every Wednesday night; but Lester, he learned about playing poker and things like that down in Texas, and if there was any place he was Wednesday night, it was right here in Gavagan's or maybe one of them joints over in the Fifth. They didn't see each other so much, and that was all right with both of them.

That is, it was all right until that business about the church sociable. The way I get the story they met about something connected with old Mrs. Walsh's estate—she was dead by that time—and spent all afternoon talking about it. Maybe that started up the report again. Anyway, that night Leslie went to a church sociable, and Lester, he goes over afterward to Bugs Farquhar's for a game of poker. I don't know if you know Buggsy. Everybody that goes to his games is supposed to bring a pint so that nobody won't feel too beat-up if he loses a couple of bucks.

Only this time things got balled up, and nearly everybody brought a quart instead of a pint, and when they got it there, it was too much trouble to take it home again, so they drank it, and they was all laid out like a massacre.

The real trouble was what happened to Leslie that night. He is at this church sociable, and they are just passing the ice cream when all of a sudden he is talking loud, and the next thing he is reciting poetry, and it is not the kind of poetry I would want to repeat in Gavagan's, neither. Old man Webster told me it was as bad as the time somebody put a pair of rubbers in the furnace. They practically had to carry him home, and they were going to expel him from the church for getting plastered, only everybody has seen him since the start of the sociable and knows he cannot have did this by himself. Only they don't know what did do it.

But Leslie, he knows all right, that it is the old report coming back. So the next day, when he got rid of his hangover, he goes around to Lester's place, and tries to get him to take the pledge like he has done hisself. Well, Lester is not feeling so good that day, as you maybe can think, so he says he will not drink no more. That night is prayer meeting night, and Leslie goes to the church to have a couple of prayers for his brother, and that is also the night when Lester, thinking that one drink won't hurt him, comes in here; only before he can get the drink, the report starts working, and he asks everybody in Gavagan's to have a prayer with him.

So they figured it out this way, that the report works when the two of them are together. And they figured out a system so they wouldn't bother each other no more. But it busted up. You know what made it bust up?

[Gross looked at the other two with the air of a man in possession of an earth-shaking secret. Witherwax said: "I'll have another Martini, Mr. Cohan."]

It was love [Gross went on solemnly]. It was love. They both picked out the same dame, like they used to back in high school. I don't remember her name, and my cousin Pershing says she ain't too much to look at; but what the hell, when a guy is in love, he don't care how a dame looks. There was a cousin of my wife's once that took tickets in the circus, and he fell in love with the tattooed fat girl in the sideshow.

So the both of them Walshes are chasing the same dame, and they are chasing each other, trying to use the report to slip one over. Maybe they meet at her house, see? So they talk a couple of minutes, and then Leslie says he's forgot, he's gotta go somewhere, and he goes off to a church if there's a prayer meeting on, and starts singing hymns or something. And Lester says he's got a date and runs out and starts loading them in or gets in a fight with a hackie. Leslie won't go to this dame's house except on Sundays or prayer meeting nights on account of he might meet Lester there, and on other nights Lester has the edge on him. But on them days he lays for Lester outside his own house, and talks to him a while and then goes to church and puts the report on him. And them two brothers that used to be just like this—

Gross held up a pair of fingers. Witherwax said: "How are they coming out with the girl?"

"Oh, her. You know how it is with dames. They want a guy that's a steady meal ticket. Last I heard she was going to marry Leslie."

The door swung open and through it staggered Mr. Lester Walsh, considerably the worse for wear. His hat had suffered a case of assault and battery; there was a tear in his coat and a long stain down it. It took him three staggering steps to reach the bar, which he clutched as a sea-sick oceanic traveler grips a rail.

"Mis'r Cohan!" he called. "Mis'r Cohan! Nurr whiskey, whiskey chaser."

He turned and faced the others with an oratorical gesture. "My bro'r's getting married toni'. Marrying my girl. But I'll fix'm. Got bes' man and whole town looking for me. Gotta get drunk for two. Nurr whiskey, whiskey chaser."

A DIME BRINGS YOU SUCCESS

Mr. Gross was leaning against the bar, rather apathetically sipping his Boilermaker, when the voices at the back table suddenly became loud.

"No you don't," Mr. Cohan was saying, with quite unusual energy. "I'm telling you once as I've told you before. This is a public place, and you can come into it, and it's against the law for me not to serve you, but not one dime of your money will I take!"

He held his hands before him as though pushing something away, then turned and surprisingly spat on the floor. The thin young man with a pale face flashed an apologetic smile across the table at his companion. "I'm very sorry," he said, "but you see how it is. Would you mind—? I'll make it up to you later."

The other, a fairly well-upholstered individual in a blue suit, produced a couple of dollar bills and shook hands with the pale young man. "Well, I think we've done all we can today, anyway," he said. "I like the policy your firm puts out, and the rates are reasonable."

"Thank you," said the pale young man, standing up. "You're covered against practically everything but fire now, but I'll look up what a fire policy on your car would cost and call you about it first thing in the morning." He smiled again, pleasingly if a trifle sadly, nodded at Mr. Cohan, and went out.

The individual in the blue suit picked up his change and stepped over to the bar. "Would you mind telling me," he addressed Mr. Cohan, "why you refused to take that gentleman's money? Is there anything wrong with him? I've just bought an insurance policy on my new car from him, and it seemed all right to me. Good strong company, and he has a very pleasing personality."

"Yes," said Gross. "I'm surprised at you, Mr. Cohan. We should always be kindly to people in troubles, and the deeper the troubles, the more kindlier we should be. I had a great-uncle once that used to go through the state prison at Geneva, passing apples out of a basket to all the poor fellows there, and he was very well thought of."

"If he passed one to that young felly, he'd be sorry," said Mr. Cohan, grimly. "That there's Lucian Baggot."

"And what of it? I'm Adolphus Gross myself and not ashamed of it."

"And is there any reason why you should be?" said Mr. Cohan, and turned to the blue-suited man. "Listen, mister; I'll say nothing against him for an honest man. He is that; but he is not the felly I'd be having feel friendly toward me. That fine lad of a Baggot broke up some of the best trade Gavagan's ever had, and all because he liked the place."

"Huh?" said Gross. The blue-suited man said: "What do you mean?"

"What do I mean? I'll show you." Mr. Cohan fumbled beneath his apron for a wallet, from which he produced a worn piece of paper. "Read that now." He turned and called to the bar boy: "Jim, turn on them sidelights. With that thunderstorm coming on, it's that dark in here a man can't tell whose drink he's drinking."

"That reminds me," said the man in the blue suit, "you had better fix me a Whiskey Sour," and he bent with Gross over the paper. It was a page torn from a pulp magazine, with the continuation of a story marching in column beside a row of advertisements —hernia trusses, albums of nude photographs, and articles which it took a second reading to reveal as loaded dice.

"Right there it is," said Mr. Cohan, pouring and pointing. "That's the thing was the ruination of a fine young felly." The others looked at an ad which read:

A DIME BRINGS YOU SUCCESS

DEVELOP A COMMANDING PERSONALITY! WIN COMPANIONSHIP, LOVE, FINANCIAL SUCCESS! THIS COUPON, PLUS A DIME TO COVER MAILING CHARGES, BRINGS YOU YOUR FIRST FREE LESSON IN OUR GUARANTEED COURSE IN PERSONALITY DEVELOPMENT. . . .

"What is it? A swindle of some kind?" asked the blue-suited man.

Now that's where you'd be wrong [said Mr. Cohan]. They done what they said for him and more, too, and there's the trouble, because he didn't need it, no more than Flaherty's dog needed five legs. I remember when this Lucian Baggot first began to come in here, a decent young felly and on his way up, the way a young felly should be; and like you said, mister, a young felly a man was pleased to know and to do things for.

He had a job with the Standard Oil in them days, down in the Henshaw Building. They all used to come in here to Gavagan's, the whole bunch of the Standard Oil boys, and have maybe a drink or two after work, and he'd come with them. It would only be a beer he'd be having then, because he was just an office boy, and not for touching the hard stuff. But he got along good with the rest—real good. You could see even when they kidded him, it was in a way that showed they liked him.

I call to mind the day when he got promoted to running one of them adding machines in the accounting department. He celebrated right in here, having a drink of whiskey to himself, and Mr. Brinkerhoff, that was the head of the department, bought the drink for him, and all the Standard Oil boys wished him health. He was that proud you'd think he had been made president of Ireland.

Listen to that thunder, will you? How would you like a drink on the house, to take the sound of it away? Well, as I was saying, this Lucian Baggot was proud as he could be over his new job at first, but after a while, you could see that everything wasn't all pork-pies and roses, because the other Standard Oil boys were treating him different. Not like they didn't like him, you understand, but when he was just the office boy, they'd be looking after him and giving him a ticket to a show or maybe a ball game, or taking him home to dinner. But now he was in the accounting department, that was all gone. The boys would have their two-three drinks, and it would be "Good night, good night," and him sitting alone there at the bar with the last of his whiskey.

Mind you, this wasn't every time. Many's the night he'd never show up at all, and when I asked for him, they'd say, "Oh, Mr. Baggot, he's got a heavy date with a girl," or maybe that two of them had gone somewhere together. Not so much different from any other young felly on a job and living by himself, he was, except that he seemed to think so. Many's the time he sat right at that bar and complained what a hard life he led, because nobody liked him no more, and how some felly he used to be friends with at the office had been married and hadn't a minute for him, and he had to spend all his evenings by himself, and at the office he could get nowhere.

I used to tell him that there was nothing happening to him that didn't happen to all. "Mr. Baggot," I would say to him. "Mr. Baggot, one of these fine days you'll be stepping off with some girl yourself, and then you'll find out that a man may choose his own wife, but his friends she picks for him, by God, just to remind him he has a leash on his neck." I used to ask him whether the people he met here in Gavagan's did not like him and sometimes buy him a drink on first sight, which was true enough.

But it was no use. He was that anxious to be popular, you'd of thought he was running for Congress, and one night he comes in here with an ad in a magazine like this one, and says he's going to send for the course. I said to him, let well enough alone, but I might as well of been talking to the stuffed owl up there, because the next thing I know, he tells me the courses have started and they're wonderful. I don't rightly understand them things, but as near as I could make out, the people in this course taught Mr. Baggot to fix his eyes on somebody without winking or yet blinking, as if he wasn't nothing but a poor dead corp, and also fixing his mind on them at the same time. He said it would distill his personality if he did it right. "Mr. Baggot," I told him, "you'll be no better for it. The only thing that's improved by distilling is honest liquor." But he only said: "It's a fine course, Mr. Cohan. I feel better for it already, and when I finish it up two weeks from now, I'll give you a practical demonstration, and you can see for yourself."

It would be two weeks, almost to the day, when he comes in here one afternoon with some of the Standard Oil boys, and this Mr. Brinkerhoff, that was the department head, is one of them. I remember it like it was yesterday, raining hard outside, like it is tonight, and all of them shaking water off their hats and laughing as they ordered drinks. Mr. Baggot was right in the middle of the bunch; when he got his, which was a Rye and Soda, as usual, he slapped his hand on the bar in front of me and motioned with his head toward Mr. Brinkerhoff, and I knew he was going to give me the demonstration.

"Mr. Brinkerhoff," he says, "you know what I think we should do?" And he starts staring at him hard, wrinkling up his forehead, so I can see he is distilling personality.

Mr. Brinkerhoff's face took on a kind of funny look, and he took a step backward, and the next thing you know, he is on the floor, with good liquor spilled all around him, and the rest of them jabbering and trying to help him up. They found out Mr. Brinkerhoff not only had a heart attack, but when he went down, he twisted his leg under him and got a broken ankle, so it was many a long day before he was back at work or in Gavagan's again.

Afterward I told Mr. Baggot that it was the most wonderful demonstration since Finn M'-Cool's wife baked the stove lids in the griddle-cakes, but if it was me I would not be wanting to distill my personality at nobody again. He looked worried over it, but he says: "Why, I wouldn't harm Mr. Brinkerhoff for the world! He's been like a father to me, ever since I came with the firm. It must have been a coincident."

"Mark my words, Mr. Baggot," I says to him, "and call it what you like," I says. "But if a thing like that happened in the old country, they would say the man had the Eye put on him."

"Oh, I don't believe in that," said he and went out. But the next thing was I noticed Mr. Harmsen, that was a great friend of Mr. Baggot's, didn't come in with the other Standard Oil boys no more, and devil a word could I get out of Mr. Baggot about it. But the others, they told me that Mr. Harmsen is in jail for having too many wives, and this is the way it happened:

Mr. Harmsen has just taken over the department while Mr. Brinkerhoff is sick, and he is just talking to everyone in it, and they are all watching him when he falls down in a fit and has to be taken to the hospital. And the phone girl at the office noticed there was two home phone numbers for Mr. Harmsen, and thinking nothing of it, calls both of them to pass the bad news to his wife, and would you believe it? He was keeping two separate apartments with a wife in each one, and the both of them met at the hospital. You wouldn't expect it of Mr. Harmsen, that was a nice, quiet felly, but some of them are the worst underneath.

All the same, I could see something else, too, and the next time Mr. Baggot was in here, I ast him, did he try distilling his personality on Mr. Harmsen, and he said yes, he did, but without thinking, and he didn't mean to do it. And—

[Outside, there was an earsplitting crash of nearby thunder, and a blue flicker of lightning briefly illuminated the windows.] That was a good one, wasn't it now? Well, it was just like that lightning with Mr. Baggot and the Standard Oil boys. One afternoon, right in here, he was talking to Mr. Cassadeo, and Mr. Cassadeo is explaining something, and Mr. Baggot is looking at him hard, trying to catch what he is saying because everyone else is talking. All of a sudden Mr. Cassadeo sits down hard, and says he is feeling faint. They got him out of here, and the next I heard was that he has one of them—what do you call them, when you go sneezing from smelling flowers?—allergies, thank you, Mr. Gross—and he cannot drink nothing no more at all, not only gin that he had in his Martini, but wine and beer and anything you could mention.

After that I got hold of Mr. Baggot, and I said to him: "It's no matter of mine what you do with yourself, but this is bad for Gavagan's business, and I'm in charge of that. If you have to distill your personality on someone, why don't you pick on him?" And I nodded my head over toward the end of the bar, where Angelo Carnuto, that was in the numbers racket, happened to be standing with one of his boys. Not that they're welcome in here, it's a respectable house, but it's public.

"All right," said Mr. Baggot, "I will," and he steps up to the bar and starts frowning at Angelo Carnuto. After a minute Carnuto turns around and says:

"What are you trying to do, put the Eye on me?" and crosses his fingers and spits on the floor and then walks out.

Mr. Baggot looks like he just heard the income

tax was after him. "You see?" he says. "That's the trouble. I can't seem to distill my personality on anyone unless I like them or want something from them. I don't know what to do."

Well, finally, he made up his mind that the only thing he could do was get away from the Standard Oil office altogether and sell insurance, which is a business where you don't know people long enough to distill personality at them. But by that time it was too late; one of the boys fell downstairs and hurt hisself, and another one got took with consumption and had to go to Denver, and of all of them that used to come in here, there was hardly a one left. Myself, I always spit when I talk to him, since they say in the old country that's the way to keep the Eye from doing harm; and his money I will not take, for the Eye might come with it.

The man in the blue suit smiled slightly. "Well, thank you for warning me," he said, "but I don't imagine there'll be much danger in a casual business deal. Seems to be clearing up; I guess I'll be on my way."

As he turned, a policeman in a wet-gleaming rain cape came in the door. "Good evening, Mr. Cohan," he said. "Anybody in here own a blue Chrysler sedan, license number—" he consulted a notebook—"CY-37-72?"

"I do," said the man in the blue suit. "What's the matter?"

"No fault of yours, but you've had a funny accident. The lightning in that thundershower hit a trolley wire and tore it loose, and the wire came right down on your car and short-circuited through it. It caught fire, and the firemen couldn't get near it because of the charged wire. Pretty well burned out. Hope you had it insured."

OH, SAY! CAN YOU SEE

Mr. Cohan set a Boilermaker down in front of Mr. Gross, who was holding Professor Thott, Mr. Witherwax, and Mr. Keating from the library, if not exactly spellbound, at least immobile.

". . . so the next day," he said, "a flock of trucks drove up and unloaded those statues on my Uncle Max's lawn. So my Uncle Max is stuck with ten cast-iron statues of an ugly guy named Hercules, wearing a second-hand tiger, all because he couldn't leave well enough alone. So when I heard about it I said to myself, Adolphus Gross, let that be a lesson to you to leave well enough alone, and I done it ever since."

He paused for effect, sipped the rye, and took a gulp of the beer.

Witherwax said: "The trouble is if everybody did that, we wouldn't get anywhere."

"I only meant—" began Gross. Witherwax was not to be stopped.

"For instance," he said, "I was reading in a book how somebody invented distilling. If they left well enough alone, we'd be drinking wine or beer and there wouldn't be any gin, and Mr. Cohan couldn't mix me another dry Martini. Oh, Mr. Cohan!"

The voice of the bartender, who was farther down, talking to a customer, became louder, as though he were indicating to Witherwax that the cause of the delay was inescapable: "No, I'm telling you I have not seen her tonight, nor last night, nor the night before that. And if ye want to talk to the rubber plant, it's your own right, because everything is free in Gavagan's saving and excepting the liquor. Jim, get Mr. Holland that step now."

He came down the bar toward Witherwax, but like the three other habitués of Gavagan's, that gentleman was watching in fascination as the bar boy produced a small kitchen stepladder, on which the neatly-dressed young man climbed to place his head on a level with the small rubber tree that grew in a pot on the bracket just above the window-curtain.

"Althea!" he said distinctly, "I'm here." He gazed at the rubber tree.

"Who is he?" asked Witherwax.

"It's a Martini you're wanting?" said Mr. Cohan. "Him? Oh, that's Mr. Holland, and all that money of his doing him no more good than if it was made of mud."

"Is he crackers?" asked Gross.

The young man had climbed down again and apparently caught this remark, for he shook his head with a melancholy smile. Witherwax said: "Ask him to have a drink with us. Nobody should be that sad in Gavagan's."

Before Mr. Cohan could proffer the invitation, Professor Thott stepped over to the young man. "Sir," he said, "I offer the proper apologies for the apparent rudeness of one of my companions and request that any injury be dissolved in a libation."

The young man hesitated, considered, said: "I suppose I might as well," and followed Thott to where the others were waiting. Introductions were made; he would have a double Stinger. It was not until he had taken the first sip from it that he turned toward the circle of expectant faces.

"I don't blame you for thinking I'm bats," he said. "I don't even mind. Perhaps I am. But she was real. You've seen me with her, haven't you, Mr. Cohan?"

"That I have," said Mr. Cohan. "And as decent a girl as I ever put eyes on. You would be sitting all the time at the corner table there, and minding your own business that had the world and all to do with each other."

Holland swallowed the rest of his double Stinger

at a gulp and pushed his glass back for a refill. Witherwax cleared his throat. "If you could tell us . . ." he said.

I don't know that it will be much help, to me or to you [said Holland], but I'll try, I'm looking for the girl I'm in love with, and I'm afraid I'll never find her because I think she's a—dryad.

[He let the last word drop separately and searched the faces of Thott, Witherwax, Gross, and Keating, as though to see whether anyone was being scornful or skeptical. No one was. Holland drank from his replenished glass and began again.]

I'll tell you and see what you think. I have a little money, you know. It's handled by one of those investment trusts, which shifts some of it from one holding to another once in a while. I believe that money should be as responsible as any other part of our economy, so instead of just sitting around drawing dividends or going in for racing cars and chorus girls, I've made a hobby of checking up on the firms my money is invested in, taking an active part as a stockholder, and informing myself well enough so that I can ask intelligent questions of management at meetings.

A little while back, the trust informed me that they had put me rather heavily into the Acme Real Estate firm—not a controlling interest, but a strong minority—and so, as usual, I went around to see how they operated. I found they were a management corporation, specializing in office buildings, so I continued my checking by going around to the buildings to see how well they were run.

One of them was the Ogonz Building, over on Lattimer Street; fifteen-story job. When I went over it, there were two things that struck me particularly—seemed to give the place a personality of its own, which most office buildings lack. One was the immense flagpole on the roof, surmounted by a big golden eagle. You can't see it at all from most of the adjacent streets because you can't get enough—what's the word sculptors use when they stand back from their statues to see how they're coming?

["*Recul*," said Thott; "or is it *recueil*? Speaking of things French, Mr. Cohan, I think I will vary my procedure by having a jorum of Hennessey."]

I got there about seven o'clock after having run over several other buildings, and the second thing that made an impression on me was the night elevator man. He looked like a cross between a gnome and a land mine, a solid figure with heavy hips, rather spindly shanks, knock knees, and a great mass of curly dark hair over a dark face. He was quite suspicious; wouldn't let me in at all until he'd checked by phone with the night man at Acme.

I didn't think that was too bad a characteristic in a man with his job, because places have been burglarized in just that way, so I let him see it was all right with me as he took me around. Of course, when we reached the roof and saw the flagpole, I exclaimed about it. His face went even darker than before and he muttered something.

"What's the matter?" I asked. "Don't you like it?"

He talked with a rather thick accent, but I gathered that he did like it, very much. What he was angry about was that orders had been given to cut the pole down. His rage over it seemed somewhat out of proportion, but as soon as he told me, I got mad, too. All the way down in the elevator, I kept getting madder at the thought of destroying that splendid pole with the golden eagle.

By the time he let me out, I was really simmering. I told him not to worry; that pole was going to stay there even if I had to throw somebody out of a job to keep it there. I meant it, too, and the next morning I went around to Acme and told the girl in the outer office that I wanted to see Sherwin, the president, about the flagpole on the Ogonz Building.

He's a big lemon-blond businessman, very pompous, who sits back from his desk, just caressing the edge of it with his belly.

"You are interested in acquiring the pole?" he said. "We are taking it down, but it is a relic of some historical value."

I said: "No, I'm just here to ask you not to take it down. I like it there. By the way, if you look at your books, you'll find I'm a major stockholder in your company."

He puffed a couple of times and said: "Well, Mr. Holland, it's not very usual for stockholders to interfere with the minor details of management. I think you may trust our discretion in protecting your financial interests. As a matter of fact, both the direct cost of continually replacing the flag on that pole and the labor cost of having a man raise and lower it each day are appreciable items, on which we propose to effect a saving."

By this time I was really annoyed. I told him that my interest was not financial but personal, and if he effected any savings that way, I was going to buy up enough more Acme stock to have control, and he could go do his saving for somebody else. He huffed and puffed around so much over that, that in order to calm him down, I asked him what it was a relic of.

He was smooth. "I've addressed the Advertising Club on that topic at one of our little five-minute informal speeches," he said. "The flagpole on the Ogonz building is a single stick of cedar from the island of Samos in Greece. It was originally a mast on the Greek sailing training ship *Keraunos,* which was visiting this country when Greece was invaded and after the war was found too unseaworthy to make the return voyage. Mr. Pappanicolou, the restaurant man, was then owner of the Ogonz Building, and he secured the mast as a flagpole. I believe there is more to the story, which I do not seem to remember at the moment, but the night man at the Ogonz Building can inform you. He was one of the sailors on the *Keraunos.*"

I thanked him for that much and went away. Mr. Cohan, will you provide for me once more?

[Keating said into the interval: "Samos, eh? That's where they had the famous temple to Hera, isn't it? The one in the grove, where the priestesses were called dryads?"]

Whether they were or not [continued Holland, sipping]. Yes, I've looked it up myself since. Anyway, the pole stayed up, and it's still there, and all I've had to do is turn down Sherwin's attempts to get me to lunch with him at the Advertising Club about once a week.

The next event in the series was that I went to a cocktail party at the Mahers and met Althea, Althea Dubois. I suppose most men think the girl they fall in love with is the most beautiful object on earth, but Althea really is. Slender and not very tall, with one of those triangular faces and rather light brunette hair. The moment I touched her hand, I knew this was it, and the next moment she was looking at me hard out of a pair of green eyes and saying: "Aren't you the Mr. Holland who stopped them from taking down the flagpole on the Ogonz Building?"

"Why, yes," I said. "Are you interested in it, too?"

"Very much," she said. "I'm so grateful to you for that, that I don't know how to tell you."

She had a little accent of some kind that I couldn't trace. It only made her all the more charming. I asked her if she were a native, and she said she wasn't, but she just loved the town and all the people and wouldn't go away now for anything. It didn't occur to me to ask her how she knew about my little duel with Sherwin; I was too interested in just talking to her, and she didn't seem to mind. So we kept right on without noticing that the party had thinned out, until we were the last ones there and the Mahers were making noises to indicate they wanted us to go home so they could have dinner. I asked Althea if she had a date and then took her to dinner at Gaillard's and we went on with the conversation, and when the waiters there began to behave the same way the Mahers had, I brought her over here.

It must have been about one o'clock in the morning before she said she really had to go. She wanted me just to put her on a Number 7 bus, and when I just wouldn't hear of anything but taking her home in a taxi, she suddenly became very quiet, standing there on the curb. As the taxi pulled up she shook herself just a little and said: "All right. The Ogonz Building."

After we were in the cab she said: "You see, I live there," as though it were some kind of confession.

I didn't see anything to be ashamed of in it; lots of those office buildings have penthouses that have been converted into living apartments. But since the subject seemed to make her nervous, I said: "Can I call you there?"

It was so dark in the cab that I couldn't see her face, but her voice was quieter than ever. She said: "No. I live—a rather peculiar life, and don't have a phone."

"But when can I see you again?"

She said: "You shouldn't—Oh, I don't know."

I began to wonder how I'd offended her or what I'd stepped into. The suspicion even crossed my mind that she might be married or being kept by somebody, but I didn't care. I wasn't going to give up that easily. So I said: "How about Thursday, day after tomorrow? I know a little Italian restaurant where we can be quiet, and we can take in a show afterward."

She didn't say anything at all for a couple of minutes. Then she put one hand over mine and said: "I'll do it. If anything happens so that I can't make it, though, I'll leave word with Mr. Ankaiosou, the night superintendent." Then she became very gay again until we got to the building. But she wouldn't let me come up with her to the door of her apartment.

Not then nor any other time. And the more I went out with her, the better I got to know her, the more I got the impression that there was something mysterious connected with the place where she lived. She always met me downstairs, and seemed as happy as she could be to be with me, but whenever the conversation approached the subject of where and how she lived, she would suddenly go silent on me, as though it was something she didn't dare talk about. By the third or fourth time I met her, I dropped any suspicion that she might be married to or living with another man. I was seeing her practically every day, and she just couldn't have gotten away; besides, she wasn't the sort of person who would do that—too sweet and lovely and genuine.

I thought it must be because of her family or something like that, but I don't think I can really be blamed for wondering. The matter came to a head one afternoon when we were out in the park—Althea loved the park. We had been kissing and were lying on our backs on the grass, close together, not doing anything except looking up through the leaves at blue sky, saying a word or two now and then.

I said to her: "Althea, why won't you ever take me home? I don't care what's the matter with it or your family. I love you."

She lifted herself up on one elbow and then bent over with her face close to mine and her hair falling down around, and said: "Dick, I love you, too, and I'll do anything you ask but that. If you come to the place where I live I'll—have to go to another, and you may not find me."

I said: "I'll have to be at the place where you live when we're married."

It was the first time I had mentioned the idea. Two big tears came out of her eyes and landed on my check, and then she sat up and began to cry as I have never seen anyone cry before.

I was simply agonized. I tempted her out of it after a while, but the day was spoiled, and she wouldn't meet me the next day either.

After that, I let the subject of her living arrangements alone and we were happy just being together and loving each other, until one day when I was at the Acme office. Sherwin was explaining that the fire inspectors had put a violation on the Ogonz Building, and that a bigger water tank to supply the sprinkler system would have to be placed on the roof, and pointing out where it would go on the plan, when I said:

"But this plan doesn't show the penthouse."

"There isn't any penthouse on the Ogonz Building," he said. "There never was."

Now that he mentioned it, I didn't remember seeing any on the one occasion when I had visited the place. All my old suspicions and a lot of new ones came into my mind with a rush, and I decided that anything was better than this uncertainty. I had a date with Althea that evening, so I went down to the Ogonz Building just before the place closed for the day, and up to the top floor. All the offices there were perfectly good offices of perfectly good firms, no chance for a living apartment of any kind. Then I went up the stairs leading to the roof.

I could see through the wire-reinforced glass of the door leading out that there was a housing for the elevator machinery and a water tank on spidery legs, but certainly no penthouse visible on that side. I couldn't see through the back of the housing for the stair well, of course, so I opened the door and stepped out and around. The sun was just setting, and there was a brisk wind that made me grab for my hat. The roof had a parapet around it about chin height. There were the ventilator heads, and there was the flagpole.

And there was Althea Dubois, walking toward me as if she had just stepped out from behind the flagpole. She looked so beautiful it hurt.

"Oh, Dick!" she said, in a kind of wail. "I warned you."

While I stood there, she ran past me and down the stairs. Before I could catch her at the top floor, I heard the elevator grinding, and when I rang the bell it wouldn't answer. I had to walk down all the way, and when I got to the ground floor there was no trace of Althea or of Mr. Ankaiosou either. I haven't been able to find any trace of either of them since. But I think she may be in some tree near where we were together, so I'm trying every one. I know if I find the right one, she'll come back to me.

The drinkers at Gavagan's Bar were silent for a moment. Then Keating said: "What did you say the night super's name was?"

"Ankaiosou; I think that's right."

Keating said softly. "Ancæus the Lesser was one of the Argonauts, a demigod. He's the only one about whose later life nothing is told. He was from Samos, and his specialty was navigation."

THE RAPE OF THE LOCK

"Meet Mr. Allen, Mr. Willison," said Doc Brenner. "He's an engineer."

Willison gloomily accepted a hand. "Does he shake for drinks?" he asked. "Make mine a Rye and Water, Mr. Cohan. Mr. Allen can maybe help us out. Witherwax here is trying to explain the fourth dimension that he read about in a book, and we can't understand it."

"But look," said Witherwax. "Suppose I draw a line around my glass there." He reached across the bar, wet his finger on the brass grating where Mr. Cohan set beer glasses after filling them from the tap, and drew a line around his cocktail glass. "A two-dimensional thing couldn't get past that line without getting wet, but since I'm three-dimensional, I can." He demonstrated by drinking the Martini. "So if I was four-dimensional, I could get around a three-dimensional barrier."

"Like the time my brother Herman locked the combination into the safe," said Mr. Gross. "It was an awful time to do it, because he was supposed to get married that afternoon and the license was in there, too."

Willison said: "But you're not four-dimensional. Nobody ever saw a four-dimensional man. Or a two-dimensional one, either."

"But Einstein—" said Witherwax.

"What has Einstein got to do with it?" said Willison.

"So his partner," continued Gross, "insisted they didn't ought to get one of those safe-opening experts because he'd blow a hole in it, and this safe had cost them a lot of money. So he used to be an opera singer under the name of Felitti before he went into business with my brother Herman, and he said if he could bust a glass with his voice, he could make the safe open by singing at it—"

"He also says the fourth dimension is time," said Witherwax.

Willison had lost the toss. As Mr. Allen, the engineer, raised his Rob Roy in salute, Willison said: "Can you do anything about this?" He indicated Witherwax.

"Why, I don't know that it's really necessary," said Allen. "He's quite right as far as he goes. Anything you can measure is a dimension. You can take Time as the first dimension, for instance, and the amount of money in my pocket as the second, and figure out how long I can stand here drinking without going broke."

"That isn't what I mean," said Witherwax.

"Me either," said Willison. "Mr. Witherwax here says if we could use the fourth dimension, we could go places and see things that we can't ordinarily."

"Oh," said Allen, sipping his drink, and then looking into it as though he expected to find a fish at the bottom. Then: "In the general case, it's quite true that the fourth dimension is a purely mathematical concept, and it isn't even theoretically possible to use it in the way you mention." He gave a nervous little laugh, finished the Rob Roy at a gulp, and signalled for another. "But I have reason to believe that three-dimensional bodies can use the fourth dimension. A funny thing happened."

Gross made one more effort and was shushed by Doc Brenner. Willison said: "If you're going to claim you can use some kind of formula—?"

"No. I'm not. And I only hope it was the fourth dimension. Because if it isn't, there's something going on that—well, I'll tell you, and you see if you can find any explanation.

About two years ago [said Allen] I was out east with International Bridge. We were putting in a pipeline in southern Iran, down where it gets a hundred and twenty in the shade, and there isn't any shade. I guess everyone's temper got pretty short, but we had a job-paymaster named Mintz, a fat man from Minneapolis, whom the heat hit hardest of all. Well, one Saturday afternoon, I came into the office to find him having a terrific row with old Hamid Abadi, the foreman of the native gang. Hamid wanted the week's money for his men and was claiming he hadn't received it as usual on Wednesday, when Mintz was out with dysentery or some sort of collywobbles, and Mintz was saying that the big boss must have given it to him, and Hamid was just trying to collect twice before skipping out.

Just as I came in, the row reached its peak. Mintz flew completely off the handle, called in one of the Persian police, and said he wanted Hamid questioned. Now, in case you don't know it, the methods of the Persian police are far from gentle. I didn't blame old Hamid a bit for turning pale at the prospect, but he was only a dirty old gang-boss of peasants, and Mintz the representative of a powerful corporation, so they were about to take him away when I cut in with the suggestion that the office record would show very clearly whether Hamid had been paid or not. Then it developed that the files were locked in the big boss's private safe, and he'd gone off up-country and wouldn't be back till Tuesday.

Well, I used to be in the Army Counter-Intelligence, you know, and in training for that, one of the courses they give you is safe-breaking. I suppose I paid about as much attention to it as the average student, which was enough to get me by. But I did know something about cracking a simple safe with a tumbler lock, and that was the kind the big boss had. So I shooed everybody out of the office except Mintz—he sat there making nasty cracks—and I went to work on the safe. I found I had forgotten most of what I knew, so that it took me over two hours. It must have been a fairly unpleasant two hours for Hamid, sitting outside there with that Persian cop, licking his chops and just waiting for the opportunity to start pulling out fingernails. But at the end of it, the safe door swung open without any intervention of reaching through the fourth dimension into a three-dimensional object.

In the safe, as you might expect, were not only records showing Hamid Abadi hadn't been paid, but also a memo from the big boss to Mari Sanjari, the secretary, saying: "Be sure to pay Hamid for his gang." Mari had just tucked everything into the safe and slammed the door when the big boss left.

The big point about the affair was Hamid's gratitude. He kissed my hand and wanted to kiss my face, which I didn't like a bit, because he smelled of turmeric. He told me how grateful he was, and pushed into my hand a little gold amulet on a chain. "It open all locked places to you," he said, in his version of English.

The thing is flat and oval and has on it something that looks like a hand, only it's a pretty crude one, holding something that might be a sword and might be a cross. But if it's a sword, the point is blunt, and if it's a cross, it's being held upside down. There's some lettering on it, what kind I don't know; it might have been made by a spider leaving footprints.

I thought the gift was a pretty touching expression of the old boy's gratitude. Even the intrinsic value of the gold made it valuable in a place like Iran. But I didn't try to refuse it; that would have been an unbearable insult to a Persian. I simply looped the chain through my own key chain and carried it around as a pocket piece. With the story of Mintz and the safecracking job, it made good cocktail party conversation.

The first time it made anything more was

after a cocktail party where I stayed late, had a few drinks too many, and no dinner but the canapés. I confess, I was more than half-seas over, maybe three-quarters. When I got home, I stuck my key in the lock, only I didn't realize till later it wasn't my key, it was the amulet Hamid gave me. The door swung right open. The instant I stumbled through, I realized something was wrong.

A gust of rain hit me in the face, and it had been a fine night outside. Moreover, my feet were not on a hardwood floor, but on cobbles, and the night was as black as the inside of a billy goat, with open sky overhead. I want to tell you that when people say a shock like that knocks you sober all at once, they're crazy. I was still more than half-fried, and everything was sort of reeling around me, but after a couple of minutes the rain on my head and getting my eyes acustomed to the dark enabled me to see where I was.

I was in a stone-paved courtyard with a building about five stories high forming an L around it, and a tree growing out of the stones at the angle where the end of the L met the next building. There was a door and some windows looking on the court, but they were completely black and silent. Behind me a high wall cut off the view, and I had apparently come through a kind of gate in it.

I thought that if I could go through that gate in one direction, I could in the other, so I opened it. Nothing happened—that is, nothing except that I found myself in a narrow street, not very long, with the shadowy forms of buildings at either end, all of them as black and silent as though this were a deserted city. I was staggering a little and when I put my hand against the wall it struck some kind of sign, so I snapped my lighter to have a look at it. In letters about four inches high it said, "Impasse du Petit Jésus," and I want to tell you that stopped me cold.

As I said, I wasn't in very good shape for figuring things out, but before I had time to figure anything out, a searchlight beam went across the sky, then another and another, and the most awful pandemonium broke out all around, all sorts of sirens, not like sirens in this country, but a high pitched "Eeeep-eeep-eeepy," and some kind of sound truck with dim lights went past on one of the cross streets at the end, "eeping" like mad. There were more searchlight beams against the bottom of the clouds, and off in the distance something that sounded like gunfire, and then a heavier explosion, and there was a vivid flash of light behind the buildings in the distance.

I was getting sober enough to decide that I didn't like any part of this combination of being soaked and maybe socked, when there was a crash as though the whole sky had fallen in, stones went whizzing past my ears, and most of one of the buildings farther down the Alley of the Little Jesus slid into the street and began to burn. I remember thinking how lucky I was they had used a low-power bomb as I ran toward the place, because a big one would have totally demolished me along with most of the buildings on the street.

Windows were coming open all around and doors too, I suppose, but because I was in the street already, I got to the bombed house first. I heard a woman's voice screaming for help from somewhere near the top of the pile of rubble, and what with the alcohol in me and the excitement, I never thought of doing anything but starting to climb toward the voice. Just as I got near the top, there was another boom which must have been gas catching somewhere, because bright blue flames began to come up, one of them catching me painfully on the hand.

Just beyond was the woman, her head sticking out, and even though she was disheveled and screaming I could see by the light of the fires that she was one of the loveliest objects I have ever put my eyes on. I wrenched at the stones and pieces of wood to get her clear. She stopped screaming and said: "Hurry, Monsieur, for the love of God. I am not hurt, but imprisoned."

I don't know how long I was at it. All I know is that I wasn't paying attention to anything but trying to get her out, and the fire seemed to be gaining on both of us in spite of the rain. Just as I got a big piece of board and pried loose the bent bedstead that was holding her down, a couple of guys in those funny brass helmets French firemen wear were there beside me, hauling us both out and down a short ladder they had run up the side of the rubble heap. Quite a little crowd had collected at the bottom and they cheered me, the only time such a thing has happened since I hit a home run while I was playing third base for my high school team.

They got a coat around the girl, who had been in a nightgown. She said: "I am called Antoinette Violanta. At present, as you see, I have no home, but if Monsieur will tell me his name and where he is staying, I can notify him of where to come to receive my thanks."

"My name's Allen," I told her, "but—well—I don't exactly know—"

"Ah, Monsieur is an American?" she said. "You speak French very purely, very correctly."

"Thank you," I said, seeing that she apparently really wanted to make something of it, and being not in the least unwilling. "Is it possible, Mlle. Violanta, that I could accompany you—"

Everybody except the firemen who were working on the burning house had been crowding round. Now one of those damned French policemen touched me on the arm. I suppose he must have noticed my hesitation about giving an address.

"Monsieur is very brave, very strong. May I see Monsieur's card of identity? *C'est la guerre.*"

I pulled out my wallet and handed him my old C.I.C. card from the war, which I've found is always good identification because it puts you on the side of the law. He looked at it with a flashlight, and I could see his eyebrows wiggle. He bowed to both of us.

"Will Monsieur and Madame accompany me to the Mairie of the Arrondisement?" he said. "A matter of records, after which quarters will be provided for you, Madame, as a person distressed."

He led the way to the damndest old jalopy of a car I ever saw, but I wasn't paying much attention to it, because I was too busy talking to Antoinette Violanta. It seemed she was a dramatic student and lived in what they called a *pension*, which is a kind of boarding house. The Mairie was a big brown building, with blackout curtains at the windows, where they took us into an official room and a clerk took down our names. The cop who had brought us whispered something to him; he asked to see my identity card again, then took it with him and went out. I sat down and talked to Antoinette Violanta some more.

After a long wait he came back and bowed to her. "Mlle. Violanta," he said, "it has been arranged to provide you with a room in the Mairie itself for this night."

She said good night and let me hold her hand for a minute. It occurred to me that I didn't have any place to go, but I wasn't allowed to bother about that, because almost as soon as she got out of the room the clerk came back, followed by another cop and a big old papa of a Frenchman with a bald head and handlebar moustache, dressed in a black silk robe. He sat down behind a desk, picked up the identity card and looked at me:

"M. Allen," he said, "you swear that the information in this document is correct?"

"Certainly," I told him. "It's official. The photograph matches, doesn't it?"

"M. Allen, you are extraordinarily well-developed for a man of such tender years."

"I don't know about the years being tender," I said. "I'm thirty-four; born in 1915."

"Evidently. And you are a sergeant in the Counter-Intelligence Corps of the American army, the 63rd Division?"

"Yes."

"M. Allen, you will oblige me by telling me where the 63rd Division is engaged."

"Why, we went in to cut off the Colmar pocket first," I said, "and then up into the Saar, with the Seventh Army."

The cops looked at me as though I had done something dirty, and the old guy banged his fist on the desk. "Assassin! Perjurer! Spy!" he shouted, "Confess! You are in the pay of the Boches!"

"I'll confess nothing of the sort—" I began, but he cut me off: "Double liar! We have confirmed the facts telephonically. In the army of our gallant allies, the Americans, there is no 63rd Division and no Counter-Intelligence Corps. A mistake? You Boches always make them, to the little adding those of a true grandeur, in the effort to distract—such as setting your birthdate at an hour which would render you three years old."

He waved dramatically at the calendar on the wall, and all at once I understood why the car we came in looked like such an antique and all the clothes of the people seemed a little funny. The top sheet was for July 1918.

I hadn't a word to say. The magistrate shook his finger at me. "Evidently the building in the Impasse du Petit Jésus was blown up by you, assassin, instead of a bomb from one of your airplanes. The ruins will be searched to discover the reason. Place him in a cell until this is done. And you, spy, remember that all is lost."

He stood up. The two cops patted me all over to see if I had any weapons, then hustled me pretty roughly down some stairs into a basement and threw me into a cell, where they locked me in. One of them called out: "Sweet dreams, species of a camel. I'll tell your sweetheart to meet you at the Luxembourg in the morning."

I groped around in the dark until I found a cot, and sat down on it to figure things out. I was fairly sober by this time, and I had the king of all hangovers, the kind you get from sobering up without having had a chance to sleep it off. I decided that if I was not dreaming, Hamid's amulet had been trying to do me a favor by introducing me to Antoinette Violanta, which was a very fine idea; but it had missed fire somehow, and landed me in the pokey as a by-product of the operation. With an espionage rap to beat, too. I know too much about the way the French handle that sort of thing to want to take a chance on getting clear, even though when I did, I could find the beautiful Antoinette. And I remembered Hamid had said the amulet would open all locked places. Well, I was behind a lock right then. So I took the amulet and applied it to the lock on the cell-door. It opened as though it had never been locked, and I stepped through into the hall in front of my own apartment. It was nearly dawn, and all I had to show for my trip was a burn on my hand and some thoroughly wet and pretty much torn clothes.

Allen finished his Rob Roy and tapped his glass to show that he wanted another.

"Very interesting," said Willison. "Ver—y interesting. And did you try it again? Or try to check up?"

As a matter of fact [said Allen] I did try writing to Paris, but you know how French officials are. They just didn't answer when I asked about somebody named Antoinette Violanta, and I haven't had the chance to go over and check in person. It wouldn't be much use now; she'd be something over fifty. And I haven't tried the amulet again because of something else that happened.

I was at the house of a girl I know, waiting for her to finish dressing before going out on a date with me one night, when I picked up a silver cigarette box to have a smoke. The lid stuck. I was looking at a magazine at the time, and without watching what I was doing, I got out my bunch of keys and stuck the thin edge of the amulet into the crack where the lid met the box, and twisted.

The box came open all right, but when I reached in still with my eyes on the magazine, I got a burn instead of a cigarette. I said, "Ow!" and looked then. And I saw Hell.

["Hell?" chorused two or three of the listeners. "What did it look like?" asked Witherwax.]

It looked the way you'd expect Hell to look if you were a Fundamentalist. It was only a peephole view, but the place was full of real, red angry flames, with little figures moving somewhere far down. Only I didn't get a chance to see any details, because I was so startled I dropped the box. It landed on the lid and closed again, and when I picked it up and opened it, it was full of cigarettes, like always.

"So you don't dare try the amulet any more?" said Willison.

Allen finished his drink. "No, it's not that. It's just that I'd rather like to get some inkling of what to expect. For example, I don't want to equip myself with an elephant gun and turn up at the court of Napoleon or the North Pole. Look." He slid off the bar stool, walked across to the broom closet at the back of the room, and, producing something from his pocket, dabbed at the lock. The door swung open, and the others standing at the bar had an impression of something bright inside.

"Well, I'll be damned!" said Allen's voice. He disappeared into the broom closet as though he had been jerked from inside, and the door banged to behind him.

"Hey!" said Mr. Cohan. He strode across to the closet and flung it open.

From the little 12-by-12 window at the back, a gust of cool air swirled through Gavagan's Bar, but the closet was empty.

BELL, BOOK, AND CANDLE

The young man in the expensive suit put his hat on the stool beside him and said: "Scotch!"

Doc Brenner paused with his Manhattan halfway to his mouth and said: "In my experience, anyone who asks for Scotch in that tone of voice is either a non-drinker taking a big plunge, or a heavy drinker who can't be bothered with mixtures." He stopped and turned his head from left to right and back, sniffing.

"I smell it too," said Witherwax. "Oh, Mr. Cohan!" The bartender had given the young man his Scotch and came in answer to the appeal. "What's that smell all of a sudden? It's like a whale died in here, a long time ago."

The young man in the expensive suit put down his Scotch and shuddered violently, demonstrating the accuracy of Doc Brenner's observation.

"By God, I wish I knew," said Mr. Cohan. "It wasn't here a minute ago, and it seems to come from around him," he indicated the young man, "but that wouldn't be right now. That's Mr. Fries, and he's got more dollars than you have dimes and can afford soap if he wants to buy it."

"You ought to have Gavagan look after the plumbing," began Brenner, but was interrupted by the entry of an individual with a mop of unruly iron-grey hair and a pince-nez, who immediately took his place beside Mr. Fries. Like the others he sniffed, then laughed, revealing a set of teeth that would have done credit to a crocodile.

"Phil, you stink!" said he. "Mr. Cohan, give me a

Stinger. It will help kill the odor emanating from my unfortunate friend here. Didn't it work?"

"Are you kidding?" said Fries. "Another Scotch, Mr. Cohan. This is the latest counter-attack. The whole house is full of it, and I can't even bear to smell myself, even if I do work in a laboratory."

"I wonder what went wrong," said the man with the crocodile smile.

"I don't know, but something better go right pretty quick. Mrs. Harrison is going to leave if I don't get rid of it, and Alice is supposed to come down for the weekend, and I don't even dare go up there and see her instead. George, if it doesn't stop I'll go nuts!" His voice rose in intensity and the knuckles of the hand that clutched the bar were white.

Witherwax said: "Pardon me, but you seem to be in a good deal of trouble. Is there any way we could help?"

"Yes," Brenner said. "Why not put your difficulties up to Mr. Cohan here? With all his experience behind the bar at Gavagan's, there aren't many things he doesn't have some answer for."

Fries made a push-away gesture and drank from his glass, but George flashed his row of teeth and said: "He's got a ghost, and it likes him."

"The ghost seems to have a rather queer way of displaying affection—" began Brenner, but Fries made another motion with his hand and said: "All right, all right, I'll tell about it. I think people you meet in Gavagan's can be trusted to keep a secret, and this is one. And maybe you can spot what's wrong, Mr. Cohan. George can't, and he's supposed to be an expert. That's why I went to him in the first place. He's studied all that sort of thing for years and even has a collection of medieval manuscripts. And it just gets worse. A week ago—"

Look here, I better start at the beginning. I own that big brown house on Baltimore Street, the one with the shutters. I don't know exactly how old it is; a couple of hundred years, I guess. It's always been in our family; was built by an ancestor of mine, about seven greats back, who was a good deal of an old rip and was supposed to be in league with the Devil. They believed in that sort of thing in those days. Maybe he's the ghost himself; but he hasn't communicated, and I don't know that it matters. The main thing is that the ghost has been in the building for a long time, one of those ghosts that throws things around.

["Poltergeist," said George.]

I know [Fries went on] but I wanted to explain. In spite of the odd happenings the ghost caused, it never made trouble for any member of the family—at least not in recent generations, though back in Victorian times when it was really fashionable to be frightened of ghosts, it may have been different. The fact is that our poltergeist established itself quite early in the game as taking a kind of benevolent interest in us.

I can remember when I was a kid, we'd always have a Hallowe'en party at home, and Donald—we called him Donald for no good reason except that it was the name of the ancestor who built the house—would put on a special show for the occasion. If we were telling stories in front of the fire, there'd be a sound of footsteps from upstairs where there wasn't anybody, or else a can that someone had been going to take down to the cellar would tip over and go rolling down, bump, bump, bump, or a candle would go out in perfectly still air. It was very thrilling and satisfactory, and unlike most families, we grew up regarding ghosts as quite amiable and friendly creatures.

Donald paid for his keep by more than merely being amusing, too. There was an aunt of my mother's who came for a visit, bringing a perfect horror of a Chinese vase that didn't match anything in the decoration. I don't know what my mother intended to do with the thing, but as it turned out she didn't have to do anything. When the family came down for breakfast, Donald had taken care of it and the vase was on the floor, broken in about a thousand pieces. And there's a family story that when some burglars broke into the place a few years back, he raised such a terrible racket that everyone woke up and the burglars had to leave in a hurry. Give me another drink; I'm feeling better.

After my parents died and my sister got married and moved away, I had the house to myself except for Mrs. Harrison, the housekeeper. You might ask why I don't sell the old place, and I'll answer by saying that nobody wants to pay anything like what it's worth for a twenty-room house, even one with a poltergeist in it, and the girl I'm going to marry—that is, if I am —[Fries looked gloomily into his glass] wants to live in it. Anyway, with me alone there, Donald apparently got to feeling lonely. When I'd get home late from the laboratory, there would be a few companionable bangings around the place, and in the morning I'd find a book he had pulled out of the bookcase and thrown on the floor—just some friendly little action to let me know he was there taking care of me and appreciated having me there, too.

You have to understand that I met Alice at a college reunion up at Williamsburg. That's where she lives with her mother, and even if it isn't the nicest thing to say about one's future mother-in-law, that mother is a horrible old harridan. She can talk the paint off a wall and is always having everyone in for a tea fight or a séance. Did I say she was a Spiritualist? Well, she is; one of the kind that's always writing letters to newspapers and making a big fuss over the business. I don't know how Alice has stood her this long. But Alice and I hit it off right from the start, and it wasn't long before we decided it would be a good idea to get married.

Her mother raised a terrible row about it, not that she had anything definite against me, but just because she can't bear to see Alice getting away from her. Of course, Alice is old enough to write her own ticket, but after all, Mrs. Hilton—that's her name now, she's been married and divorced about six times—Mrs. Hilton is her mother, and she didn't want to hurt her. So we finally agreed that after we were married, she'd come and live with us in the big house.

I figured that in a twenty-room place there'd be space enough to keep out of her way, and Alice felt the same. Just to give the thing a dry run, I asked them both down for New Year's weekend at the place. That's where the trouble started; that's why I smell like essence of decayed cabbage tonight.

[He gave it a dramatic pause, and Brenner said, "What do you mean?"]

What do I mean? I mean that Donald likes Alice all right but didn't want any part of mama. There weren't any thumpings or things like that—he must know she's a Spiritualist and would run him ragged if she got the chance—but it was unmistakable. The first night she was in the place there was a wind and one of the outside shutters banged and she didn't get a wink of sleep all night. The next night the water pipe in the bedroom over hers burst and she woke up swimming. Then when she went to bed, the edge of the rug was rolled up just inside the door and she tripped over it and nearly broke an ankle. Things like that; the kind of accidents that could happen anywhere. Only I knew they weren't accidents; they were Donald expressing his disapproval. He was letting me know that if that woman came to live there, there'd be hell to pay.

I suppose he was protecting me from Mrs. Hilton, you see, and I haven't a doubt he was right, and if we did have her living with us, there'd be hell to pay in more ways than one; but you can see the fix it put me in. If I told Mrs. Hilton what was really going on, she'd be all over the place with mediums and assorted Spiritualists before you could turn around, and

I wouldn't dare call my name my own. If I didn't tell her, Donald would keep on giving her the works every time she came, and it would be just as bad. It's a shame you can't reason with a poltergeist.

So I went to George here, because I knew he'd been quite a student of that sort of thing, and he told me—

["I told him," said George, "that there wasn't anything to do but exorcise the ghost—put him right out of existence He said he didn't want to do that to an old friend of the family, and I told him it was pretty much of a choice between the poltergeist and Alice the way things stood. So he agreed to try it."]

Yes, I agreed [said Fries] and now I wish I hadn't. George dug out some old medieval manuals and came around to exorcise the ghost. It was very impressive, with bell, book, and candle, just as they say. He hadn't got more than three-quarters of the way through the ceremony, though, when one of the glass crystals fell off the chandelier and hit him on the head.

A ghost is supposed to be powerless in the face of an exorcism, so we sat down to figure that one out, and when we did, one of the chair legs gave way under George. Then we knew Donald had it in for George as badly as for Mrs. Hilton; probably on account of the exorcism, so we came over here to Gavagan's to figure it out. We decided that the poltergeist belonged to me and my house, and if anyone but a professional was going to exorcise it, it would have to be me.

You see, neither George nor I dared take a chance on letting the thing get out by calling in someone else, because if Mrs. Hilton got wind of it, she'd be down here like a ton of bricks, and the old battleaxe wouldn't want us to exorcise the ghost at all. I got George to show me how to do it and memorized what I had to say and then I tried it. It went off smooth as greased ice, with no crystals falling on my head, and there wasn't a sound in the place afterward, so I imagined the exorcism had succeeded and called up Alice long distance to ask her and her mother down for the weekend.

Luckily they couldn't make it and asked for a rain check until next week. Because the exorcism hadn't worked at all. When I came down in the morning about half the books in the bookcase were pulled out and thrown around the floor and the pages of some of them were torn. George agreed with me that it was a warning, and said I must have done something wrong, but I went over the whole process with him watching, and I had it perfect.

We puzzled over it for a long time. Then he said: "What kind of bell did you use?"

I told him the little bell that stands on the dinner table when I want to call Mrs. Harrison from the kitchen.

"Wrong," said he. "I've seen that bell, and it's brass. If you really want to exorcise a ghost, you'll have to get a silver bell."

Well, I got a silver bell—they're harder to find than you might think—and that night I tried the exorcism again. It worked no better than the first time. That is, there weren't any noises, but during the night a big piece of plaster dropped out of the ceiling in my bedroom and hit the pillow beside my head. George and I knew it was another warning, more in sorrow than in anger; Donald could just as easily have dropped that plaster on my head, only he didn't want to hurt me, just to discourage me from trying any more exorcisms.

So George and I checked over the whole procedure again. It couldn't be the bell was wrong, and George said it was absurd to believe that Donald was immune to exorcism. We had a long argument about it. Finally, he said, "What book did you use?"

"A Bible, of course, just as you told me," I said.

"Yes, but what Bible?" said he.

"The family Bible," I told him. "It's almost as old as the house, and I don't think there's any doubt about it."

He said: "But it's a King James Bible, isn't it? A Protestant Bible?"

"Of course," I said.

"That's probably the trouble, then," said George. "Most Protestant churches don't have any such thing as exorcism. Maybe some of them do, but to be on the safe side you need a Douai Bible. A Catholic Bible."

Well, I got one, and I tried all over again. That was last night, and now look at me—or rather, smell of me. I've turned into something no respectable goat would associate with, and the whole house smells the same way, and Alice and her mother are coming down, and Mrs. Harrison threatening to quit, and what I'm going to do, I don't know, and I want another Scotch—

Brenner said: "Why not give up the idea of exorcising Donald? From what you say he seems to be an intelligent sort of poltergeist, and I'm sure he'd understand."

"Mrs. Hilton!" said Fries in a strangled tone of voice, and drank again.

"I've looked it up in the best texts," said George, with a frown. "I can't imagine what the trouble is." He addressed Mr. Cohan. "Can you?"

"That I can," said the bartender readily, crossing his arms and leaning back. "One thing you'll be wanting and not having is a blessed candle, and that you can get at any parish house for the asking. But I'm thinking that even if you had it, it's little good the candle would be doing you. A black Protestant, and not in holy orders, go on with you! All you'll be doing is making magic, and your pollyghost will love the smell of it."

"But look here," said Fries. "I can't very well turn

Catholic overnight to get rid of it. And Alice and her mother are coming."

"That, young felly, is your problem," said Mr. Cohan. "Would you care to be paying for your drinks now? That smell is bad for the trade."

ALL THAT GLITTERS

"A good evening to you Mr. Councilman," said Mr. Cohan, ducking his head deferentially, and without orders, set out on the bar two glasses and a bottle of Irish whiskey.

Doc Brenner halted in the midst of trying to explain relativity to Mr. Witherwax, and both of them gazed at a big man, with an unlit cigar in one corner of his mouth and a figure that was making definite approaches to the pear. Without appearing to have noticed Mr. Cohan's greeting, this individual strode frowningly past to the end of the bar, removed the cigar from his mouth, and spat with great violence in the brass crock that was placed there.

The act seemed to cheer him up enormously. He turned a face crinkled with tiny red veins toward the others. "A fine good evening it is, Mr. Cohan," he said heartily, "and who is it I have the pleasure of meeting in your elegant establishment?" His hand came up; the whiskey went down; the other hand swished a chaser after it, and he beamed.

"Sure, Mr. Councilman, and these are good friends of mine and Gavagan's," said Mr. Cohan. "Mr. Witherwax, Doc Brenner, this is me friend, Councilman Maguire of the Fifth."

"And president of the Fifth Ward Fidelity Democratic Club," said Maguire, shaking hands. "Always glad to meet a friend of Mr. Cohan's. Any time the two of you would be in the Fifth, just drop in. Mr. Cohan, set up the glasses; it's a pleasure to be buying a drink for people in your place."

Doc Brenner said: "It's quite a way over here from the Fifth."

"So it is," said Mr. Cohan. "But Councilman Maguire is not the man to forget his old friends—nor his duties, neither."

"What duties?" asked Doc Brenner. "Spitting in that nightmare at the end of the bar?"

The cast-iron smile disappeared from Maguire's face, and he glanced quickly at Mr. Cohan, then rumbled in his throat.

"Tell them, Denny," said Mr. Cohan. "It will be a fine lesson to them. The two of them are after me half the time to get rid of that gobboon."

Witherwax said: "It don't belong in here. Look, I been reading a book about interior decorating, and it says that with a bar like this, you got to have furnishings in the same period." He swung his arm around. "It don't match nothing."

Brenner said: "It's insanitary. Mr. Councilman, I'm surprised that the city doesn't pass an ordinance against things like that in public places. It's all right if you have one in your home, but suppose somebody comes in here that has tuberculosis? Answer me that!"

Councilman Maguire glanced at Mr. Cohan, who nodded affirmatively; downed his second jorum of Irish, and appeared to make up his mind. "I will answer you that," he said, solemnly. "I will that, and Mr. Cohan here will bear me out. Insanitary that crock may be, if you say so [he nodded at Brenner], and no beauty, neither [he nodded at Witherwax]; but you wouldn't want to see a Republican administration in this town, would you? You would not. But that's what you'd be getting, if it weren't for that pot there, and me coming over at least once a month from the Fifth to spit in it. Look here now, will ye look at this? It will tell you the whole story."

He reached into his breast pocket and produced a wallet, from which he carefully extracted a small photograph.

Brenner glanced, turned the photograph over and handed it to Witherwax. "I don't see anything startling about it," he said. "It's a picture of you all right, but rather foggy, and not a good likeness."

"Right you are," said Maguire. "It's what isn't in the picture that tells the story."

"How is that?" asked Witherwax. "That's the City Hall in the background, isn't it? But it's no secret that you're a member of the Council. And what's that under your foot?"

Ah, there you have it! [said Maguire, bringing the flat of his hand down on the bar.] Sure, I knew you were smart as soon as I saw you in Gavagan's. That there under me foot is a shoeshine box, and it's not that it's there that tells the story, but that there's nothing over me foot. Did you ever hear of a man putting his foot on a shoeshine box, just for the fun of it, now? You did not. Mr. Cohan, have another go at the glasses, and I'll tell you how it was, and why it is that I come into Gavagan's Bar, just to be spitting in that brass crock there.

It all started four years and more ago, when me old grandmother got a letter from Ireland. She says to me: "Denny," she says, "this is good news for ye. Your great-uncle Tom is dead and gone, and you're the head of the house of Maguire."

"And what good does that do me?" says I. "From all I hear of my great-uncle Tom, he had nothing to leave anyone but his good wishes, and it will be a cold day in July when they take them at the grocery store."

"Hush, will you?" says she. "Have I not told you many a time that the head of the house of Maguire had a leprechaun to be working for him?"

So she had, for sure, all the time when I was a boy, and me laughing a little bit behind me hand at the old lady. I says to her: "And what use would a leprechaun be to me here in America, where I can go round the corner and buy me a better pair of shoes than any leprechaun could make? And not feel the price of them, neither! Besides," I said, "me great-uncle Tom Maguire will not be the last of the name left in Ireland."

"I'll thank you not to make mock of an old woman," says she. "Maguires there are in Ireland, and I hope there'll be more; but not another Maguire of Ballymaclough. Your grandfather was the last of them, except for his brother Tom that never married. And you'll not be making mock of the little people, neither. They can bring you good luck or they can ruin you."

And she started telling me a story that I could see was going to take the best part of an afternoon. So being a busy man, I said I would put in a good word with the immigration people for this leprechaun when he landed, and I left. And that was the last thought I gave the matter till after me grandmother was dead and in her grave, God bless her soul. I never would have thought of it again but for this picture you see here.

Now it is my experience in politics that the people, they like a leader to look like a leader but to sound like one of themselves. So I made it a habit, being as I had me office at the City Hall, to stop on me way back from lunch and get a shoeshine from one of the boys that hang around there, and pass the time of day with them. Those boys, they know a devil of a lot more than you'd think about what's going on, and many's the time I've learned things from them, like when they saw Prossiwitz, that's the Republican councilman that was, whispering on a park bench with Spencer the contractor, the dirty rat.

I favored this one lad of a bootblack. He was a little one; not over four feet high, with ears too big for the head of him, and he looked like he was never proper fed. The thing that took me was the brogue he had; as though he just stepped off the boat from old Ireland herself. Me. now, I came over here when I was a little lad, and I lost all me brogue before I was sixteen.

This lad, now I asked him what his name was oncet. He said it would be Diarmait, which is the name of one of the kings of Ireland, and a strange name for a bootblack. I told him so, and many's the time I used to laugh at him about how he'd grow up to be a councilman himself, and maybe mayor.

One day, when I was talking to him like that off and on, not looking down too much, but watching the birds that fly round the park, and looking for maybe someone I knew, he stops shining my shoes. "Maguire," he says, and when I looked down at the tone of voice he used, I could see he was serious. "Maguire," he says, "ye are a Maguire of Ballymaclough. Ye should know already that I'll never grow up to be a mayor or a councilman neither."

That should of told me the story, but I was only listening to the last of this rigamarole with one-half me ears, because just at that minute, who do I see coming across the park but this felly Angelo Carnuto, that was in the numbers racket, and him a man I'm not wishful to talk to any time. So I give the boy Diarmait a quarter and took meself off, and forgot the whole business.

It would be a week later or more when this picture come up. I was having me shoes shined again and smoking a cigar as you can see for yourselves, and a fine autumn day it was, when one of these photographers comes along, the kind that takes your picture and hands you a ticket, and you send in the ticket with a bit of money and get the picture. Now a photographer like that has a vote like any other man, so I took the ticket from him and stuck it in my pocket, not thinking about it at all, but only about the election that was coming.

That night I went around to the Fifth Ward Fidelity Democratic Club, where they was having a rally. Seeing that I was running that year, the secretary of the club come around to me with something about getting photographed for some posters with me face on them—not that it's much of a face, but people like to see who they're voting for. Well, I was that busy with one thing and another, so I reached in my pocket for the ticket and told him to get that picture, maybe it would do. And it was this, this picture here.

Look at it, now. Do ye see a sign or a bit of the boy Diarmait, that was shining me shoes? Ye do not; and neither did I. When I saw it, it come back to me about the time the lad had spoken, and then I began to understand, and I thought to myself: "Denny Maguire, one of two things. Either that day, you had a drop too much, or this is the leprechaun of the Maguires of Ballymaclough, and no mistake." For you could no more photograph a leprechaun than you could photograph the thoughts in your head, when some people can't so much as see them.

The more I considered it, the more like it seemed, with the little wizened up face of the brat, and his ears too big and too pointed. It fitted together; with all the shoes in America made by machinery, what would he be doing but shining them that was already made?

With that, another thought come to me. I remember how me old grandmother, God bless her, used to say that every leprechaun had a pot of gold hidden away somewhere, and he would have to give it up, if you held onto him till he did. At that time I was needing some money. You will remember that was the year when the Republicans had Judge Gregory up for mayor, yelling their heads off about reform; and it come to me that a few dollars might make all the difference between winning an election and losing one.

So the next day, on me way back from lunch, I stopped for a shine. It was a doubtful thing to do now, because there was a little rain falling, and nobody else at all around the front of the City Hall but me and the lad Diarmait. When he bent over my shoes I reached down and grabbed his arm.

"Let me go, you big ape," he says.

"Not till I get your crock of gold," says I.

"What do you mean, crock of gold?" says he.

"Would I be shining shoes here in the rain if I had a crock full of gold to live on?"

"I'm thinking maybe you would," says I. "Come on, now, I know who ye are. Hand it over."

He wept and he pleaded, and said it was all he had between him and the workhouse, but I would not give up a bit for that, and the end of it was that he opened up his shoeshine box, and there it was, the big brass crock you see at the end of the bar, only it had a lid on it then.

"Take it," he says. "Take it, and that's the luck of the Maguires of Ballymaclough until ye get some sense in your fat head, or else the house is bossed by a Maguire that knows his business better than you do."

I took off the lid of the pot and thought I'd be wanting little more luck than I saw inside there. It was full to the brim with gold pieces; all kinds, some of them looking like old Spanish, some English and other things. It was a fortune in there. I could hardly lift it.

There I stood with it and thought. I could not spend the gold pieces as they were, for it's against the law, and if I turned it in to the gov'ment, like the law says, I'd lose half the value of it. Not that I'm for breaking the law, you'll understand, but the law is against people trying to cheat the gov'ment, and this was something special that had come to me as honest as the day is long. So I thought I would take my pot of gold somewhere and sell the pieces one by one, which is not against the law at all if you find one of those collectors.

But the more I thought of it, the less I liked the idea of taking that pot of money home, what with three children and the old woman around the house, and no more did I like the idea of taking it up to my office in the City Hall, with an election coming on and Republicans all over the place. Then I thought of my old friend, Mr. Cohan here, and how he was always one to do a favor for an honest man, and I called a taxi and came right out here.

When I got out of the cab, the pot seemed a lot lighter than when I got it. I set it on the bar and asked for a drink, and told him to have one for himself, and would he mind taking care of the pot for me the while. He lifted the lid and took a look in, and then he gave me a look like I had lost my wits entirely.

"Are ye pulling my leg, maybe?" he says. "And why should I take care of a pot of beans for ye?"

Then I looked myself, and would you believe it? The pot that had been full of gold pieces as an egg is of meat had nothing in it at all but baked beans. My mouth came open like the mouth of an oyster, for I could not understand at all how such a trick had been played on me. I told Mr. Cohan the story and about how the lad Diarmait was a leprechaun, and he says: "Did you spit in the pot?" "No," says I. "Was I supposed to?"

"Yes," says he. "It's well known in the old country that unless you spit in a leprechaun's gold to hold possession, it will turn to something worthless. Oh, oh, and now you'll be having bad luck, I'm afraid."

There it was, and no help for it, and the luck was as bad as could be, for we lost the election. Is that not true, Mr. Cohan?

"Every word of it," said the bartender. "And there's the pot for proof."

"But what have you got it here now for?" asked Brenner, looking in the direction of the brass crock.

"Didn't I tell you?" said Councilman Maguire. "It was after the election, and a poor day that was, too, I come in here to see Mr. Cohan, and we were talking about the misfortunes of the Maguires. And he—"

"I made him tell everything that had passed between him and the boy Diarmait," said Mr. Cohan. "Because a leprechaun will be wonderful attached to a family, and not bringing bad luck to them if they'll give him half a chance."

"Then it come to me," said Maguire, "that the leprechaun said something about getting sense in my head, and Mr. Cohan here says that maybe if the gold was gone, there'd be some luck left in the pot yet. So he pulls it out and puts it at the end of the bar there for a spittoon. And I spit in it. And would you believe it? The very next week it was found out that Spencer the contractor had Prossiwitz, that was the Republican councilman, on his payroll, and wasn't that a fine thing for a man that was elected on the reform ticket? He had to resign, and when they held a special election, I come over here and spit in the crock and the right man won the seat. So now I come every time there's an election. A little more out of that bottle, Mr. Cohan."

GIN COMES IN BOTTLES

Mr. Witherwax had made a discovery. "Listen," he said, "it works. There was this guy from Hungary and this Roberts, see? They started right in there in the lobby and understood each other perfect. It's like the manual says; more than half the wars and troubles in the world are because people don't understand what they mean. What about that piece in yesterday's *Journal,* huh? Where it says the Russians and us don't mean the same thing by democracy? If they had this Esperanto, they couldn't make no mistakes like that."

"Oh, yes, they could," said Doc Brenner. "It's not a question of understanding what a word means, but how far you carry the idea the word represents. Like 'water'; I might want a bathtub full of it and get a glass of it to drink. That reminds me, Mr. Co-*han;* I don't want any water tonight. I want an Appetizer Number Three."

"Yes, but—" said Witherwax.

"What was that you ordered, old man?" It was the stooped and tweedy Professor Thott who, as usual, had drifted up as quietly as so much ectoplasm.

"Appetizer Number Three, the real dry whiskey cocktail," said Brenner, and then quickly, before Witherwax could get under way again: "Now if you want a real universal language, why not one like English, which already has hundreds of millions of speakers?"

Thott nodded: "And can be learned quickly by

anyone who'll take the trouble to study the basic form."

"The manual says," persisted Witherwax, "that English is too irregular and too hard to spell. And besides—"

Mr. Gross belched ponderously over his Boilermaker. "My wife's nephew Adrian," he said, "when he was in college, roomed with a guy that said Russian was going to be spoke by everybody. This fella was one of them Reds, I think. But that was before he got bit by the yak."

"And besides," said Witherwax, "the manual says it's gotta be a language that don't belong to nobody in the beginning. Otherwise, some people know more about it than anybody else, and then they're boss, and you ain't got no international brotherhood."

"Russian wouldn't do at all," said Thott. "Yes, Mr. Cohan, you may give me an Appetizer Number Three. In fact, I can scarcely conceive of a worse candidate for a world language—"

"That's like I said," said Witherwax. "Once you get talking like them Russians, you have to think like them."

"No," said Professor Thott, judicially. "The fault of Russian is its syntax."

"Another Boilermaker, Mr. Cohan," said Gross. "I once had a business partner that got an infection in his syntax—"

"This drink is good," said Thott. "In Russian you first have to learn an enormously complicated grammar. Then you find words don't mean what you think they mean, because Russians use a lot of arbitrary colloquialisms—"

"That's just like the manual says," said Witherwax. "If we want to have international brotherhood, we gotta get a language that everybody understands all the time."

"You mean with no homonyms?" said Doc Brenner.

Mr. Gross belched again, and held up two fingers to indicate another Boilermaker. "Are you saying that the language a fella speaks can make a fairy of him?"

"I do not know—" began Doc Brenner, and stopped as a newcomer leaned across the bar next to him and addressed Mr. Cohan:

"Has that unhappy servitor of mine been in here? You know, Joe Kozikowski. Make mine a Scotch and, a double Scotch."

"That he has not," said Mr Cohan, pouring. "Maybe one of the gentlemen would have seen him. I will make you acquainted with them. Mr. Medford: Professor Thott, Doc Brenner, Mr. Witherwax, Mr. Gross."

There were murmurs of politeness. "And what would have happened to poor Joe, may the blessed Virgin preserve him?" asked Mr. Cohan.

"That's what I'd like to know. I want to get him back on the job," said Mr. Medford.

"And a credit to you it is to take such care of the poor felly," said Mr. Cohan. "Meself, I had him here for a couple of days and it was Gavagan's own orders to fire him, for he would be breaking the bottles and pouring the Kümmel in with the Kirsch to make one bottle the less of things that looked all the same to him."

Medford sighed heavily. "I know. But I like the kid, and now there's a special reason."

"My brother Julius, that's on the force—" began Mr. Cohan, but Medford stopped him with a horrified gesture.

"I don't want him arrested," he said. "He hasn't done anything wrong. Just the opposite. Besides, I've already called Missing Persons, and they wouldn't touch the case for me because I wasn't a relative, and if anybody wanted to quit a job, he could. As for those private eyes, I wouldn't want anyone to have one of them looking me up. The next thing you know, you're being blackmailed."

Witherwax said: "I read it once in a book that everybody had to behave like he wants everybody else to behave."

"The Kantian categorical imperative, that is called," said Professor Thott.

"Who is this Joe Koz-something?" boomed Mr.

Gross. "A man that is in trouble should not be left alone."

"Joe's not in any trouble that I know of," said Medford, waving his double Scotch. "He works for me—or used to. But he knows something, or has discovered something, and I'll pay him handsomely to find out how he did it."

"The thing about this Esperanto—" began Witherwax.

Doc Brenner laid a hand on his arm. "Mr. Cohan, another Martini for Mr. Witherwax, while Mr. Medford tells us about this Joe."

> Mr. Cohan knows him [Medford replied readily]. Another one of these—I can't fly on one wing. He's the son of the fellow that used to be janitor of the building where I live, over on Sixteenth Street. The old boy used to call himself Stanley Kozikowski and say he was in the Polish army during the war, but I always rather doubted that story. He had a funny accent that might have been Polish, but might have been a good many other things, too, and he was darker in the face than most Poles. I never knew him to be going to any of those Polish gatherings, either. He just stayed home in the basement apartment with Joe and gabbled with him in their own language, whatever it was. This Joe was a feeble-minded kid; I don't think he ever got beyond third grade and that was in a school for backward children. That is, they said he was feeble-minded; what happened makes it seem he wasn't so much feeble-minded as living in another kind of world, if you get me, with only part of him in this one.
>
> Well, a couple of months ago, the Jap who was working for me got his Ph.D. and quit. I needed someone to take care of the apartment, and I didn't want women running around, so I took the line of least resistance and offered Joe the job. He doesn't have much behind the eyes, but I figured he was capable of handling things like sweeping the floor and washing the glasses,

and beside being amiable, he's willing as the day is long. My Nisei used to cook for me, and Joe couldn't do that—he'd be likely to put tomato catsup in the salad dressing because it was the same color as paprika—but I don't mind cooking as long as someone can clean up the dishes.

The scheme worked out pretty well. When you have people working for you, you have to use them for what they can do, and it isn't always the same with any two, even when they have the same job. One will turn out to be a saw and the other one a claw-hammer, if you understand what I mean. Joe was certainly a blunt instrument. No matter what you said to him, he'd smile beautifully across that sun-tanned face and say "Yesss, Misster Medford," pulling out the s's, and do what he thought was right, which wasn't always what I wanted.

I remember the first time I sent him out to market for me. I wanted some chick-peas to make minestrone—I'm fond of Italian cooking—so he brought home a chicken trussed for roasting and a can of peas. After that I wrote out a list he could hand to the storekeeper, and I found I had to run charge accounts, because I discovered that a one-dollar bill and a five meant exactly the same thing to Joe. But upon the whole, he was a good and faithful servant, and it was convenient to have him living in the building.

That is, up to a month ago. Joe had finished the dishes that night and gone downstairs, and I settled down with a bottle of Port and a book, when I heard him come back in. For a while, he didn't come into the living room at all, and I was just getting up from my chair, wondering whether it was Joe after all, when he got through the door. Half-wit or not, I've never seen anyone look so miserable. He wasn't crying; maybe he didn't know how, but his whole face was twisted with misery and his feet dragged.

"What's the matter, Joe?" I asked.

He just stood there for a minute with his face working. Then he said: "He gone."

I said: "Who's gone? Your father?" It was pretty clear that he was the only person who could be.

"He gone," said Joe.

I thought, of course, that the old man must have died, so I started for the elevator. Joe tagged along behind, unwillingly I thought, and repeating at intervals: "He gone."

But he wasn't dead, at least in the building. The place where he lived was as neat as a new cocktail shaker—that reminds me, Mr. Cohan, you better furnish me something for drinking purposes. [Doc Brenner silently pointed to his own glass and that of Professor Thott.]

The guy had just vanished, and all Joe Kozikowski would do was stand there, croaking, "He gone." Well, it was obvious that if the old man had gone somewhere. Joe was going to have a hard time getting along, because there'd be a new janitor in the place. I have an extra room at the apartment, which I had been using mostly for storage, so I took the kid back upstairs and managed to get the idea over that he was to live there. He was pathetically grateful; actually got down on his knees before I could stop him, and would have bumped his head on the floor if I hadn't stopped him.

["I see," said Doc Brenner, "why you don't think he just quit on you. Unless you did something to wipe out the previous good impression."]

Not at all [said Medford, drinking], it was something he did. At a cocktail party. For no reason at all, I thought it was time I threw one. I like to give parties that are off the beaten track one way or another, and although Joe was working his head off for me—I couldn't get him to quit working till he was ready to fall asleep after I gave him that room—he wasn't quite up to doing tricks with canapés like my Jap.

A friend of mine named Clark, who's a chemist, suggested that I make cocktails that were really dry, no ice in them at all. The trick is to get some dry ice—most of the big dairy companies sell it—and drop it right into the shaker with the liquor. It makes the coldest cocktails in existence, because the temperature of the dry ice is so low, and doesn't dilute them a bit, because the dry ice turns to gas without any liquid form. Spectacular business, too. When you drop the dry ice in the shaker, it fizzes and a devilish-looking smoke pours out and flows around the room, which is something to make conversation all by itself.

What I forgot, though, or what Clark didn't tell me, is that those dry-ice cocktails, without any ice to dilute them, have real authority and use up liquor fast. Right in the middle of the party, with about thirty people on hand, all talking at the top of their voices, I started to fill the Martini shaker again, and found I had only about half a bottle of gin left.

I went into the kitchen, where Joe was arranging canapés from the caterer's, and said: "Joe, can I depend on you? This is an emergency."

"Yess, Mr. Medford," he said, as usual.

I said: "I want you to go to the liquor store and buy six bottles of gin. Here's twenty bucks. This is special. You understand?"

"Yess, Mr. Medford," he said.

With Joe it's always a good idea to run a check-back, because you never can tell how much he actually gets of what you're saying. So I said: "All right, Joe, what are you going to do?"

"Sstore, get special gin."

"*Six* bottles," I said, holding up that many fingers. "And fast."

"Yess, Mr. Medford," he said in a way that sounded almost intelligent.

"Okay, boy, on your way," I told him, and went back in to try to hold my guests with my glittering eye until the reinforcements arrived.

They were a long time coming. It didn't matter too much, because there were plenty of Manhattans and Scotch; and besides, the unusual strength of the cocktails was getting everyone comfortably fried. I noticed myself that when anyone dropped a match on the floor, I had a slight tendency to stumble over it, and decided I'd better pull up. But even so, I saw someone pick up the empty Martini shaker, and then one of the girls went home, and I began to worry about the party laying an egg after all.

But just as I reached the point of desperation, Joe showed up—with one bottle.

"For God's sake," I said. "Where's the six bottles I told you to get?"

"Thiss all," said Joe. "Special gin."

I cursed myself for having used the word "special" on Joe, but there wasn't anything I could do about it now except send him back again, and I was in too much of a hurry to get the Martinis replenished to bother. Now about the rest of it, I want you to remember that I had tipped over one or two myself, and my powers of observation weren't quite as sharp as they had been, and I was in a hurry.

But that bottle of gin was special, all right. I would guess it was an imperial quart, and it was in one of those earthenware bottles, with a stopper sealed over with a wax seal. I remember hoping my idiot child hadn't brought me some of that Hollands gin, which is no good for cocktails; but there was nothing to do except try it, so I dropped the dry ice into the shaker, poured in the vermouth, snaked the stopper out of the bottle, and put in the gin.

Somebody said something to me just then, and I turned my back on the table where the shaker was to answer. I could hear the stuff sizzling away behind me, and pretty soon the vapor began to come out. The first thing I noticed was that it was a lot thicker and darker than on the earlier rounds. It came flowing down past my legs and around our feet like a fog, and the girl

I was talking to stopped what she was saying to look at it, and said: "Oh, Mr. Medford, that's going to be a strong one!"

I turned around. The shaker was still fizzing and the smoke coming out, thicker than ever, but more of it going up toward the ceiling than down. It was a kind of black, but a thin black, so that as it billowed up I could see the pattern of the wallpaper through it. The talking in the room was dying down; everybody was watching it. I remember looking at Clark, my chemist friend, and wondering whether he knew what had gone wrong; but he was staring, as goggle-eyed as the rest. Someone said: "I don't like it," and someone else: "It's a great trick; how in the world does he do it?"

I was just wondering that myself, when the smoke stopped coming out of the shaker. Only it didn't fade away as the vapor from the other dry-ice drinks had done. It seemed to bunch together up above the table and grow more solid in what seemed like a bulbous approximation of a human figure. If I hadn't had so many drinks at the time, I'll swear there was one portion of the cloud that looked like a ferocious human face. I think one of the girls saw it, too; she gave a little scream. At the same moment, there seemed to be an unintelligible rumbling sound, like a train in the distance coming nearer, from the thing.

I didn't know what was going on, but it wouldn't do to let the party get out of hand; so I put on as much nonchalance as I could and stepped over to the table, saying: "Well, I want Martinis; a hell of a lot of Martinis."

Just at that moment Joe Kozikowski came through the door behind me with a tray of canapés. He looked up, gave a yell, dropped his canapés on the floor and bolted through the kitchen door. I haven't seen him since.

At the time it didn't seem to matter. By the time two or three of us got the mess of the canapés cleaned up and I looked around again, the spook or smoke or whatever it was had disappeared. The funny part of it was that, when I went back to the table, the Martini shaker was full of Martinis clear to the nozzle; and so was the shaker that had held Manhattans and the bucket for the ice for Scotch and sodas. Everybody was starved for Martinis before, but now everybody had to drink them.

I suppose it's not polite for a host to get boiled at his own party, but that must have been what happened, because when things cleared up, I was lying on the couch with the bath-mat over me and a head the size of a New York railroad station. It was several hours before I got clear enough to try to figure out what had happened. Then I realized there wasn't any Joe around; he had vanished just like old Kozikowski, leaving everything he owned behind.

I don't know how he'll get along where he's gone without someone to take care of him; but maybe where he's gone, he won't need anyone to take care of him. I guess there never seemed to be more than part of him in this world, and after I saw the bottle he brought, I was sure of it. It got broken in the rumpus, but what there was left of it had little symbols, all dots and curves, worked into the material. Clark says they're Arabic. The only way I can possibly figure it is that Joe went some place of his own and got a bottle of gin, only instead of g-i-n, gin, he got j-i-n-n, jinn, right out of the Arabian Nights. I'd be glad to get Joe back.

Mr. Witherwax said: "Like I was saying. If everybody spoke this Esperanto, nothing like that could happen."

THERE'D BE THOUSANDS IN IT

Mr. Witherwax, who had been pursuing his investigation of literature, was summarizing the result across a Martini: ". . . so this guy says the trouble is that nobody hasn't worked out how all these inventions are going to change people's lives, like putting coal miners out of work, see? He says there ought to be a law against new inventions till some scientific committee figures them out, see?"

"You can't stop people from making inventions," said Doc Brenner.

"My nephew Milton," said Mr. Gross, "he invented a cigarette-smoking machine once."

"A what?" asked Brenner.

"A cigarette-smoking machine. For them companies like the Lucky Strikes that want to know how many puffs it takes to smoke their cigarettes, so they can put it in the advertising."

"He says," continued Witherwax, "that invention has become the Frankenstein in civilization, sort of a menace—"

"You're mixing up Frankenstein with the monster," said Brenner, "like most people who haven't read the story. Frankenstein was the man who made the monster, and—"

". . . but he couldn't interest any capital—" said Gross.

Mr. Cohan, Gavagan's Bar's bartender, said heavily; "Now, now, gentlemen, if you will not all be talking at once, there will be more of you listening, which with a drop to drink makes the better time. Will you be having anything now, Mr. Gross?"

"Another Boilermaker for me."

Doc Brenner shook his head. "Still working on this one—It's just an attempt to rationalize prejudice on the part of a conservative who fears change."

"You can sling the English better than me," said Mr. Witherwax, "and I ain't got the book here to prove it, but it says how about electric lights? Since we got them, people can stay up all night, and maybe that's why so many people get nervous, because they ain't living natural, see?"

Brenner swished his drink around in his glass. "It's pretty, but there isn't the slightest bit of evidence that any invention has really proved harmful. Of course, if the atom bomb—"

"Oh, yes, there is," said a voice.

Four pairs of eyes swiveled toward a youngish man sitting a little farther down the bar. A glass of neat vodka stood before him.

"What did you say?" asked Doc Brenner.

"I said there was evidence of a harmful invention. I have it on the best authority, since I am both the inventor and the person harmed."

"See?" said Witherwax accusingly to Brenner. "What invention was this?"

"It's my dressing machine."

"Your what?"

"My dressing machine. Thoroughly practical, I assure you. There'd be thousands in it if I could only go into production on the orders I already have. But I can't."

"Ah," said Mr. Gross, "I know how you mean. When them patent lawyers are after you, you got trouble, like with my nephew Milton—"

"No difficulties of that nature at all," said the youngish man. "I have all the basic patents necessary. It's quite another matter, and I fear a rather emotional one. By the way, my name's Lawrence Peabody."

There was a shaking of hands. After Mr. Cohan had been summoned to perform his ministrations, the youngish man settled himself:

After being graduated from Harvard [he said] I looked about for something to do. The pater was generous enough, you know, but he didn't want me to be one of the idle polo-playing set, and I rather agreed with him. I had my engineering degree and a chance to go to South America with the Templetons, but somehow the idea of building bridges in a jungle with insects crawling around my vitals failed to appeal. I wanted to live in the city; so I came here with the idea of setting myself up as a professional inventor.

It's not a bad life, you know. I was able to afford a good tool shop and, in between diversions, managed to fool around with a few things like a rho-meter—["What's that?" said Witherwax to Gross behind his hand. "It's something for a rowboat," replied the latter]—and an erasing key for typewriters, which had enough promise for National Industrial to buy up the patents and pay me a retainer. They gave me various odd jobs, improvements on inventions they already had under way, and in the meantime I worked on the big idea: this dressing machine.

You see, I have always been one of those unpleasantly lazy people who have to be blasted out of bed in the morning and who stumble around in a daze for an hour or two after rising. As a result, I've always found dressing such a terrible chore that I often stayed in bed far beyond the hour I should. I thought if I could find a way to cure that, there would be a market for my invention.

["I read in a book once that all the great inventions are made by lazy people," commented Mr. Witherwax.]

The remark is not original [continued Peabody] but the point is well taken. I suppose I must have labored over the thing for a couple of years; but, when I was finished with it, it worked. It works still.

["How?" asked Gross, who appeared to have forgotten his nephew Milton.]

It's really very simple [said Peabody, drawing imaginary lines on the bar with his finger]. I have a big wall closet in the bedroom, half of which is taken up by the machine and the other half by clothes on racks. The bed stands with its head next to the door of the closet, and there's a console arrangement right here at the side of the bed, with the controls set into it. Now before you go to bed, you hang the clothes you want for the next day, in proper order, on the end rack of the machine, right here. In fact, you can set it up to take the clothes for ten days in succession, if you have that many. When you wake up in the morning, you simply kick off the covers and press button number one of the control, right here. A pair of lug arms come out here and grab you, very gently, of course, and slides on your undershirt.

["How about your pajamas?" said Brenner.]

Don't wear any. I use an electric blanket, so it isn't necessary. Then you press the next, and it puts on your shorts, then your socks, shirt, pants, and so on. Finally, you press the red "Release" button here, and the machine turns you loose, all ready for the street, except for tying your shoes. I haven't been able to make an attachment that will do that effectively. Then the arms swing the empty rack around to the end of the line and the rack of clothes for the next day falls into place. If you want to repeat suits, you leave a vacancy on the second rack.

["Ahem," said Doc Brenner. "As a strictly luxury item, I can see some utility in it, but I should think it would be confined to people who can afford a house on Fifth Avenue and another in Newport."]

You don't understand [replied Peabody]. The marketing expert at National Industrial thought so, too, at first and was very skeptical over the whole thing. In fact, almost the first person he succeeded in interesting was Pontopoulos, the movie man. He thought it might appeal to that magnate's rather Oriental ideas of luxury.

It was a brilliant piece of self-deception. Pontopoulos was interested, but only professionally. He perceived at once that the machine was the answer to one of the most expensive problems in the show business—getting the chorus dressed and on the line at the proper time without having a special dresser for each girl; or man, when one happened to be dealing in chorus men.

I'll never forget it. His face took on a glassy look, and he offered me a cigar out of his own pocket, which I understand is practically unheard-of for Pontopoulos. He's usually surrounded by two or three yes-men, who handle the cigar distribution, and they don't give strangers the Belinda double-Coronas that Pontopoulos himself smokes. But he could see the whole thing at once: the costumes arranged on racks for the whole chorus a day ahead of time, everything in place; the girls lining up in the dressing room; the machine accepting each in turn and sending her out, untouched by human hands but perfectly and beautifully groomed for her act. There'd be thousands in it.

Pontopoulos agreed to buy my dressing machines as fast as they could be supplied, not only for his movie studios, but also for his chain of television stations and the two or three musical comedies he was putting on in New York, in the hope they would run long enough to enable him to make movies of them without paying the writers anything extra.

It was about that time that Cynthia decided to come down and do some shopping and see a show or two. Have I mentioned Cynthia? Her full name is Cynthia Crane, and if you don't mind, I'm rather in love with her. We're going to be married—that is—if. [Peabody drained his vodka at a gulp and, pushing the glass across the bar, tapped it with his finger. Mr.

Cohan had no difficulty in understanding the signal.]

You know what the hotel situation is—or don't you? There's that convention of the White Rose Society on, and Cynthia couldn't find a room anywhere for money, so I decided to give her one for love—that is, to let her use my apartment while I put up at the club. Perfectly satisfactory arrangement until the night before last—would have been still, but for the dressing machine and the fact that the Radcliffe alumnae threw a party for Cynthia. Since it was a hen party and apt to run rather late, I was at a loose end, so I set up a little do of my own at the club —nothing expansive, you know, but a few chaps in for dinner and a little serious drinking in a private room. Since most of us had belonged to the old glee club, I hired a guitarist with the idea of doing some howling over the drinks after the food was gone.

Well, we were giving "The Spanish Cavalier" a good beating, when—no, wait, I'd better make it clear what happened at the other end of the line. Apparently, the hen party was a good deal like most Radcliffe reunions; that is, the girls blotted up quite a bit of the stuff themselves—

["Strong drink can be a curse to women," said Mr. Gross solemnly.]

Indeed it can [continued Peabody] and especially when they go in for it in the form of sticky liqueurs, as they nearly always do. I don't mean to suggest that the girls were badly under the weather or anything, but one of them named Georgia Thompson thought she would avoid questions if she spent the night with Cynthia instead of going home to her own family.

It seems that she took the day bed in the living room, where Cynthia had been sleeping, while Cynthia herself went into the master bedroom, my room. It was a warm night, you remember, and as nearly as I can make out, Cynthia just flopped down on the bed in her nightgown. She must have thrown out her hand across the console and hit buttons number 5 and 6. Before she could do anything more, the machine turned on, grabbed her, and put the pants and the jacket of one of my suits on over her nightie.

She knew about the machine, of course, but naturally she screamed and thrashed around. In doing so, she struck one of the other buttons. The machine promptly put one of my shorts on her, over the jacket, and held her gently, waiting for the next order.

[Doc Brenner snorted into his drink.]

I assure you it's no laughing matter [said Peabody, looking pained]; at least not for me. By this time Georgia was awake, or at least as awake as one can be after having a good deal to drink and sleeping for about ten minutes. When she saw Cynthia in the grip of the machine, she screamed, too, and tried to help her. In doing that, she managed to touch a couple of other buttons, so that the machine put on one of my undershirts and another pair of pants over what Cynthia was already wearing.

This seems to have been too much for Georgia, in the condition she was in. She sat down on the floor and had a fit of the giggles, while Cynthia hung there, suspended in the machine, growing angrier and angrier, not daring to do anything herself but trying to persuade Georgia to do something.

["Them laughing jags is terrible," said Mr. Cohan.]

Give me another vodka [said Peabody]. I don't quite know how long this phase lasted; Georgia was finally persuaded to get up and call me at the club. As I said, we were in the middle of "The Spanish Cavalier." I couldn't hear too well, and she couldn't either, so the conversation took a good deal longer than it should, with Cynthia a prisoner of the machine all the time, and half my clothes on her in the wrong order. It must have been horrible.

I finally managed to understand what was wrong and told Georgia to press the "Release" button. But with everybody in the room singing at the top of his voice in the background, she understood it as "threes." Now, there is a whole row of number 3 buttons on the console, right here. As soon as Georgia pressed them, the machine turned up Cynthia's legs and began putting all the socks I owned on to her, one pair after another.

Meanwhile I was pretty worried—Georgia had remarked over the phone that Cynthia wasn't exactly pleased with the turn events had taken—and as soon as I could tear myself loose from that gang of hyenas and find a taxi, I rushed home.

I was too late. The girls had somehow managed to find the release button for themselves. When I got there, all I found was an empty apartment, with my clothes strewn all over the bedroom floor and some of them torn.

Georgia called me up the next morning—that's yesterday—and said Cynthia had gone back to Brookline, perfectly furious with both of us. This afternoon I heard from her—a letter. She says she still loves me, although it's a strain, and she's willing to marry me. But I'll have to break with National Industrial and promise never to do any inventing again. She won't go to South America and build bridges with me, either. And the old man won't put up the money for us just to sit around.

I think I'll have another vodka.

Mr. Gross said: "Now that cigarette-smoking machine my nephew Milton invented—"

THE BLACK BALL

Mr. Witherwax was saying: ". . . and it says in this book that you could get to lift an elephant or maybe listen to what somebody was saying a couple of hundred miles away, just like you was in the room. All you got to do is get to be one of these chelas."

"Why don't more people do it, then?" demanded Mr. Gross. "A fellow that could lift an elephant could make a lot of money with a circus or something."

"Mr. Cohan, give everybody another round," said Doc Brenner. "I can tell you why, Mr. Gross. It's not so easy as it sounds. In the first place, you have to find a genuine guru, or yogi, and most of them are fakes."

"Yeah," said Witherwax, "and then you gotta spend ten years sitting on spikes or something like that, and you only get about a cup of rice a day, and no Martinis, and this book says you dasn't even think about women. By the time you done all that, what the hell, you wouldn't care whether you could lift an elephant or not, so it doesn't matter."

"That's about right," said Brenner. "It's like looking in one of those crystal balls. They say the people who really have one that works get so excited over what they see that they want to keep on seeing and can't make any use of it."

"The statement it not universally true," said someone.

All three turned to look at a tall man with an air of histrionic dignity and a spray of grey around the edges of his hair, who had just placed on the bar beside him one of the handled leather cases in which bowling balls are transported. "And what would you be having, Mr. Leaf?" asked Mr. Cohan.

"A Rob Roy," said the tall man. He turned to the others. "I am at present defending a client, a most unworldly man who arouses my deepest sympathy. I have every reason to believe that he not only possessed a genuine and functional crystal ball but was an adept in its employment. Yet use was made of his discoveries."

"You're a lawyer?" asked Brenner.

"I am an attorney," said the tall man.

Mr. Cohan said: "Make you acquainted. This is Counsellor Leaf, Mr. Witherwax, Mr. Gross, Doc Brenner. The next round is on the house."

Hands were shaken. Mr. Gross said: "Ain't you the Madison Leaf what defended my wife's cousin Irving, the time he got accused of putting the porcupine in the mayor's bed?"

"Ah, yes, a fascinating case. *People* vs. *Potasz,* as I remember."

"It was—" began Mr. Gross, but Brenner extended a hand. "I'd like to hear about this client with the crystal ball, if you can say anything about it before the trial."

"Yeah, me too," said Witherwax, and Mr. Cohan said: "Me brother Julius, that's on the force, says you can get into a lot of trouble telling fortunes."

Madison Leaf delicately poised his second Rob Roy, the one that was on the house, and looked around until he was sure that his audience was giving him its full attention.

> Gentlemen [he said gravely], I have accepted this case without fee because I am convinced of the essential innocence of the unfortunate Mr. Jackson—that is, his innocence of the matter charged. It is true that he changed his name from the one originally given him to Bokar Rapurjee Jackson; but that is not a crime in this state, and it may even be described as a legitimate device for the exercise of his peculiar pro-

fession. As to his claims to the cannonball, I have been forced to advise him that they rest on legally dubious ground. No doubt a claim could be made out under the precedent in *Untervoort* vs. *Vandermyer*, as given in the 43rd volume of the Wisconsin reports. However, judgment would doubtless encounter the opposition of the Indian government, and as the U.S. Circuit Court decided in the matter of Mayfine—

[Witherwax said: "I don't understand these complications."]

[Madison Leaf bowed.] Quite correct. Under the influence of such agreeable company and Mr. Cohan's excellent beverages, I had momentarily forgotten that I was not addressing a professional audience. I beg your pardon.

Mr. Jackson applied to me in—no, that is not quite correct; I shall have to go back and lay the foundation. Very well; there was a gentleman, and I use the word advisedly, named Frederick Washington, now the late Frederick Washington, a gentleman of color, of dark color; and a most remarkable character. My connection with Mr. Washington began when he besought my good offices in composing certain differences between the group of which he was the leader and another group of similar ambiance.

[Witherwax gazed admiringly at Madison Leaf; Gross whispered behind a hand to Brenner: "Does that mean they were doctors, with that about the ambulance?"]

I perceive you do not quite apprehend [said Madison Leaf, taking what might be called judicial cognizance of the interruption]. I will explain. The late Mr. Washington, at the time he sought me, was engaged in the promotion of a sport, or game, having to do with predicting the order in which certain figures would recur in the reports of the New York Stock Exchange. This sport is somewhat extensively engaged in, and the rewards for success are considerable.

I understood from Mr. Washington that he began to engage in this sport as one of those who risk certain sums of money on their ability to forecast series of numbers. In this endeavor he had become so very successful that he had accumulated an amount of capital which permitted others to make wagers with him.

[Mr. Cohan frowned. "Me brother Julius says the whole numbers game is a racket," he said.]

[Madison Leaf regarded him from the distance of miles and centuries.] To refer to a man's business as a "racket" is an actionable statement [he said]. I may say that I contemplate no action, however, and as the heirs of the late Mr. Washington may be somewhat difficult to discover, I do not think you are in danger.

Mr. Washington was naturally aware that other entrepreneurs were engaged in the promotion of the same sport. The reason he applied to me was that he wished to suggest the drawing of an agreement, under which players in one geographical part of the city became automatically patrons of his game, while the remainder would operate through another gentleman, who had been in business for some time—Mr. Angelo Carnuto.

I pointed out to Mr. Washington that such an agreement would probably be without legal force, if written. "Look," he said. "I can ruin this Carnuto's racket any time I want, but peace is a wonderful thing, and I would like to have more of it."

I concurred that it is always better to settle differences by agreement than by any other means. I also remarked that I would be glad to act as Mr. Washington's emissary before Mr. Carnuto, but that it would be necessary for me to understand the full strength of the position I was representing. It was therefore desirable that he inform me of what means he proposed to use in ruining Mr. Carnuto's business, provided no agreement were reached.

Somewhat to my astonishment, he demurred, and in a highly evasive manner. I opened the interview by imagining that he had crude physical violence in mind, but Mr. Washington's approach convinced me that it was something subtler and perhaps more dangerous. I therefore informed him that unless he gave me his full confidence, I could not act as his attorney. He threatened to retain someone else; I advised him to do so, merely remarking that as I had performed some legal services for Mr. Carnuto and possesed his confidence, few other emissaries would find him so approachable.

At this point in our conversation, which, I may mention, took place in Mr. Washington's office, there entered one of his assistants. This gentleman was in a state of considerable agitation. He said he had received a telephonic message to the effect that unless Mr. Washington laid off—as he put it—his intestines would be wound around a doorknob.

Mr. Washington was evidently not a man of great physical courage. His countenance assumed a singularly unpleasant color. I may say that the event was not entirely fortuitous. It is a lawyer's duty to be prepared for all eventualities required by the humble service of his client—

[Gross belched loudly. Madison Leaf threw back his head and then apparently decided that this was not intended as a comment.]

Mr. Cohan [he said], will you please give us more of the same prescription? It is an attorney's duty to become aware of all facts that may benefit his client. I had not neglected that duty. When Mr. Washington summoned me, I was already somewhat aware of what he might have in mind, since, as I have said, I was not unacquainted with Mr. Carnuto. In fact, I had informed Mr. Carnuto that I proposed to call on Mr. Washington, and suggested to him that if our conference were interrupted by such a telephone call as the one actually received, a peaceable settlement might become easier.

Mr. Carnuto might, indeed, have adopted a threatening attitude earlier. But he was most anxious to adjust matters so that this sport might be carried on in a manner pleasing and profitable to all parties concerned; and the plain fact was that, while Mr. Washington's business was known to be operating in a manner gratifying to himself, Mr. Carnuto's own business was showing a startling decline in profits. Analysis showed this to be due to the fact that players in the Negro section of the city were showing an extraordinary ability to select the winning numbers. Mr. Carnuto was convinced that the appearance of Mr. Washington on the scene had something to do with this but feared that the mere elimination of the gentleman, without discovering what lay behind him, would only intensify the difficulty.

You may judge, therefore, that I was deeply interested when Mr. Washington originally remarked that he could ruin Mr. Carnuto's business. After he had a little recovered from the shock of the telephone call, therefore, I remarked that it was fortunate indeed that he had asked me to advise him; that I understood this to be practically a declaration of war between the two; but that I might still be able to avert trouble if Mr. Washington would honor me with his confidence.

Mr. Washington became sulky. I said nothing. The assistant who had brought the message said: "He want me to call him back by four o'clock, boss. What should I ought to tell him?"

Mr. Washington addressed me. "If I told you, you wouldn't never believe me," he said. "But I'll show you, and then you can tell Angie I sure got something."

We got into his car and proceeded to Rathburne Street, in the Negro section, to a small store in the middle of the block. There were curtains in what had been the show windows, which were far from clean. Across the door was rather crudely painted the words: "Church of the Living Light."

Inside, the floor space was cut off by a curtain, in front of which a fat colored woman sat behind a kitchen table that had been painted with red enamel. She regarded me in an unflattering manner, which became still more unflattering when Mr. Washington said that we must see Mr. Jackson at once, but she made her way through the curtain. Presently she came back and announced: "The Master will see you."

Beyond the curtain there were four or five rows of folding chairs, and at the back of the room a low dais, one step up. On this was a table, and on the table a crystal ball about six inches in diameter. The only light in the room came from beneath this ball and shone through it up the face of a man who stood over it. He was quite tall, a light-skinned Negro, made to appear taller by the dais, the light, and the fact that he was wearing a turban.

He screwed up his eyes as Mr. Washington came in and pronounced with an accent that I would describe as solemn: "Brother, have you brought another brother to the sacred light?"

Mr. Washington's directness was admirable. He said: "This ain't no sucker, Bokar. This is Mr. Leaf, the great big lawyer. He's going to fix things up with that Carnuto for us, only he's got to have a demonstration."

"What kind of demonstration?" said the tall man, and sat down.

It was already apparent to me that this so-called church was a cover for an illegal fortune-telling activity, a fact of which I took mental cognizance for possible future use. I suggested that it would be very convincing to me if Mr. Jackson could predict the action the court would take in the case of *Chase* vs. *Bascom Corp.*, which I then had pending on appeal.

"No, sir," said Mr. Jackson. "This here ball

won't show me nothing but figures. Got to be something with figures in it."

"Very well," I said. "What will be the stock exchange quotation on Republic Oil next Friday?"

Mr. Jackson seated himself before the ball and gazed into it intently. After a minute or two, still gazing, he said: "It's gonna be 44.375."

I made a note of this figure and then suggested that to convince Mr. Carnuto, it might be as well if I were also furnished with the numbers that would win the game on that day. They were readily furnished, and we left.

In the car, I asked Mr. Washington about the ball, which to me resembled a type that is made commercially by a firm in Pittsburgh. He said that Mr. Jackson had secured it in India, where he had gone as a sailor during the war, and at the same time he had changed his name. When I inquired further as to how so valuable an object had been released, Mr. Washington again became evasive, and shortly afterward we reached the place where he dropped me off.

Gentlemen, I am an officer of the court, and accustomed to weighing evidence. I admit that it is only surmise on my part that Mr. Jackson had deserted his ship in India, passed himself off as a Hindu, and stolen the ball. Some knowledge of something like this is required to account for the fact that Mr. Washington had a hold over him, over and above the obvious psychological dominance.

The question of whether a series of numbers could be correctly predicted, however, admitted of evidential proof. The evidence already at hand indicated that Mr. Washington was producing deleterious effects on Mr. Carnuto's business. I was now in a position to complete the chain.

I accordingly wrote out the numbers Mr. Jackson had given me, sealed the paper in an envelope, and left it with Mr. Carnuto, asking him not to open it until Friday. I informed him of Mr. Jackson's possession of the ball, advised him to consider what would have been the result had I wagered an important sum of money on these numbers instead of the small amounts Mr. Washington had clearly been placing through intermediaries. I suggested that in the event these proved to be the winning numbers, it might be advisable to accede to Mr. Washington's request for a division of territory.

I fear that in so doing, I applied the wrong type of stimulus to a man of Mr. Carnuto's somewhat forthright disposition. He agreed. When Friday arrived and with it the exact predicted figures both as to Republic Oil and the numbers, I accordingly telephoned Mr. Washington to tell him his proposition would be accepted. There was no answer, nor was there during the succeeding days. In fact, the next time Mr. Washington came to my attention, it was by way of an item in the newspapers. Some boys swimming in the Freeport River discovered that the unfortunate gentleman had apparently stepped into a tub of fresh concrete on the bank of the stream and then fallen into the water.

Upon this discovery, I went around to the Church of the Living Light but found the premises occupied by a grocery store, whose occupants denied all knowledge of Mr. Jackson or his establishment. In view of Mr. Carnuto's attitude, I hardly thought it advisable to pursue matters further. In fact, I heard no more of any phase of the matter until very recently, when I received a message from Mr. Jackson. He was in jail, having been arrested on a charge of espionage, and desired me to defend him.

To say that I was astonished would be putting it mildly. But I am not the type of lawyer who refuses a case because a client is poor and friendless and the charges against him serious. I hurried to the house of detention, and as soon as I was allowed to interview Mr. Jackson, informed him that I would be glad to take his case.

"As your attorney, I shall of course assume your essential innocence," I told him. "But I think it would be wise to tell me exactly what happened."

"It was that Washington," he said. "He was a bad one. I told him we were going to have trouble if he told anybody where he got the numbers from, but he must of told that Carnuto. Somebody did."

I did not think it well to pursue this subject, so I told him to proceed with the detail of why he had been arrested.

"I was just trying to get my ball back, that's all, and those dumb soldiers pinched me."

I asked him to give the circumstances. He said: "A couple days after you was in my place, one of the boys called me up and said this Carnuto found out about me and my ball and he was coming to get the ball. People like that know too many people. I figured there wasn't any good place I could hide out around, and I sure didn't want them to get that ball. So I remember that out at old Fort Osterhaus, where they got the park, there's a whole lot of piles of cannonballs from the Civil War or something, and I painted my ball all over black and took it out there and put it in one of the piles instead of one of the balls was there. It fitted just like the skin on a frog, and I dumped the regular cannonball into the river. Then I went away to New Orleans for a while, and when I read in the paper how this Carnuto got hisself killed, I come back. But when I went out there to Fort Osterhaus to get my ball, there was a lot of soldiers around, and they throwed me in jail. All I want is my ball."

I am sure, gentlemen, that you are aware of an item of news which was evidently overlooked by Mr. Jackson in New Orleans—that in the interval between the disappearance of Mr. Washington and the date when Mr. Carnuto was assassinated by some of his associates, Fort Osterhaus had been taken over by the

Atomic Energy Commission for the installation of one of their most secret projects. I can understand how the guards would take a rather strict view of Mr. Jackson's nocturnal presence, especially when he explained that he was looking for a crystal ball in one of the piles of cannonballs. It must have seemed a singularly transparent excuse. However, I do not anticipate any difficulty in clearing him; there is no real evidence against him for anything but a simple trespass.

There was a momentary silence. Brenner said: "But what's the bowling ball got to do with it?"

"Why," said Madison Leaf, "I am now on my way to Fort Osterhaus to offer it to the commandant there in exchange for Mr. Jackson's ball, if that object can be found. It will not unduly disturb the decorative scheme."

"Why don't you wait until you get him out of jail and take him along to show you where it is?"

Madison Leaf looked dignified. "That might result in his putting in a claim for what is really abandoned property," he said. "If the ball cannot be found after he is released, the legal aspect will be much simplified. And after all, I am handling the case without fee; I believe myself entitled to some slight compensation." He downed the last of his Rob Roy and picked up the bowling ball. "Good evening, gentlemen."

Gross gazed after him. "If my wife's cousin August could get hold of something like that—" he began.

"He'd turn out to be one of those guys who get so excited that he couldn't use what he saw, most likely," said Brenner. "Mr. Cohan, I want another Scotch and Soda."

THE GREEN THUMB

Young Mr. Keating from the library joined the group at the bar, ordered his usual Rum and Coke, and settled himself to listen to Mr. Gross's account of how his uncle Moritz got arrested for keeping a live eel in his bathtub in a hotel in Columbus. He had just reached the point where room service was refusing to send up a box of earthworms for the eel when the narration was interrupted by a sound which caused everyone to turn toward the rear. A pair of female shoulders in a neat print dress was shaken, and the sound repeated itself as an unmistakable sob.

"Crying jag?" suggested Mr. Jeffers.

"Not that she got here," said Mr. Cohan. "I wouldn't be giving her more than one Alexander now, and her as decent a lady as I ever saw. But this Gavagan's will not have; it's bad for the trade."

He walked firmly but gloomily around the end of the bar and placed both hands on the mourner's table. "Begging your pardon, ma'm—" he began.

As she half turned her head, fishing in her purse for a handkerchief, Keating started. "Why, it's Dotty Eichman!" he said and took a step toward her.

"Better not," said Mr. Willison. "Women cry because they enjoy it, and you'll get no thanks for spoling one of the finest pleasures in her life."

"Oh, come on over and meet her," said Keating. "She's a nice kid, and maybe we can keep her from bawling."

Dotty Eichman had her face under control. She

was a brunette and pretty. Keating said: "Hello, Dotty. May I present Mr. Willison?"

"How do you do?" She extended a rather limp hand. "Won't you sit down?"

"You're sure you don't—" began Keating.

"Oh, I was just being silly. I'll feel better if I can talk to somebody about it. Have Mr. Cohan bring over your drinks, and I'll have another Alexander."

Keating and Willison accepted the proferred chairs. The former said: "What's the matter, Dotty? Feuding with your in-laws?"

"No, with Tom." She managed a wan smile in the direction of Willison. "My husband."

"Dotty and I are always getting each other out of jams," said Keating. "She was at Mareeba in Australia when I was base adjutant and we had a private agreement to protect each other. Every time one of the fly-boys began to pitch woo, I was engaged to her, and every time one of those Aussie hostesses began to turn on the heat, she was engaged to me. Only I never could persuade her to make it real."

"You can be glad I didn't," said Dotty. "It's like being under a curse." She sipped her Alexander.

"What is, if I'm not too inquisitive?" said Willison.

"What's happened to me." She addressed Keating. "You remember the time they brought in that colonel?"

"The one with the queer name—Poselthwaite or Throgmorton or something like that?"

"That's right," said Dotty. "I've been working it out, and that's when it must have started. No, wait, it didn't either start then. It started way back when I was born, and my parents wanted a boy, so they took out their disappointment by trying to make me as much like one as possible. They never taught me to cook or sew or do anything girls do, and when it came time for me to go to college, they wanted me to take a course in engineering. But I just didn't have the aptitude for it; I couldn't remember the formulas or do the mathematics. All I liked to do was tinker with the machines, so one day I just dropped out and enrolled in a motor mechanic's school. That was all right, too, because I was doing something a man ought to be."

Keating interrupted. "She was good at it, too. It got her a captaincy in the Wacs, and she was line chief at Mareeba."

"Well, anyway," Dotty said, "you see? I was glad to be doing something in the war, and everybody couldn't have been nicer to me, even if I was a woman over a group of men. And then that night they brought this colonel in."

"I remember his name now," said Keating. "It was Pendermatter."

"That's right, so it was," said Dotty. She turned to Willison. "I don't know whether you know how it was in Australia. Sometimes planes would get forced down in the desert, and unless the fliers were guided back to civilization pretty quickly they would die. Even when everything else was all right, they wouldn't know where the waterholes were. So the American and Aussie governments finally worked out a system of rewards with the bushmen for every flier they brought in alive. So much for a Jap, with the rewards for our people graduated according to their rank. The reward the bushman liked best was a button in the shape of a sunflower with 'Vote for Landon' written across it. It took a major for them to get one of those."

Keating interrupted again: "We ran out of Landon buttons, and the government had to have more made. The contractor must have thought we were crazy."

> [Dotty finished her Alexander.] Those bushmen are pretty primitive, but they're smart. They can't count above seven, but they very soon got to recognize the different insignia; and if anyone tried to shortchange them with a Roosevelt button or a St. Christopher medal, they'd blow up and threaten never to bring in any more, so we had to meet the going price. Then this night, one of them brought in this colonel—what was it? Pendermatter. He had started out for some sort of big civic do down in Adelaide and had his best Sunday uniform on

with all sorts of decorations, so that he looked like a Christmas tree with the lights turned up.

I came out of the officers' club just as they brought him along. There was this little group, two or three Aussie interpreters and Pendermatter and a bushman. The Abo was bouncing up and down and arguing at the top of his voice. Of course I went over to see what was going on. One of the Aussies said the bushman thought that Pendermatter was just about the second son of God in the American army and was demanding a very special reward, something better than anyone ever got before for a downed flyer. "They've already offered the blighter two Landon buttons," he said, "but he won't have them. It has to be something new, and we can't get him to be specific."

The bushman let loose another flood of oratory. The Aussie said he was describing himself as a descendant of the great Bamapama, the greatest medicine man in Australian legend, and saying that only a man with his special powers could have found so high and beautiful an object as Pendermatter, and that was another reason why he was entitled to a special reward. Well, there had been a party at the officers' club and I was dressed up, and part of it was one of those little charm bracelets that wasn't worth very much, so I helped out by offering it to him. The minute I put it in his hand, his eyes bugged out and he began to chatter again, wagging his head. The interpreter said: "Thank you, Captain. You appear to have solved our difficulty. Wait a bit, though."

The bushman was picking over the charms on the bracelet. He stopped at one that was a miniature of an old-fashioned cookpot, looked at it and then at me, and began to jabber again. The interpreter said: "He says he's going to make a number one magic when he gets home, so that every time you touch a cookpot, your fingers will have virtue."

I giggled and said something about how I

couldn't boil an egg without an assistant, and the interpreter said something about he wondered whether primitive peoples didn't have an order of knowledge that civilization had lost, but I recognized that as a buildup to asking for a date, and walked away and forgot about it. For then, anyway.

You know, Walter [she turned toward Keating], Tom's family didn't care too much about his marrying me. Very sweet to him and all, but the idea of anyone in a Social Register family marrying a mechanic really got them down. I met him when he brought the car into my garage for a checkup on the lube system and took a chance on going to dinner with him that night. I just wasn't at home with his family, though. I don't mean I behaved like a social goon or anything like that—my parents weren't from the slums or anything, even if they did bring me up to be a mechanic. I knew it was all right when I went places with Tom by the way other people treated me, not Tom's family, but the others. That is, it was all right down to the time they'd find out I was making a living by being a mechanic in my own garage. Then they'd lower the boom.

One night when we were out in the car, he parked it and said: "Dotty, I've been coaxing you to marry me, and I want you to more than ever. But there's a string to it now. There won't be any money."

It didn't even annoy me. I simply said: "What of it? If I marry you, it won't be for money."

"I'll have to go to work," he said. "The mater has laid the law down. If I marry I'll have to earn my own living, and I've been looking around and the best I can get is in an advertising agency at fifty a week."

What could you do with a man like that? I kissed him and said the garage was doing all right, and we'd have to be pretty slow not to get along on what I was making out of it. Then I said yes, I'd be glad to marry him.

You might think that would make him happy. Not at all. He told me I'd have to give up the garage if we were married. He started in with his mother about how she was old and not very well, and she'd just about die if her daughter-in-law was working in a garage and her name came out of the Social Register. Well, I got rid of that line by asking him whether he wanted to marry me or stay married to his family, but he only started in on another one, and this one was hard to beat. He said that he'd never really had to work, and now he couldn't let me be the support of the family tree and feel he was doing his part. He wanted it to be an honest marriage, and wanted me to stay home and have children and take care of the house like a normal wife. Well, we argued over it for hours. I remember the roofs of those factories out along the boulevard line were getting green with the light before the sun comes up before he started the car again. But I loved the big ape—I still do—and I ended up by giving in to him. So I sold the garage and put part of the money into furniture for the apartment—he let me do that—and part of it into a hospital fund to pay for a baby if we ever have one, and I took the rest and invested it in a course at the Éclat School of Cookery.

I wanted my cooking to be a surprise to him, so I went to the Éclat in the afternoons while he was at work, and didn't say a word about it to him. Maybe that was a mistake. Anyway, we kept on eating out, and I began to notice what he ate. I hadn't before; food was just food and good or punk to me. You find things out about the people you marry, and what I found out was that Tom liked the plainest kind of food; just a piece of roast beef, or some spaghetti with tomato sauce, or baked beans, or a lamb stew in a casserole. He always took me to places where they served that sort of thing. I thought at first it was because we didn't have much money, and once in a while I'd suggest going to a nice place, just to celebrate, but when we did, he'd order the same things. He just likes that kind of food.

At the Éclat they teach the most elaborate French dishes and sauces, and I did pretty well with them, and I thought if I could get away with that kind of cookery, the things Tom liked would be easy. So I got a Fanny Farmer cook-book and left it around the house and told Tom I was reading it and learning to cook. That made it all right, so I got some beans and the other things and told Tom I was going to give him a dish of home-baked beans for dinner the next night. The big lug got so excited he took part of the afternoon off and brought home a bottle to celebrate the occasion, and I guess we both got a little bit high. I thought it was because of not quite knowing what I was putting in the beanpot that the beans came out the way they did, not looking quite right.

They tasted all right to me, but Tom took a couple of forkfuls, then stopped, with a kind of funny look on his face.

"What's the matter, don't you like them?" I asked, and I was afraid I knew the answer already.

I did. He put the fork down and sort of smiled and said: "They're wonderful, darling. Only I guess I had a little bit too much to drink to be eating such rich food."

Well, I took some of the baked beans to the Éclat next day to find out what I'd done wrong. Pierre looked at them suspiciously, put in a fork and tasted, and his eyebrows went up. "In what week of the course are you, madame?" he said.

"The fourth," I told him.

"Of the advanced course, without doubt?"

"No. The elementary."

He yelled for Marcel, who came over and tasted the baked beans, then pinched his thumb and finger together beside his nose. Pierre said: "I have already discerned in madame the evidence of a talent that may some day rival that of the sacred Escoffier. Imagine, only four weeks, and she has already produced a perfect *cassoulet de Midi!* Madame, go home; tell your dolt of a husband that it has been his misfortune to refuse a dish of a rare excellence, and if he has no more appreciation of your artistry, I will marry you myself."

Of course a compliment like that from Pierre was dandy, but I didn't want to marry him; all I wanted to do was please Tom. So I tried again, and kept it real plain. I just fried some pork chops in a skillet and had some boiled potatoes and a salad. He ate it, but he didn't seem very enthusiastic, and I don't blame him; that's not the way to treat pork chops. So I tried the kind of lamb stew he likes in a casserole, and it was worse than the baked beans. He wouldn't eat it, but when I took it to the Éclat, Pierre said it was *mouton rouennaise* and a masterpiece.

It kept on like that. I couldn't figure out any rhyme or reason to it. Tom liked the steaks and chops I cooked, but we can't afford them very often, and every time I cooked something in a casserole, he wouldn't eat it. And then one night he invited his parents over for dinner and they accepted. It was supposed to be a sort of peace offering, and I thought maybe if I fixed a good dinner, we'd get along.

So I fixed some roast beef. I thought I couldn't possibly go wrong with that, and it was simple, too, and I'd slip a lemon pie into the oven when the beef came out, and then we could maybe get together. Tom's mother is one of those tall, thin women who wear a lot of frills and insist on being so feminine you can hardly stand it, and I could see when she came in that she was ready to drop the axe if I got one bit out of line. She looked around the place as though I were keeping Tom in a jail, and offering cocktails didn't help much, because she would only take one, and then she asked for the napkin I'd forgotten to give her. She said something about being old-fashioned and believing a woman should devote herself to her home.

So it was up to the roast. The moment I took the lid off the roasting pan, I knew something was wrong because it didn't smell the way it should, and when I cut into it I was sure. It was much darker than it should have been, and the texture wasn't right either. They stopped talking when I served it, and Tom and his father each cut off a little piece and ate it and then began on the potatoes. Tom's mother, who had never taken her eyes off them for a minute, said: "I'm afraid none of our family care much for game meat, even though it is venison, especially when it's been hung so long it's a little bit high." I could have burst into tears right there, and I was so nervous I couldn't eat a bite myself, and I did something wrong with the lemon pie and it fell, and the only good thing about the meal was the coffee. After we finished it Tom said he thought he'd see them home, and I came over here to figure out what was wrong.

I think I know now; I've got it arranged. My fingers have virtue; too much virtue. Every time I cook something in a pot or a casserole or under a lid, it turns into the most elaborate French dish, and Tom won't eat it. The only cooking I can do is in a frying pan.

"Very interesting," said Willison. "Very interesting. With a talent like that you could easily be a *cordon bleu.*"

"But I don't want to be a *cordon bleu,*" wailed Dotty. "I just want Tom. And now I think of it, I want another Alexander."

"If you'll shake it yourself, I'll have one with you," said Willison. "You ought to be able to make something special of it."

"Okay," said Dotty. "Did you hear what he said, Mr. Cohan? Load the shaker and bring it over here."

She stood up, grasped the container in firm mechanic's hands, and agitated vigorously. The liquid that foamed into the glass was a whitish blue. Keating said: "An Angel's Kiss, by God!"

"Mr. Keating," said Mr. Cohan, "swearing in the presence of ladies is not allowed in Gavagan's, or I'd do it myself. That day man is always putting the Crème de Violette where the Crème de Cacao belongs, and I must of grabbed the wrong bottle."

CAVEAT EMPTOR

Mr. Witherwax, in a state that might be described as a low dudgeon, brandished his Martini in one hand. "I hope they send him up for a million years!" he said.

"Who?" said Mr. Gross, shaking raindrops from his hat and motioning to the bartender for his usual Boilermaker.

"Finley. The real-estate agent. Wait till you hear what he did. I told you I was moving, didn't I? Well, I took the day off to see to it, and got to the new place with the moving van about noon, and we were just beginning to get the stuff inside, when up comes another moving van with a lot of stuff belonging to a family named Schultz, from somewhere over on the East Side, and they want to get in the same place. They had keys, too. What do you think I found out?"

Mr. Cohan, who had finished serving a thin, sad-looking man farther down the bar, sidled over. "Don't be telling me, Mr. Witherwax, that Finley rented it to the both of you?"

"That's right," said Witherwax. "It's an awful mess; making us pay six months in advance because apartments are so hard to find. It'll be all right for me, because my lease is good on account of it's dated first, but we had to get this Schultz from his office and then the owner, and the moving men standing around on the sidewalk picking up overtime, and the stuff wasn't all in yet when I came away. I don't know what Schultz is going to do."

"What happened to Finley?" asked Gross.

"Skipped out. When they went to his office, they found he hadn't been there for two days. He's probably got half a dozen other suckers the same way. They're going over the books now."

Gross said: "That reminds me of my wife's Uncle Cicero. He bought a lot of bronze for junk once, and then found it was part of the statue of Abraham Lincoln—"

"If they ever find him—" said Witherwax.

"They will," said the thin man in a surprisingly penetrating voice. Three heads turned to look at a hatchet-faced man with black hair and a thin black moustache sweeping back from his beak of a nose, not unlike Robert Louis Stevenson in his later, more tubercular years. "It's the seller they always find in these fraud cases. I only wish I could find the buyer."

"Why?" asked Witherwax.

The thin man smiled a wan smile. "Well, because it was I who committed the fraud—or tried to. I have reason to believe that it was committed on me instead. I think it was legitimate. I tried to defraud the Devil."

Mr. Cohan shrank back against the bar and hurriedly crossed himself. Gross exhibited a bovine placidity. Witherwax said: "The Devil, eh? How do you know it was the Devil?"

I don't [said the thin man]. It was only *a* devil of some kind. And I didn't even see him—or it. I'm just sure. Mr. Bartender, I don't know your name, but please give these gentlemen a drink and put it on my check. I have to tell somebody about this, or—well, I have to tell somebody about this.

It started when my friend, Cal Haugen—that is, he used to be my friend—became interested in medieval sorcery. I thought it was a lot of nonsense. Especially the books, which he said were grimoires, manuals of diabolism and magic. They claimed to be medieval, but he admitted to me once that most of them were printed during the eighteenth century and predated to bring higher prices. All the same, he treated them seriously and used to try out the formulas, drawing pentacles on the floor and making incantations. Used to say that the books were imperfect guides, but the only way to discover something was to follow what leads you had, then find out where they had taken you, like Henry Hudson trying to reach the Northwest Passage and finding the Hudson River.

None of the formulas worked—at that time, anyway. I remember the night when we laid off experimenting to have a couple of drinks, and Cal remarked that it was a damn shame the infernal powers were so slow on the uptake; if one of them appeared, he'd be glad to sell off his soul, which was likely to be lost anyway, whereas he certainly could use some money.

He was kidding, but there was an undercurrent of seriousness about it that made me think he might really be hard up, and when I asked, he said, yes, he was. I could let him have a hundred and I told him so, but with the mood of our experiments still on us and, in a way, because we were both a little embarrassed, I said I'd have to have an option on the purchase of his soul.

By that time we were down to the fourth or fifth drink. Cal pretended to treat the whole project with deadly seriousness; wrote out a memo all full of whereases and all the other legal-sounding hocus-pocus we could think of. In it, he agreed to sell me, Albert Conrad, one soul for five thousand dollars at any time within a month from date. We each signed it with a drop of blood. Then we had some coffee.

I hadn't drunk enough to make the coffee ineffective in keeping me awake, so I borrowed one of Cal's grimoires to read myself to sleep on. When I gave my attention to it, I thought I could see why the Devil, if there were a personage who could be summoned up to appear to fleshly eyes, took a dim view of the methods set forth in the grimoires. They were full of formulas for the sale of souls, but every one had an enormous joker in it somewhere, so the sorcerer who conducted the sale could escape at the last moment. You'd think that even a half-witted devil would spot it every time, but apparently the people who wrote the grimoires didn't believe that a demon would be one unless he were less than half-witted.

That didn't seem logical to me, and at first I thought of calling up Cal and telling him I'd discovered where he made his mistake. But it was late; the drinks and coffee had left me comfortable and a little bit tired, and it was too much trouble to move. And as I sat there thinking about it, it occurred to me that I had in my pocket an option for a perfectly genuine soul-sale, with no trickery or intention of trickery about it. If I could somehow call up a devil, I could offer him a soul in all sincerity; not my soul, but I didn't suppose the Devil would be particular about that. The keynote of the whole business would be the one thing the grimoires missed, the genuineness of the offer. And after I collected from the Devil, I could pay Cal his five thousand.

The whole thing was fantastic, so I laughed and went to bed. Next day I did call Cal and tell him why I thought the incantations were a failure. He was disposed to argue about it at first, but after a while said I might be right; if sincerity of purpose were a requirement for getting into the Church, or Heaven, it probably would be desired in the other department, too, and there wouldn't be much more use invoking the Devil without it than invoking the Holy Spirit.

[Mr. Cohan, who had moved as far away as he could without getting out of earshot, crossed himself again.]

The more I thought of it, the better my chances looked to achieve a position perhaps unique in human history—thanks to the agreement Cal had signed. Now I know perfectly well that the medieval alchemists and magicians were self-deluded even when they thoroughly believed in what they were doing, and their experiments were a tissue of absurdities. But it seemed to me that in the course of all the centuries they worked on it, they could hardly miss arriving at some few clues to the real thing. After all, the astrologers did found the science of astronomy. Besides, as Cal put it, the formulas in the grimoires were the only guideposts there were; I had to follow them as far as they would lead.

You see, by this time I had already made up my mind to try it. It was a lot of trouble. The formula called for a magic sword, and I didn't have a sword of any kind, but I got a poker and worked away on it with a file and a sharpening stone until I achieved a fairly respectable point, and I thought maybe that would do. A sulphur fumigating candle supplied the brimstone; it smelled terrible and nearly choked me. I found I had to practice for hours with a brush before I could make even fairly good copies of the Hebrew letters of the Tetragrammaton.

But I assembled all the properties, and at midnight, as the grimoire advised, started my incantation. It's quite impressive, even when you translate it into English. I used the medieval Latin of the original, of course; I didn't want to vary the formula any more than I had to; and I kept in mind all the time that this was a perfectly genuine offer. And I succeeded.

[Gross emitted a prodigious belch: Mr. Cohan almost dropped the bottle he was holding, and Witherwax's mouth fell open. "You mean you saw the Devil?" he asked incredulously. "Mr. Cohan, another round."]

No. I don't mean anything of the kind. I told you in the beginning I didn't actually see any devil. But I know I raised one. The lights in my pentacle took on a bluish cast that I simply haven't any means of accounting for; I found myself suddenly shivering all over, though the room was quite warm, and I had the most horrible sensation of depression and utter despair, as though everything in the world had failed and I had lost my last friend. The strangest part was—well, you know the feeling when you're reading, concentrating on the page, and someone looks over your shoulder? It was like that, only intensified a dozen times. I looked all around the room and even turned around two or three times. There was no one there, but I definitely felt someone in the room with me.

I thought that as long as I had gone this far, I I might as well carry on. So I said: "I offer you the soul of Calvin Haugen in exchange for money —lots of money."

I don't know what I expected to happen, but nothing did except that the lights gave a slight flicker. Not a sound; nothing to see. If it hadn't been for that feeling of *presence* and the awful depression, I would have said this was quite as much a failure as Cal's own experiments. But I remembered the bargain had to be sealed, so I wrote out another contract and put a drop of blood on it, then pronounced the formula of dismissal.

As soon as I did that, both the despair and the conscience of someone being in the room with me vanished, and I found myself wondering what I had been so excited about. One of my lights had burned out, and the contract lay on the floor where I had placed it. The whole thing was a disappointment; I could see how the medieval demon-raisers must have thought themselves bilked if this was all they got after the emotional tension and build-up and the danger of trouble with the Church.

But I wasn't through with it yet by any means. I don't usually dream much, and when I do, the dreams are the confused and disorderly kind most people have. But that night I had a perfectly clear, logical dream, just like watching myself on the screen of an extraordinarily clear color television. I was going to the bank and drawing out everything I owned—there was a close-up of my hand writing the figures—and then going to the office of a broker named Wolff and telling him to buy stock in a firm called the Cal-Tex Oil Company. Then I saw a date pad and myself telephoning Wolff to sell out just four days later.

The whole thing was so vivid and precise that I looked up the Cal-Tex Oil Company in the morning. There was such a firm all right, and its stock was selling around $1.75—a notorious dog. There was a broker named Wolff, too, with an address in the Benson Building. But I didn't follow the advice of the dream. After all, it seemed to me a pretty slender basis for investing everything I owned in a stock that might be good for wallpaper if it were carefully kept.

However, that night I had the dream again, just as clearly pictured as before, only this time with a couple of small differences. The picture of me drawing out the money was accompanied by a series of red flashes, as though the dream were being insistent on what I should do. At least I took it for that. And the next sequence was changed; instead of going to Wolff's office, I was putting the money in an envelope and sending it to him with a letter by special messenger.

I don't know what caused the variation in procedure, but this time I decided to follow directions—that is, except about taking a chance on everything I owned. I couldn't quite do that, but I did sink most of the wad.

[He paused; Mr. Witherwax said expectantly: "And did you lose the money?"]

No, I didn't, though I might as well. You see—wait, I'm getting ahead of myself. The first thing that happened was that on the morning after I sent Wolff the money, I nearly fell over when I looked at the paper. Cal-Tex had hit a gusher of simply mammoth proportions in an entirely new oilfield; its stock had already scored one of the most sensational rises in the history of the market and was still climbing. It was real then; I hadn't imagined the visitation, and I had actually succeeded in bilking the devil.

Or so I thought until Cal called me up. I hadn't called him because—well, because I felt I had played him a rather shabby trick, in spite of his professed agnosticism and his willingness to sell a soul he didn't think he had. But now he called me up, very excited, and wanted me to come over at once.

As soon as I got inside the door, he almost shouted. "You were right! It worked; I know it worked; but it's nothing I want to monkey with any more. The damndest thing."

He went on to tell me how, the night after I had tried my invocations, he had tried it himself, keeping steadily in mind his perfect sincerity of purpose, just as I had. The thing happened pretty much the same way; he had the shaking chill and the feeling of someone in the room without being able to see anyone, and the terrible melancholy that would have made suicide a positive pleasure, only it seemed to him that his lights had taken on a reddish tinge instead of the blue mine had. It frightened him; he hadn't imagined that Hell was a depressing place. He pronounced the formula of dismissal almost at once.

But as with me, that wasn't the end of it. That night he had had a dream, just as vivid and precise as my own, only of a far different kind. What he saw was the option contract for the sale of his soul that we had worked out the other night, and then his own hand writing "Cancelled" across it, and both of us signing our names.

I said: "As a matter of fact, I'll even take up the option. I've just had some luck with money and if you want the five thousand—"

He said: "As a matter of fact, it's something I wouldn't really dare to go on with, even though I don't quite believe in it. Those few moments were pretty horrible and vile. I want to get out of the whole thing, and as it happens, I can—even pay you off your hundred. The strangest part of all is that I've had an amazing piece of luck. A broker named Wolff called me up this afternoon about my account. I'd never heard of him and didn't know I had any account, but it seems that someone sent him two thousand dollars by special messenger yesterday, with instructions to invest it in Cal-Tex Oil, and the stuff's gone up like a rocket. I can't imagine who did it; probably that nutsy uncle of mine out in Arizona, with all the dough. He wouldn't give you the time of day if you asked him, but he likes to surprise people. Have you got that crazy document with you?"

I began to see it then. I saw it all, almost in a flash, and it turned out I was right. I don't know how the bookkeeping system of the infernal regions operates, but when Cal summoned up a devil the night after I did, it must have become clear to them that I wasn't Cal Haugen, and the soul I was selling didn't really belong to me; I only had an option on it. That was why the dream changed the second night. I was directed to send the money in, instead of going in person, so Wolff couldn't identify me. I wasn't a person to him, just a name on a sheet of paper. And of course, the devil had arranged it that I would make one of those stupid mistakes people sometimes make. I was thinking of Cal Haugen, so I'd put his signature on the letter to Wolff instead of writing my own name. But there wasn't anything I could do about it at this point. Even if I told Cal the whole story, he would have said I deserved it for trying to sell his soul instead of my own, and he would have been right. I saw a Bible on the table as I went out; the grimoires were gone.

Mr. Witherwax finished his Martini. "Did you try the formula again?" he asked, munching the olive.

"Yes. I wanted to find out whose soul I *had* sold.

But the formula didn't work this time. Maybe I've sold my own and they aren't going to give me a chance to call it off."

Mr. Cohan crossed himself again.

THE WEISSENBROCH SPECTACLES

Mr. Gross laid a package on the bar and said: "My Boilermaker, and double on the whiskey, Mr. Cohan." He turned a head like a basketball toward the door. "Is that rain? That's all I needed. That *mamzer* of a nephew—"

Young Mr. Keating from the library glanced at Mr. Gross and raised his voice firmly to forestall the oncoming anecdote. "I'll check the closed stacks, Doc, but I don't think we have a really good one. However, I can ask interlibrary service."

The snub-nosed Dr. Tobolka appeared to hesitate between the difficulty of dealing with a Gross anecdote and that of following Keating's lead and inventing a reason for not listening. At this moment, Gross sipped his Boilermaker, emitted a ponderous belch and then a groan of positively subterranean depth.

Tobolka said: "Are you all right, Adolphus?"

Gross said: "If I was any worse, the undertakers are taking me off without even waiting till I fall down. It's my soul." He patted the protuberance just below his sternum to indicate that this was the seat of his soul.

"What's the matter with your soul?" asked Tobolka.

"It's hurt. On account of this." He indicated the package, about three by four feet and flat. "It was all because of that television. Myself, I'd rather be at Gavagan's than looking at it, but you know how it is with kids. While they're supposed to be doing their homework from school, there they are lying in front of it and watching a cowboy shoot off his gun fifty times without having to put no bullets into it, and this Miss Marks comes around—"

"I beg your pardon," said a man who was sitting on a stool a couple of places down from Gross, "but is that the Miss Marks who teaches at Pestalozzi School?"

Gross regarded him with gravity. "She is that one, and why she would be spending her time teaching I I cannot tell you, because what she ought to be doing is in the movies, but I guess maybe there is some reason why she does not, because I heard she got a tryout at the Striped Cat night club and they did not want her after the first show."

"Sorry to interrupt," said the man. He was young, well-dressed, and good-looking, with a smile that flashed on and off as though controlled by a switch. "I was just about to meet her, and—"

"Make it no matter," said Gross heavily, downing the last of his Boilermaker and shoving the glasses toward Mr. Cohan for a refill. "Like I was saying, this Miss Marks comes around and says that if the kids don't do their homework from school no better, they wouldn't get passed, and I better do something about this television they're watching all the time. And my business has been keeping me late, and my wife, how can you expect a woman to keep the kids from doing what they want?"

Gross breathed deeply and looked around with a certain belligerence. Nobody contradicted him, so he went on: "So this is where that nogoodnick Hershie, my nephew, comes in. I am telling him about this, and he says he has got the answer so that I will not have to lose all the money I spent on this television. He says he has got a very valuable picture which is painted by a Frenchman, only he can't sell it himself because he don't know the outlets, but it is about an even trade for a used television set. So I take him up on it. See?"

Gross looked around again. Keating, obviously

anxious to get the worst over with, said: "And this is the picture?"

Gross emitted a kind of growl and applied himself to his second Boilermaker. "And you know what?" he said. "I take it to Irving Schelmerotter, he's the dealer that buys for the Munson Museum, and he takes one look at it and says it's saloon art and to hell with it. So now all I got for my television set is this picture, and the kids will be wild because the television set is gone, and my wife will be nuts on account I got stuck."

Before he could lapse into gloom again, Tobolka said: "What is it a picture of?"

"A knife," said Gross.

"A what?" said Keating. "Why should anyone paint a picture of a knife? Or for that matter why should they hang it in a saloon?"

"No, you don't get it," said Gross. "It's a wood-knife, without no clothes on."

Mr. Cohan leaned across the bar. "You wouldn't be wanting to show it to us now, would you?" he asked.

"I have to cut the string," said Gross.

"String we got, and better than you have on it now," said Mr. Cohan.

"Okay, since you ast me," said Gross. He cut the string and peeled off the paper. Then he hoisted the picture in its ornate gilt frame on to the bar and balanced it, looking at it with an air of melancholy pride.

"Oh," said Keating and Tobolka in unison.

The painting was one of a wood nymph of extreme, not to say flagrant, nudity. She sat on her curled-up right leg, which in turn rested upon a tree stump. Her left leg was thrust out to the side and rear. Her body was upright, with her head tipped back and her hands clasped behind her neck beneath a coiffure of approximately 1880. She was gazing at a painted sunbeam with a smile of ineffable idiocy. A pair of gauzy wings, although absurdly small by aërodynamic standards, testified to her supernatural origin. They failed to balance a pair of mammae of transcendental size and salience.

"It's by a Frenchman, see?" said Gross, and indicated the corner where the signature "Guillaume" was visible.

Keating donned a pair of glasses with heavy black frames and said, "Reminds me of the old White Rock ad; the one they had in the magazines thirty years ago, before some advertising man whittled her down."

"Whittled her down?" said Gross.

"Yes. I compared some of the old magazines with the modern ones, and Psyche used to be a hell of a lot more pneumatic."

"Okay," said Gross. "But what am I going to *do* with it?"

"Your art dealer was perfectly right, my friend," said Tobolka. "An unusually perfect example of saloon art, even though Guillaume is a recognized painter. I suggest you get Mr. Cohan to hang it behind the bar as a permanent exhibit."

Mr. Cohan shook his head. "Gavagan would never stand for it," he said. "This is a family bar, this is, and he wants to keep it that way. Would you be wanting your sister to look at a thing like that while she was drinking her Whiskey Sour, now?"

"I beg your pardon," said the young man from down the bar. "May I see it?"

"Help yourself," said Gross.

The young man climbed down from his stool and came around to face the picture. He drew from the inside pocket of his coat an eyeglass case and with a flourish produced from the case a pair of glasses, which he hooked over his ears. They had frames and bows of thin, plain metal, oxidized black, and the thick octagonal lenses gave them an old-fashioned air. An air of satisfaction spread across his face as he contemplated the major features of the composition. He peered at the signature, then turned to face Gross.

"Sir," he said, "I am not a wealthy man, but I would be willing to give you eighty-five dollars for this painting."

In the background, Keating gave an audible gasp. Gross lowered the picture to the floor and said: "You couldn't make it a hundred, could you?" he said. "I got to do something for the wife and kids after that television—"

"Eighty-five," said the young man, the lines setting firmly around his mouth. "Take it or leave it." He produced a checkbook and riffled it slightly.

Gross said: "One man to another, this is practically highway robbery, but you got a deal, Mr.—" He extended a hand.

"Bache," said the young man, shaking it, "Septimius Bache. How shall I make out the check?"

"Just make it out to Mr. Cohan here, and he gives me the cash, see?" said Gross. "My name's Gross, and these here are Mr. Keating and Dr. Tobolka."

There was more handshaking. Bache said: "In honor of a succesful operation, I think you should serve out a round, Mr. Cohan. I'll add the amount to my check. And oh, yes, will you take care of the picture for me back of the bar for the evening? I'm expecting to meet someone. Gin and Bitters for me; the Hollands gin."

The picture was passed across the bar, there was the exhilarating sound of liquor making contact with glasses, and Tobolka raised his drink in salute.

"Pardon me a perhaps very personal question," he said. "But if you're willing to tell, I'd like to hear why you bought that picture. Not that the price you paid for it was extravagant. I'm no expert, but from what I understand, this is about the market price for a picture of the period. But why this particular one?"

Bache fingered his glass, glanced around the bar as though to see whether anyone else was listening, and then gazed at his drink. "I'll tell you," he said. "The same thing that brought me in here tonight. You see, I'm—" He hesitated, and sought strength in his Gin and Bitters. "Well, I suppose you'd say I'm a sort of a fetishist."

Mr. Cohan frowned. "There'll be none of that in here, young fella," he warned. "Not since that Englishman that me brother Julius arrested outside this very bar for molesting."

"But I don't molest. It's just that—"

"Him and his mackintoshes . . ." Mr. Cohan added darkly.

"Oh." Bache seemed a little brighter. "Mine isn't that sort of thing at all. It's what you might almost call a *normal* type of fetishism. Are you a psychiatrist, Doctor Tobolka?"

"No. I'm not even that kind of doctor. I'm a biologist."

"Oh. Well, I—I'd thank you for another Gin and Bitters, Mr. Cohan—I've been to see one. I was getting worried and run down, and after seeing a Marilyn Monroe movie I couldn't sleep very well, and after I saw Gina Lollobrigida—"

Keating said, "And this makes *you* queer?" He started to sing an approximation of a tune, which seemed to have the words, "I'm a fetishist, aren't we all?"

"Better you should go across the river and see some burlesque," said Mr. Gross. "Tempest Storm and you'll never sleep!"

"Now, gentlemen," said Mr. Cohan. "True enough there's no ladies in here at the moment, but—"

"But the trouble," Bache went on awkwardly, "was that I couldn't get interested in other girls, and I thought there must be something wrong with me. Well, this psychiatrist gave me a lot of tests and asked me some questions, and after a while said there was nothing abnormal about it, and I might as well recognize the fact and let it contribute to my own happiness. Only if I picked out a girl to marry, I had better see that she was—well-endowed, because I wouldn't really get along well with any other kind."

Gross drew in his breath noisily. Tolbolka motioned for another round, gave a little laugh, and said: "It seems rather like a—er, a counsel of perfection. That is, unless you go to an art school and ask one of the models to marry you on the spot. I understand that even bathing suits are fitted with artificial aids these days."

"Falsies," said Keating. "That's what they call them."

"True," said Bache, "and you'd be surprised at the number of women who use them. However, I have an unusual advantage." He smiled slightly, took off the spectacles, returned them to their case, and tapped it with one finger before restoring the case to his pocket. "I have my ancestor's spectacles."

"Your ancestor's?" said Tobolka.

"Well over a hundred years old. In fact, about a hundred and seventy. In my state, I wouldn't part with them for anything."

"I should think glasses that old wouldn't be very good," said Tobolka.

"Oh, my eyes need only a slight correction for close vision, as when I was looking at that picture, and they're all right for that. But that is only the minor use to which I put them. As tonight. You know a Mrs. Jonas?"

"Ain't been in yet tonight," said Mr. Cohan.

Bache said: "I know. I'm waiting for her. She was going to bring in this Marian Marks who, she says, is just the girl for me. That's why I came prepared."

"I don't see—" began Keating.

"It's a rather long tale," said Bache. "But I'll tell you. I'll tell you while I'm waiting. Only it's a rather dry tale, too, and I think we ought to have something in the form of a libation to see us through it."

You see [Bache went on] about 170 years ago there used to be an old spectacle-grinder somewhere in the Vogelsberg mountains in Germany, named Hein Weissenbroch. This Weissenbroch was not only a craftsman; he was close enough to the court at Erfurt so that some of the enlightenment came off on him, and he wanted to make what were thought of as scientific experiments in those days. One of his ideas was that of making spectacles out of rock quartz.

["But," said Tobolka, "quartz has such a low index of refraction!"]

Exactly, Doctor, exactly. You have to make the lenses so thick to get a major correction that it isn't worth while. Not to mention that clear rock crystal is expensive and hard to find. But in the first place, Weissenbroch didn't know this, and in the second, he wouldn't have cared anyway. He was interested in experimenting, not in proving what everyone knew already. And rock quartz has a better transparency than glass, and gives you less chromatic aberration. I've looked it up.

He used to combine hunting for birds with his fowling piece and prospecting for quartz. One day, when he was out with a peasant named Karl Nickl, somewhere near Blankenburg, he came on an outcrop that had a vein of fine clear quartz. His only equipment that day was the fowling piece, but he explained to Nickl that he wanted a crowbar or something of the kind to pry loose some of that quartz and make a pair of spectacles. Nickl protested that this vein belonged to the kobolds and shouldn't be disturbed. He was a little hazy about any penalties for interfering with the kobold quartz, but he was so vehement about letting it alone that Weissenbroch dropped the idea for the time being. It doesn't pay to get those peasants down on you. You're apt to get lost in the mountains.

After they got back with their bag of game, Weissenbroch was still fascinated by that kobold quartz, but he didn't say anything more about it. A few days later, without saying anything to anyone, he went back up the valley where the outcrop was, taking a crowbar, and pried out a good clear piece to take back with him. Well, he split off part of it, being careful not to let anyone know what he was doing, because he didn't want stories about raiding the kobold quartz to get around, and ground a pair of spectacles. They were designed to give only a slight correction, but that was about all anyone used in those days.

They looked like perfectly ordinary spectacles. But when Hein Weissenbroch put them on, he got the shock of his life. If he looked at the wall of his shop or around in it, they were just glasses and pretty good glasses, too; but when he went into the living room and looked at the floor, the carpet disappeared.

"How could it?" said Keating.

Tobolka said: "Some sort of diffraction-grating effect, I suppose. Go on, Mr. Bache."

And when his wife came in from the kitchen, her clothes had also become invisible. Weissenbroch's first reaction was that she had gone mad and was going about her housework naked. They must have had a towering row about it, though the letter only hints at that.

["What letter?" said Tobolka.]

I'm coming to that. Weissenbroch was finally able to determine by feeling that, although he could only see textiles as a sort of shimmery shadow through the glasses, they were still there. He had sense enough to keep from telling anyone else about this, even his wife, but not sense enough to keep away from the local inn. Unfortunately, he found there just what he hoped he would find; a couple of local *Mädchen*, not to mention the barmaid herself. From various hints in the letter, I gather that Weissenbroch became so exhilarated that he was impelled to drink a quantity of schnapps, and his conduct toward the women in question partook of the disgraceful. It was fortunate that he did not break the spectacles. What he did do was get himself taken before a magistrate and fined several marks. It was a large sum for his time.

Now, as I remarked, Hein Weissenbroch was a man who had been in touch with the enlightenment movement. He used to correspond occasionally with Goethe and Schiller at the court of Saxe-Weimar in Erfurt, and there is a record that he ground the last pair of spectacles that Schiller wore before his death. It was undoubtedly from someone at the court that he heard of the arrival in France of my ancestor, Dr. Benjamin Franklin, as ambassador of the colonies.

["Are you really a descendant of Benjamin Franklin?" said Keating, with something like admiration.]

So they tell me [Bache went on]. Well, Weissenbroch knew of Franklin as a scientist, of course, and thought that he might be able to explain how the kobold-quartz spectacles had worked. Possibly he figured he could always go back to the quartz lode and get more of the material. Anyway, he wrapped the spectacles up and sent them to one of his friends at the Saxe-Weimar court, with a covering letter addressed to Franklin, and a request that the package be forwarded. It was the only thing to do in those days; the mail service wasn't so good.

I would judge that my ancestor made good use of the spectacles. There are still some of his descendants in France, you know. But he never mentioned them either, and we wouldn't have known about them except for Weissenbroch's letter, in a spidery eighteenth-century German hand.

["What did he do about Weissenbroch?" asked Keating.]

We don't know. All we have is Weissenbroch's letter, with a marginal note by Franklin. It says: "Tell M. Weissenbroch d. n. atz. enuz. e. p., 4.13." Nobody knows what he meant by those abbreviations. And all we know about Weissenbroch is his letter to Franklin and his correspondence with Goethe and Schiller. The line of communication was cut. You see that was about the time when the Landgrave of Hesse-Cassel began selling his soldiers to King George for service in the American colonies. The court of Saxe-Weimar took a very dim view of it and wouldn't have anything to do with Hesse-Cassel for a while. And Weissenbroch lived in Hesse-Cassel.

Mr. Cohan leaned across the bar. "And would you be telling us now, that when you have them on, it looks as though nobody had no more clothes than a monkey?"

"I'm telling you exactly that," said Bache, producing the spectacles again and seating them on his nose as he surveyed the bartender. "For instance, they tell me that you have a large wen on your abdomen, just northeast of your navel and below your belt buckle."

Mr. Cohan turned a color that would have done credit to sparkling Burgundy; but before he could make an appropriate answer, the door opened and the brass-blonde Mrs. Jonas walked in, followed by a taller, younger woman.

"Hello, Mr. Cohan," said Mrs. Jonas, steering her protégée down the bar toward Bache. "Sorry if we kept you waiting, Septimius, but we didn't want to get caught in that shower. Marian, this is Septimius Bache; Septimius, I'd like you to meet Marian Marks. I think you two have a lot in common."

Miss Marks certainly lived up to the advance notice Gross had given. Hollywood could have used the face that smiled from under a pile of red hair, and the rest of the ensemble down to a pair of very well-turned ankles appeared to be in accord with what was visible. But Septimius Bache's face was curiously blank and his voice was curiously cool as he barely touched the hand she offered.

"Oh, yes," said Bache, looking through his spectacles. There was a little pause. "Would you—uh—care for a drink?"

"A Stinger, please," said the girl.

Any conversation was abruptly halted when the door opened again and another girl came in, who might have been the antithesis of Marian Marks. She was short, and shell-rimmed glasses sat on a decidedly plain face beneath round-bobbed black hair. In contrast to Miss Mark's rather gorgeous turnout, she was wearing a short coat over a shapeless smock. She handed Mrs. Jonas a package.

"Professor Thott said he had to mark term papers, but he knew you'd be wanting the geranium slip, so he sent me over with it," she said.

"Thank you, Ann," said Mrs. Jonas. "You know Marian Marks, don't you? Ann Carter, this is Septimius Bache."

Bache took her hand. "Won't you stay with us a while?"

"No," said the girl. "I've got to get back to the university. Thanks just the same."

She turned, but Bache took a step after her. "As a matter of fact, I've got to go in that direction myself. Do you mind if I walk back there with you?" He turned to the others. "Glad to have met you, Miss Marks. See you later, Ellie."

He walked beside Ann Carter to the door, gazing down at her through enraptured eyes. As it swung to behind them, Marian Marks said: "Well! Not that I mind his walking out on me just after an introduction like that, but I wonder whatever he sees in her?"

BY AND ABOUT

Fletcher Pratt (1897-1956) and I began collaborating on imaginative fiction in 1939. Pratt was then an established author of science fiction, history, biography, and military and naval books. I was just getting started as a free-lance writer. After some years of work as a technical editor, educator, and consultant, I had co-authored a textbook and sold a few science-fiction stories and articles.

The Hitlerian War interrupted our collaboration. In 1946, at the war's end, Pratt and I decided to develop a series of barroom tall tales, along the lines of Lord Dunsany's stories about Jorkens. I do not recall which of us first had the idea of reporting the events at Gavagan's or whether we were ever consciously influenced by Dunsany's example. Unbeknown to us, across the ocean, Arthur C. Clarke was launching a similar project with his tales of the White Hart.

The first Gavagan's Bar story was "The Better Mousetrap." This was rejected by two magazines, rewritten, rejected some more, and finally sold to *The Magazine of Fantasy and Science Fiction*. Meanwhile, we had collected several more such tales and enjoyed speedier success as we got into the swing of things. In most of the stories we worked over our notes in consultation. Then I wrote the rough draft, and Pratt did the final.

The setting of these stories is an old-fashioned bar in the 1950s. In those days, the dollar had several times its present value; and dimes, quarters, and half-dollars were made of real silver. Beards were scarce; men wore their hair short, often in the now-rare crew cut. Commercial television was new. Manhattan cocktails were popular. Women's lib, gay rights, and ethnicity were not yet burning issues, but the Cold War was. The sexual revolution was largely in the future, and "Negro" was deemed a more polite term than "Black" for persons of that race.

Pratt and I worked on and off for six years with these tales. The last was "The Weissenbroch Spectacles," written in 1953. Of the twenty-nine Gavagan's

Bar stories, only twenty-three appeared in the original *Tales from Gavagan's Bar*. The other six, written after that book went to press, were published in magazines. Twelve were published in *The Magazine of Fantasy and Science Fiction*, three in *Weird Tales*, and two in *Fantastic Universe Science Fiction*.

I have given the stories a light editing to remove inconsistencies of style and content, because Pratt punctuated by ear alone. "Oh, Say! Can You See" was retitled "Ward of the Argonaut" by the magazine; I have restored the original title. "Methought I Heard a Voice" was originally published as "When the Night Wind Howls" (from Gilbert and Sullivan), but I think the present title (from Shakespeare) more fitting.

With the approach of the Civil War centennial, Pratt became so busy with books about the war between the states that he had no time for either fiction or these reports before his premature death. Hence, we never got around to reporting the story about a vampire with a sweet tooth, who attacked diabetics only. This unwritten story may be "The Moon and I," for which there is an otherwise inexplicable entry in my opus-card file. It apparently never got to the rough-draft stage, for I have no carbon copy. This tale was to have drawn on Pratt's knowledge of professional boxing, he in his youth having been a fighter in the flyweight class. Although he did not mind discussing his pugilistic days, he refused to publicize them, since he disapproved of a writer's exploiting details of his private life.

The present volume is published under an arrangement with Doctor Clark, my college roommate and a longtime friend of Pratt. Readers who would like to know more about the life and writings of Fletcher Pratt will find a biographical sketch of this versatile author in my book *Literary Swordsmen & Sorcerers*, published by Arkham House in 1976.

L. Sprague de Camp
Villanova, Pennsylvania
May 1976